ABOUT THE MADNESS OF CHIEF INSPECTOR MARY SWEET

Mary Sweet, a London Police Inspector, has been committed to a Psychiatric Ward in Jolly Old England. Following the murder of her husband, Hubert Sweet, Mary was promoted to her Husband's position as Chief Inspector of Great Britain. But she was forced to take leave when she thought the King of England was actually Queen Elizabeth II. When she was working at the Coronation for King Charles III, she thought she heard that the Crown Jewels were hers and not the rightful Queens.

Trying to protect those Jewels, Mary tries to steal them. When all the alarms in The Tower of London go off, she thinks she's going to be beheaded by a Dead King. But instead she is arrested and sent to the London Asylum for the Insane where, to her relief, she fails the Mental Health Examination. Thrust into a large ward on the outskirts of London Town, she works with the other patients there and founds "The Mary Sweet Psychiatric Investigation Unit" (or PIU) and is quickly appointed to protect the New King and Queen by Her Royal Highness Queen Elizabeth II and her Royal Consort, Prince Philip. Following an escape from that Insane Asylum, Mary and her Teams are flown back to London on the Direct Order of the Royal Family and the British Prime Minister.

The PIU Team Members escape from the Psychiatric Unit with the help of a talking Mouse, Detective McMouse, as well as Teams of talking Dogs and Cats, and Ghosts from English history. When Mary and her Teams expose a plot to take control of all of Great Britain, as well as the world, by Russian Spy and General Gusto Gatwick (a retired British General), Mary and her Teams are forced to fight on the streets of London to once again protect innocent bystanders and catch not only the General but other Spies that are working for him.

When the General escapes, Mary – now plagued by her mother, Gertrude and the cook Simpsa – goes insane yet again. But when Gertrude and Simpsa are exposed as more Spies working for General Gatwick, Mary and Detective McMouse kill them both.

Following the General to France, Mary and her Teams now must stop the General from killing not only French President Macron and his family but, because Macron has been made to believe that the British government has declared War on France, he has the French Government declare War first.

The General, having escaped back to Moscow in Russia, works with President Vladimir Putin to confuse the situation even more with a 'Maskarova', the Russian work for 'Mask'. Ordering a pre-emptive nuclear missile strike on Great Britian, the United States and much of Europe, Chief Inspector Mary Sweet must now find the Nuclear Missile Bunker buried beneath the Kremlin and right near Red Square. As the Clocks tick down, Mary and her Teams of Humans, Animals and Ghosts work together to defeat the General, take him, his Spies and President Putin prisoner before the world goes Mad again.

A Note from the Author, Tom Richards: "As the First Novel in the Mary Sweet Crime Series, this was absolutely the most fun I've had writing any book in my long career as a writer. It's no spoiler to say that Mary and her Teams win the Day. And when they do, Mary and her Teams are awarded a variety of Medals by King Charles the Third, as well as promotions. In this hilarious tale, you'll meet so many people from history like General Patton, Sherlock Holmes and Doctor Watson, King Arthur and his Knights of the Roundtable, Sir Lancelot and his wife Guinevere on top of the Flying White Steed Goldenrod, King Henry VIII, his wife Queen Anne Bolyn, Her Royal Majesty Queen Elizabeth the Second and the Royal Consort Prince Philip and Napolean Boneparte. I hope you enjoy reading this as much as I enjoyed writing it.

All the best and Blessings to all of you!

Tom Richards

Eyeries, Beara, Bantry, County Cork, Ireland

www.storylinesent.com

Email: tomrichards141@gmail.com

14 October 2023

What Readers Say About The Madness of Chief Inspector Mary Sweet:

"A Great Read and Well Done! I've not read a crime novel before, but this was the most fun I've had reading any novel or non-fiction book in a long, long time" – Reader in Ireland

"What a wonderful combination of a Ghost Story, a Crime Story, a Romance and an adventure story. I love books with strong women featured in them, and Chief Inspector Mary Sweet is so strong, she won the day! I almost fell out of my chair I was laughing so hard." – Reader, the United Kingdom

"Ghosts? In a crime novel? Why not, that's all I can say! The world is full of Ghosts. I must say that I particularly enjoyed the adoption of Sherlock Holmes and Doctor Watson in this great 'ghastly' story. Well don and thank you!" – Reader, the United States of America

First published in 2023 by Storylines Entertainment Ltd
Beara, Bantry, County Cork, Ireland P75A342
© Copyright Storylines Entertainment Ltd
and Tom Richards, 2023 All Rights Reserved

Cover by Touqeer Shahid.
Find him on fiverr.com at Touqeershahid95
Set in Garamond
Images courtesy of The National Aeronautics and Space Administration
and other Public Sources
All music and songs used by the author are in the Public Domain.
Edited by Frank McQuaid. Find him at
http://httpfrankmcquaidliteraryagency.org/

ISBN: 978-1-915959-38-6
Rights Acquisition: for information on rights acquisition contact
Storylines Entertainment Ltd.:
tomrichards141@gmail.com
Go to www.storylinesent.com for more information and to purchase other
books written by him

BY THE SAME AUTHOR
Fiction for Adults
Dolphin Song *
Always Come Home *
Lost Lovers *
Happiness and Heartbreak
UnBaptized *
Annie's Joy **
Remembrances **
Book 2 of the Mary Sweet Detective Series **

<u>Fiction for Young Adults & Children</u>
Hotfoot
Hotfoot 2: Lucky's Revenge
The Lost Scrolls of Newgrange
The Den Adventure
Sue the Two-Headed 'Roo and You
Jungle Juice Jim (in progress) *

Non-fiction
A Survivor's Guide to Living in Ireland
* Denotes Feature Films or Television Series of these Novels
Soon in Production
** Denotes Novels in development

MEET THE CHARACTERS IN THE MADNESS OF CHIEF INSPECTOR MARY SWEET

Chief Inspector Mary Sweet – when we meet her, Mary is in her early 60s and is looking forward to retirement. In charge of a Police Station in London Town as an Inspector, many men and women report to her. But life changes when her husband, Chief Inspector Sweet, is gunned down along the River Thames and Mary's life is threatened. Due to so much stress, she is taken to a local hospital where a doctor tells her to take a needed break. But life changes again when she begins to hear and see things, including a talking Mouse (Detective McMouse) and Hubert's Ghost. Admitted into the London Insane Asylum, Mary's condition grows worse. Now truly mad, she begins the process of recruiting of Insane Inmates and forms the Psychiatric Investigation Unit (PIU). After they all escape from the Asylum helped by talking mice, dogs and cats, Mary is ordered to protect the King and Queen of England from certain assassination by General Gusto Gatwick, a retired British Officer, but Mary finds out that he is actually working for the Russians to destroy the world and take control himself.

Chief Inspector Hubert Sweet – late 50's, a hard-charging Inspector. He plans an early retirement with Mary. Romantic by nature, he does everything he can to look after her and his mother-in-law. He can't stand Gertrude but such is life! He is murdered by General Gusto Gatwick

Father – Daniel Johnson is 81 years old this Christmas Eve. It was easy for the imposter and thief Gertrude Jansen to forge Mary's Birth certificate

Mother – Mary's real mother's name is Abigail Johnson. She's only 79 years old

Gertrude Johnson, Mary's 89-year-old mother – suffers from Dementia and lives with Mary in a walk up in a wonderful part of London. Mary has inherited plenty of cash from her dead husbands. Gertrude is constantly getting into trouble because she refuses to take care of her medication. A retired school teacher, she also thinks that she's something of a detective and always tries to help Mary solve various cases – which results in more stress.

Simpsa Simon – late 30s. A simple woman she hates to work.

General Gusto Gatwick – who is a relation by blood to the Prince. A pilot by profession and now retired, the General says he fought in WWII but everyone knows that he's lying. Determined to become Mary's sixth and final husband, all that Gusto wants is her money. (Dramatic Question: is he the perpetrator of all the crimes including the attempt on King Charles and Queen Camilla.) When the attempt fails, Mary has to track down and arrest the suspect. This puts more stress on her as Gertrude helps her. Mary goes crazy and that's the INCIPIENT INCIDENT.

Jennifer Markova – is also a suspect because she escapes from Scotland Yard. They think that she's the potential killer of the King. But she is a Captain with Interpol and a Spy for England and Europe

Pavel Markova – her husband. The General killed him but Jenn was told that Hubert Sweet killed him. So she killed Hubert seeking revenge and justice

Police Officer Bernie Bridgestone – will help Mary to crack this complicated case. He has a relative in the Insane Asylum

Detective Tom-Jon McMouse – this is the little fella that truly cracks the case when he identifies Jennifer as a Spy, catching her red handed with a van load of bombs and guns. He is finally understood by one of the Insane people. When she hears what he's squeaking, she tells Mary and that's when they make their plan to escape and save the King and new Queen from doom.

Betty McMouse – Tom-Jon's wife

Doctor Tonya Gale – woman from Zambia (she knew Mary and Hubert when they were on their honeymoon – left her a big tip that allowed this woman to go to medical school).

Doctor Cheryl Watts – Ward psychiatrist treating Mary

King Charles the Third – the King of Britain and the Commonwealth

Queen Camilla – second wife of King Charles

Princess Diana – first wife of King Charles who sets up a Charity to clear the mines from London's parks, streets, museums and Prince Albert Hall. The General has placed these mines there as a diversion. He sets one off in Albert Hall during a performance of the 1812 Overture. This is conducted by the famous Austrian director Andre Rieu.

Dodi Fayed – the Princess's Husband

MEMBERS OF THE PSYCHIATRIC INVESTIGATIVE UNIT

- Nurse Edith Penrose – beautiful, nice and a great dancer. She's the one that finally insists that music is played when Mary brings in Doctor Watts' CD player
- Nurse Jeremy – a white guy who is prejudiced against dark skinned people. He hates to dance or do anything perceived as kind. Turns out he lost his wife to Alzheimer's which is why he is working there. He secretly loves Nurse Edith. When she finds out, they fall in love and agree to marry. Together, they help Mary and her Team escape.
- Kack White – Jeremy's wife who comes back as a Ghost along with Maud, Tony's wife.

The Psychiatric Unit Investigation Team (PIU)

- George Smith – retired Sargent London Police Force. Now a Detective responsible for collating all information and data from all sources and interpreting them.
- Maud – his wife. Fluent in Russian, French and Ukrainian. Translates Flash Messages from Targets.
- Tony Enwenopa – committed for the purported killing of a police officer which was never proven. He's been committed when his family died following a fire in London over 5 years ago. Tony has Dark Skin, and Nurse Jeremy hates him for that. They finally become best friends when they discover that they've both lost their families. An EMT in a London Fire Brigade
- Maria – his dead wife who comes back again. And Jess and Monica, their twin girls.
- Nimmy Ursula – a black woman from Nigeria is a new team member. Admitted only last night, she's been Involuntarily Admitted when Nurse Gale accused her of trying to run over her in London. Completely false!
- Francis Assisi – his real name. aka Colonel Francis McOuvre

Ghosts

- Sherlock Holmes
- Doctor Watson – great-grandfather of Doctor Cheryl Watts
- Queen Elizabeth the Second
- King Henry the Eighth
- Anne Bolyn
- Hubert
- Sir Lancelot and his horse, Goldenrod
- Kack White, dead Nurse Jeremy's wife

IN FRANCE and RUSSIA

- General Napolean Boneparte and his ancestor, General Pierre Bonaparte – one a Ghost and the other a living man

- The Little Sparrow as a Spy for Mary and Team
- The Secretary of Defence for President Macron, George Charles de Gaul. Who dies from apparent arsenic poisoning.
- His wife, Clarrisa, who also dies
- Major in the British Army
- Colonel in the British Army
- Motorcycle Sargent in the British Army – both men actually employed as Spies for the General
- Douglas Martin – Chief Advisor to the British Ambassador for France.
- Lieutenant Brian Jones – Carrier Pilot from the USS Dwight D Eisenhower

Animal Detective Units

- Chief Inspector Claws Catnip
- Mama Bluebell
- Cats and Dogs

London Asylum Staff

- Nurse Tullisha Gale – the Head Nurse. She hates most people for no good reason. It turns out she was brought up that way. She particularly hates Mary Sweet because Tullisha was a former London Police Officer and Mary fired her years ago for being bigoted against people of colour and was also responsible for the mysterious deaths of many Alzheimer's patients in that Sanitorium when she stopped feeding them. Just out of spite.
- Nurse Cleve – Tullisha's Lover who is eventually murdered by her

DEDICATION

To Frank McQuaid & Jin Alanso Detectives that this author Depends On To Private Investigator Bridget Whitely, The Chief Inspector of this Novel which I now name Mary Sweet And to Nimmy Oyede Nimotallahi Ajoke My Lifetime Friend from Nigeria

TABLE OF CONTENTS

CHAPTER I

Mary Sweet and Her Husband's River Thames Murder (Was it Suicide or Murder?)

Mary Sweet woke up with a pounding headache as she swung her legs out from beneath the light summer blankets. She reached for her husband but then remembered that he had to go to work early that morning. 'I shouldn't have had that last glass of red wine,' she thought to herself as she rubbed her temples. Looking across the bed to the nightstand, she saw a glass and the empty bottle of red wine. 'Hubert is such a wonderful husband. The best one I've had yet. I'll have to tell him to stop buying me those bottles of red. Yet, I love the taste and a few glasses puts me to sleep after a tiring day at the shop.'

Finally getting out of bed, she walked to the window and pulled back the thick curtains. "God, why the hell did I do that?" she cried as she covered her eyes from the bright sun. "Now, Mary, pull yourself together. Take your shower, have a cuppa, and get dressed. I'll be fine, I hope."

Stumbling out of the bedroom, she walked into the bathroom and turned on the shower. Slipping off the pink robe her mother had given her for Christmas, Mary eyed it then threw it on the floor. "Bloody thing is so fuzzy it makes me itch," she said as she climbed into the shower. "I told that old bitch that I didn't need another robe. Mind, it's not her fault if she doesn't listen to me. Her doctor says she has dementia but could live to see one-hundred years and get a letter from the new King." She shampooed her hair and when she finished washed the soap out of her hair. Then she washed herself and finally finished, stood in the shower feeling the hot water sluice down her back. "I'm getting fat, not that Hubert thinks so," she said as she patted her belly. "Too many pork pies and chips for lunch. Mary, you'll just have to go on a diet again."

As she turned off the water and stepped out of the shower, her mother screamed up the stairway. "Mary, you old tart, where's my breakfast! That rat of a husband of yours forgot to feed me."

Mary closed the door, trying to ignore her mother's screaming. "You'd think I was a servant around here. I'm no one's servant. I'm a Police Inspector, aren't I. So Mum, get your own damned breakfast or wait until the maid gets here."

Throwing the towel in a hamper, Mary walked naked into the hall.

"There's the tart, standing in my hallway naked!" her mother Gertrude screamed at her. Standing only feet away, Mary's mother was dressed in a Victorian costume of a bygone era. Her dress was bright blue and she wore old fashioned shoes and silk gloves. Her hat with its ribbons and feather made her look like she was out of the television series Selfridges. "Don't just stand there, you ass," Gertrude screamed again. "I want my breakfast right now!"

"Mother, I'm going to get dressed. After that I'll get you your breakfast. But first, we'll both have a cup of tea and you can take your medication."

"I won't you fat stupid bitch!" Gertrude yelled as she wagged a finger under Mary's nose. "You're not my doctor! My doctor is a nice man. Why, he even asked me to marry him."

"That's wonderful, Mum. Now let me get dressed."

Walking into the bedroom, she closed the door and locked it. But Gertrude pounded on the door. "Get out of there. That's my bedroom. Mine, do you hear me? Your father and I used to fuck in that room which is why you're here! Mary, all I wanted was a boy but I had you, God help me."

When the banging stopped, Mary finally got dressed. She took the Police Inspector's uniform from where it hung in the closet. Putting it on for what seemed like the millionth day in a row, she looked in the full-length mirror and frowned. Sticking out her tongue at the damp greying blonde hair and her pallid complexion, she sighed.

"Repeat after me, Mary Sweet. You're retiring in six months. You'll be sixty-five years old. You have a wonderful husband who happens to be your boss, Chief Inspector Hubert Sweet. You've been married five times now, and you'll have one of the happiest retirements our police force has ever seen."

Taking out a tube of lipstick, she wrote on the mirror in bright red lettering:

1. RETIREMENT NOVEMBER 2023 WITH HUBERT
2. DON'T LISTEN TO MUM. SHE'S CRAZY
3. DRINK LESS WINE. GO ON A DIET. GET EXERCISE
4. BE NICE TO HUBERT. HE'S MY ONE TRUE LOVE. ALL THE OTHER HUSBANDS, BLESS THEM, WERE JERKS

5. GO TO CHURCH MORE OFTEN. PRAY MORE FOR STRENGTH AND LESS STRESS. PRACTICE YOGA ONCE A WEEK. BE KIND TO MUM, TOO. 

Finished dressing, she put on her Police Inspector's cap and marched out of the bedroom. As she walked down the steep steps, she couldn't help but notice the ancient wallpaper. "Pink flock. I hate pink and I hate flock wallpaper! My mother! She thinks she can scream, can she? Wait until I get to Hyde Park at lunchtime. I'm going to scream my ass off!"

In the kitchen, she found her mother sitting at the table, holding a fork and knife. "Oh, you good, good girl! Are you making my breakfast now?"

"In a minute, Mum. Let me put on the kettle first then I'll make us a cuppa. Then we can have breakfast." Looking at her watch, Mary saw that it was not quite eight o'clock in the morning. "Good, that no-good maid will be here soon to make Mum some breakfast."

Then, through the open kitchen window, she could hear the next-door Church bells begin to chime. "Bong, bong, bong…"

"Goddam that Church! Those bells could shake the house apart." She looked up at the teacups that hung from hooks above the sink. She reached but it was too late. One fell then hit the plates directly below them. As the Church bells kept chiming, the entire shelf with all the plates fell away from the wall and shattered on the old tiled floor. "I told them! How many times have I told that old vicar that I'd sue that ridiculous Church if those bells broke our China again! That's the last time, dammit. Look at this mess."

Gertrude still sat at the table holding her knife and fork. "Was that the breakfast bell, dear? Has the ship come to port? I don't even remember buying a ticket for the good ship Titanic."

"No, that's not a ship's bell, Mum. Those were the Church bells ringing. Let's get us a cup of tea now."

As she bent down to get some new cups out of a cabinet below the sink, the back door opened. Her maid, Simpsa Simon, strode in with a smile on her face. "Oh, isn't it a lovely late spring morning!"

"It's summer, as far as I'm concerned," Mary seethed. "Simpsa, this isn't summer time. Not yet. You were due her over thirty minutes ago. Seven-thirty each morning. That's what your contract says and we both signed it."

Simpsa frowned a little. Stepping across all the broken China, she patted Gertrude's hand. "You're hungry, aren't you, pet? Let me sweep all the rubbish out from beneath your feet and I'll make you some breakfast. Tea, toast, rasher, pudding and a fried egg. How's that?"

"Simple, Simpsa!" Gertrude replied. "I'd love that."

"Mum, you can't have that and you know it," Mary said as she crossed her arms across her official uniform. "The doc says you can have a boiled egg or poached, but nothing fried. It clogs your arteries."

"Fuck the doctor!" Gertrude yelled. "I'm eighty-nine years old and I'll be ninety at Christmas. The doc can go get stuffed!"

"Look, you two, I have to go to work. Simpsa, remember to give Mum her meds. She's supposed to take all of them, not some of them."

"But Gertrude hates the red ones," Simpsa whispered. "I put those down the toilet then give her the rest."

"All of them, do you hear me? All!"

Mary kissed Gertrude on the cheek then walked out the back door. Looking up at the tall church spire, she sighed. "Let it go, Mary. It happens every hour. Just get some new China and store them anywhere else but those shelves. Hubert will have to put them up again. Maybe I'll tell him to tile above the sink instead? Wouldn't that look pretty? Anything but pink!"

As she crossed the street she looked at the time again. It was ten minutes past eight and she had to be at the station at 9AM. Smiling to herself, she began to jog down the road. Passing two bin men, one of them whistled at her.

"G'morning, Inspector Sweet!" he said as he doffed his cap. "My, aren't those legs of yours as purty as Lady Di's."

"Thank you, Tom. You two have a wonderful day."

Then Mary turned into the local park and stopped jogging. Putting her face up to the sun, she began to plan her day. Today would be a day of briefings as her husband told the entire station how they would plan for the King's Coronation. And at lunchtime, they'd have lunch together at a restaurant that looked out over the River Thames.

As she left the park, Mary didn't notice a man in a military uniform looking at her. His eyes blinked in the sunlight and he licked his narrow lips. Smoothing his long moustache with a gloved finger, he took out a pen and paper from his pocket. Then he looked at his watch and noted the time on the paper.

Mary. 0815 GMT. Local Park.

Smiling to himself, he began to whistle an old military marching tune as he sat on a bench. An old woman sat down next to him and began feeding the pigeons from a brown paper bag filled with breadcrumbs.

"Why, 'til the General Gusto Gatwick, ain't ya?" the woman asked. "Fine day, isn't it General? And a fine week it's supposed to be for the Royal Coronation."

"A fine day and week, I agree, Madam," the old General replied. "I think I'll take my constitutional now." He rose from the bench and putting his hands behind his back, began to walk toward the exit from the park. "That Mary Sweet. Her name should be Mary Gatwick but that Chief Inspector Hubert beat me to her. That, I must say, could be fixed if God wills it."

Outside the park, he looked into the distance. He could see a woman in a uniform walking up the long street. Smiling again, he looked into the bright blue sky. "That's the Luftwaffe at high noon!" he said to no one. "Oh, that I had been a pilot back then. I'd have been a Spitfire ace and then would have run for Parliament. And, if my plan comes off, I could still be selected by Parliament as the new King of England!"

A Bobby walking his beat along the street saw the General and bowed slightly. "Morning, General Gatwick. Hope you have a fine day, sir."

The Bobby saluted and the General stood to attention and returned it. "Sir, it's going to be a wonderful day and a wonderful, wonderful Coronation. With luck, we'll both live to see the next Coronation."

The Bobby, London Police Officer Bridgestone, walked over and stood by the General. "With luck, sir. Hear that Prince Charles has a lousy ticker. If the poor man dies, the new Queen won't last long either. The fate of England lies in the hands of God."

"God and the Angels on High!" spoke the General. "God save our righteous King and Queen."

A long black limousine pulled up. The Bobby opened the door and the General climbed in. "Good-day, Policeman. Have a cuppa on me."

Handing the Bobby a few coppers for opening the door, the General walked away.

"That General is insane. He's retired yet he talks about the King and Queen dying? That family will outlive me and that General, that's for sure!" Glancing at his pocket watch, the Bobby started walking down the street. "Ten more minutes and our Chief Inspector will brief us on the Royal Coronation. Can't be late or Inspector Mary Sweet will eat me for dinner!"

His walk turned into a jog and the jog into a run. When he saw the Station, he entered the open doors in a sweat. And as he did, a small mouse looked up at him. "Stop running so fast, Bobby," it squeaked. "You're not late and the Inspector won't eat you for dinner. She's back on a diet and all she'll have for lunch is cheese which she'll share with me."

Then the Church Bells near the Station bonged nine times. The mouse went through a hole in the hallway wall. As it turned around, all it could see was polished black shoes walking quickly toward a tall door. "Glad I'm not a human being. Humans are insane! All I want is cheese and a comfortable bed to sleep in. And a wife. I need one of those so we can make tiny, tiny mice."

Then the dark red door closed. Inside the large room, sitting at desks, were most of the Police Officers who were scheduled to be on duty during the King's Coronation. Mary Sweet stood at the top table. When Hubert Sweet walked in, Mary saluted then turned to her team of London Police Officers.

"All rise! Salute the Chief Inspector."

After all of them did, the Chief took his position next to Mary.

"Officers of this station, please sit down. What you are about to hear is for your eyes and ears only. Let no one else know what we discussed, not even your close relatives or friends. What's critical is this. We have been following a number of people who are of a variety of nationalities. Most of them are French and are pretending to be tourists. One of them was arrested just yesterday for a charge of murdering our Ambassador to Italy. When he was interrogated, he admitted that he worked for the French Secret Police Force. Their single mission while in England? To kill the new King and Queen."

A police officer stood up. "Sir, is there any truth to what that man or woman said or was it some sort of lie to throw our force off the scent of the real killers of the Ambassador."

Inspector Sweet stood up. "We're not sure yet, but thank you, Police Officer Bridgestone. We've asked the French Police Department as well as the French Embassy to give us some background on this character. If he's telling the truth, then the Royal Family is in extreme danger."

At the back of the room, a woman put up her hand. "Inspector, I apologise but I must go to the WC. I'll be back in a moment."

When she left the room, the female Police Officer went to the toilet. Seeing one other police officer washing her hands, the London cop went into a stall and closed the door. There, she took out the small recording device that she'd concealed in her jacket. Taking a mobile phone out of her bag, she dialled a number. When the General came on the line, she whispered into her phone:

"General, listen to this. Sir, your ruse worked. They think it was the Frenchman this Station caught who killed the Ambassador. We both know it wasn't him. He's a simple French tourist who had way too much beer to drink. Instead, it was me, just as you ordered. Sir, what is your next order now?"

"Next, Jennifer, you will follow the Chief Inspector when the meeting is over," the General hissed down the line. "If my observations are correct, and they always are, he will have lunch with his wife at a restaurant overlooking the River Thames. When he is finished, you know what to do, don't you?"

"I do, Sir. And the money for this next murder?"

"Already in your Swiss bank account, just like the last one. This action is much riskier than the previous one, so I have paid you double what I paid last time. I've paid the entire fee because, my lovely Jennifer, I trust you and love you."

"But you won't marry me, will you, General. Even though you promised to."

The General laughed. "Jenny, I'm far too old for you, we both know that. You also know who I truly love. Now get back to work. Phone me when you spot them having lunch."

The Police Officer hung up her phone. She counted to ten then flushed the toilet and walked out of the stall. No one was in the room with her, so she stood at the mirror and put on more lipstick. "That General takes me for a fool but I'm no one's fool. He's not the only one who can betray women he says he loves. I can too. And someday, if that man isn't careful, that's exactly what I'll do."

When the woman left the WC, the small mouse that was fed by many of the Police Station staff and officers climbed up onto the sink counter and looked in the mirror. It sniffed at the faucets where that spy had washed her hands and carefully scraped off some lipstick from the counter. Placing it in a very small plastic bag that he always carried, the mouse looked into the mirror and talked to himself.

"That's no London Police Officer or my name isn't Tom-Jon McMouse. I'm the son of the great Mouse Detective, William R Mouse. I'll take this little pouch to the lunchroom and leave it with an Investigator I know. If he can understand what I squeak, she'll analyse this lipstick to gather that brat's DNA. Then we'll have a real lead in what could be the biggest case in English history!" He brushed his thick whiskers with both paws then washed his face in a puddle of water that that Jennifer Spy had left on the counter. "Oh, I heard everything she said, so I did!" the little mouse said to the mirror. "I just wish I knew the Queen and King's English rather than just squeaked in an English accent."

Finished, the mouse climbed down from the counter and made his way out of the WC through a small grate. Then, as quick as any Detective Mouse in that English Service, he scurried to the Lunch Room and there, he waited.

CHAPTER 2

The Lunchtime Affair

After the Briefing at the Central Police Station, Mary came out of that important meeting hungrier than she'd been in a long time. She took the Tube up to Charing Cross, then started walking. "I'm not going to jog right now," she said to herself again. "I'll walk as fast as I can instead." But when an old woman with a cane passed her as did a woman dressed in a torn jacket, Mary knew she'd been followed by her Grandma and that ass Simpsa.

"Go home!" Mary shouted at the top of her lungs. "I'm meeting Mister Sweet in a few minutes. Don't you have anything better to do that to follow me around?"

"We're not stalking you, daughter Mary," Gertrude sneered. "I'm taking my constitutional! We've both been invited to have lunch at a really posh restaurant right on the Thames. Isn't that so, darlin' Simpsa?"

"Tis true, surely, Misses," she said to Mary. "We're going to have a big meal and lots of wine and even pie a'la mode!"

"That General is rich!" Gertrude hissed. "Why you wouldn't marry him when he asked you is beyond me. You should never have married that pompous ass Hubert. He's not right for you. You never had any children with him."

"Leave me alone!" Mary shouted again. "We never wanted children. I'm going to a restaurant, too. So excuse me while I run way in front of you."

As Mary broke into a slow run, she heard the chiming of the bells in Westminster Cathedral and she knew her husband was already at the restaurant. "Now I'm late because of those two bitches," Mary said as she kept running. She ran right over Tower Bridge, past all the tourists, then took the steps down to a tiled path right beside the Thames, the great river of London. Mary stopped running, took a breath, and sat down on a bench. Across the River she could see the old-World War Two cruiser, The Belfast. The deck was thronged with tourists. River barges, speedboats, and cruisers full of other tourists moved up and down the River as Mary took a lipstick and mirror out of her bag. When she was finished she started walking again down the River, past all the tourists and homeless people.

"There's those wonderful homeless women I read about in the paper," Mary said then called to them. "Grace, Mary! It's me, Mary Sweet! How are you?"

The women walked over and one took out a pouch of tobacco and rolled a cigarette. Then the three women sat down on a bench. "Are you still homeless, ladies," Mary Sweet asked as she reached into her bag for her purse. "I have a few pound in here I've wanted to give you."

"That's not necessary at all!" Grace said, waving her hand at Mary. "Both me and Mary, we got great jobs sweeping streets in London City. For us, it's a lot of money so we're spreading that luck around."

"Here, Inspector," Mary said and held out a shiny new Fifty Pence piece. "Look closely and you'll see that it's been struck with the New King's head. Isn't that amazing? We got it when I bought this new pouch of tobacco and some papers."

Mary Sweet took the large coin and examined it. King Charles was stamped on the back just above the image of his mother, Elizabeth the Second. "That's the nicest fifty pence piece I've seen in many years," Mary Sweet replied. "I'll pick up one or two at lunch, I hope. Now forgive me, ladies, but do please keep that blessing. I know when you were both homeless that a stranger helped you right near here. He was a Yank on holidays and he gave you both some tobacco and whatever cash he had in his pockets. He told you he'd have given you more, but there was no ATM close by. And then, Mary, you gave him a special Fifty Pence Piece which I'm sure he took home. He probably has it someplace very special because you told him not to use it or give it away."

"Aye, and so I did," Mary remembered. "A very kind Yank, that older man. He was absolutely miserable, that man, because as I remember he'd recently lost his good wife."

"It really is about paying it forward, isn't it?" Mary Sweet said. "I wish I'd met that Yank. He could be dead by now by his own hand. You told me that story and how deeply in love with her he was. Do you know, I saw a small ad that he ran in the London edition of the The Big Issue. He was looking for you two and asked that if anyone saw either of you, to email him. I don't think I still have that article in my bag but it's at home. Ladies, do you have a phone number now?"

"Sure we do. We both have brand new mobile phones that the City Council bought for us." Exchanging phone numbers, all the ladies stood up. That's when Mary Sweet heard the bells of Westminster Abbey chime again.

"Oh my God, I'm really late! I'd better get going or Hubert will think something happened to me."

As the former homeless women waved, Mary rushed down the Thames. She saw the front of a French Restaurant, 'L'Amour', and then Hubert was waving for her from the front door. "Darling, I'm so sorry I'm late. I was chatting with some women I know and the time…"

"Don't worry about it, sweetheart," Hubert said as he kissed her on the cheek. "It's so nice outside in the sunshine I thought we'd have lunch at this nice table with the checkered tablecloth."

A waiter came up to them with a small bottle of champagne and as he poured it into two glasses, Hubert pulled a chair out for his wife. "Sit down, Mary. Take a load off your feet. You look like you've been running."

As his wife sat down, and he waiter began service each of them salads with lobster meat, a woman who was leaning on the railing next to the River, right across from the unsuspecting couple, took a small pair of binoculars out of the backpack she carried. This time, she wasn't dressed as a Police Officer but as a tourist from France. She wore a bright yellow raincoat and a matching French cap. On her feet she wore short yellow boots. When she looked through the lenses and saw the couple enjoying themselves, she smiled at herself.

"They have no idea who I really am," she snickered quietly in her accent that was decidedly French. "Ooo-la-la! Look at that salade and the lobster that's in it. That Mary Sweet, said she was going on a diet and she is! Bon chance, Mary!"

When she had finished spying on them, she took her mobile phone out of her pocket. Using a telephoto lens which she snapped onto the phone, she took a number of pictures. When she was finished, she sent them to the General. After only a few minutes, her phone rang.

"I know they're outside, you idiot! I can see them through the window."

"I know you can, but I wanted you to be sure they're …"

"Quiet, be quiet for once. I'm having lunch with the guests we've both invited. Gertrude is here and she agrees that I'm the perfect sixth husband for sweet Mary."

"You only want her money," Jennifer hissed down her phone. "That's all you ever wanted from me and you've left me behind in the mud. Now I'll say this, Bon Generale. If you marry that damned Mary Sweet I'll come into your house at night. I'll slit both of your throats. Then I'll shoot you both many times with my small automatic Beringer rifle."

"You wouldn't dare. Don't you know who I really am?"

"You're no one! Not even le Generale. I looked you up at all the military colleges in the world. You're a phony, Sir whatever your name is. You are nothing! Nothing at all. You're just scum."

"That's not true. I was the head of my class in the Admiralty Naval College in Portsmouth. You looked up the wrong name. I am the world-famous Gusto Gatwick, son of the great Admiral Gusto Gatwick! Now get off the phone and carry out your orders or you will be the one who will be shot!"

When the line went dead, Jennifer smiled. She reached into her deep pocket and took out her petit rifle. Attaching a long-distance sight to the top of the short gun, she turned around and found a man in her gunsight. He was walking his small dog along the River Thames and had no idea at all what was about to happen.

"Help! Help! Messier Homme! Help!" she shouted. The man looked up and saw her as she began to wave. Handing the dog lead to his wife, he began running down the concrete path next to the River. Jennifer looked again through the gunsight. As the man was passing steps that led down to the River, she pulled the trigger.

A racket of tat-tat-tat-tat and smoke filled the air next to the Thames. A woman screamed and then another one. Someone shouted and pointed at Jennifer. Again, she pulled the trigger. Bullets struck the concrete path at the women's feet. They both turned and ran away from her. Next, Jennifer shot an old priest she saw limping across the street. Then she shot a man with his child. They both fell, leaving blood in the streets.

At the table outside the restaurant, Hubert and Mary both rose at the same time. Simultaneously, they reached for their weapons hidden in their jacket pockets. Mary started to fire at the yellow-attired murderer just before her husband started to fire. Both of them missed. The yellow clad figure who must have been a woman returned fire with an automatic weapon. Behind them, the restaurant window shattered. They could hear screaming inside.

"My Mum's in there!" Mary yelled as she kept firing. "You stay here. I'll call reinforcements and the Ambulance Service. There may be more of them so watch your back. I'll be with you in just a minute."

Ducking, Mary ran toward the entrance of the restaurant. When the waiter came out, a spray of bullets hit him. He bled all over his black and white uniform and, spinning in a complete circle, crumpled to the ground. Mary shot over her shoulder then entered the restaurant.

"Mum! Simpsa! Go out through the back door!"

"I'm not doing that! I haven't finished my expresso yet!"

The General rose from the table. "Madame, give me your weapon. Take the women out the back door. I will stay here and help the Chief Inspector to apprehend that female murderer."

"No way, General. You're not trained in situations like this nor have you fired a sidearm in years. Go out the back with the women. I'll ask the restaurant owner to call for reinforcements, too."

The owner heard her and, picking up his phone, dialled the emergency number just as the interior of the restaurant was strafed with any number of bullets. "Get down, everyone!" Mary screamed. She waved at all the restaurant patrons and they hit the floor. The chef came out of the kitchen carrying apple pie a'la mode. Just as he did, a bullet ricocheted off the marble floor and struck his tall white hat. Dropping the dessert, he hit the floor then brought up his hands. They were filled with blood.

"Le morte! Le morte!"

"No, you're not dead. It's just cherry sauce that fell onto the floor," Mary yelled again. She took the radio out of her jacket and made a direct call to her Police Station. "This is Mary Sweet. We're under attack right now by at least one terrorist! Do you read me, over!"

Her radio crackled then someone came on the line. "It's Police Officer Bridgestone. We've already been radioed by a Police Car in your area. Help's coming right now as well as the Ambulance Service from all over London."

Then Mary heard an explosion. Looking out the open window that was now free of its glass, she saw that the yellow clad woman was holding something that looked like a short tube. "Oh my word. She has something like a bazooka with her." The tube fired again and the shell rocketed toward her. When it hit the back of the restaurant, every person in there screamed again. Glass shattered, sending fragments flying everywhere. She could only watch as four other people, or was it five more, hit the floor, dying in front of her eyes. Another shell rocketed into the restaurant and more innocent people died. Mary could smell gas and knew it was only time before…

"Hit the ground! Now!" Then there was a terrible explosion. The entire room was covered in flames. People ran out of the restaurant, their clothes on fire. Gunfire killed them as they left.

"Everyone, move toward the front of the building. Stay low! Help's on the way.

She glared at Gertrude, Simpsa and the General. They were all sitting on the floor behind their table. All of them looked scared to death. Mary ran out the door, looking for her husband. "Hubert? Hu? Hu? Where are you? Hu!"

"Here!" She turned and saw him crouching behind a car that was on fire. Running as fast as she could, Mary took a position right behind him. Breathing in deep, all she could smell was petrol, sulphur and smoke.

"Backup's on the way," Mary breathed. "They'll be here any minute now."

"Yes but by then many more people will be dead." Hubert looked over the smoking bonnet of the Black Taxi that was on fire. "Wife, you stay here. I'm going to kill that murderer."

"Husband, you stay here and cover me. I'm a much better shot that you and you know that!"

As Mary began to creep around the side of the burning car, Huburt put his head up over the smoking bonnet. "You in that yellow coat! Put your hands up. It's all over." In the distance they could all hear the wailing of any number of Police sirens. Then they heard the squeal of tires on the street and then saw the blue flashing lights of the cars. "See? Now give up!"

Mary and Hubert could hear the woman laugh. "Give up! Are you crazy! It's you who must give up. See?" They both watched as the women held up a bulky backpack. "I still have much ammunition. Ce bon, yes?"

She aimed the small tube up the street, and they watched her pull the trigger. Within an instant the leading Police Car exploded into flames. "I'm going to kill that bitch," Mary said as she reloaded her weapon. "When I count one, cover me."

"Okay, I'll do it. You say one and I'll go." Hubert grinned at her. "One."

He ran as fast as he could across the street. All that Mary could do was cover him. She shot every round in her magazine. When the last bullet was fired, she saw that she'd hit the woman in the arm. The yellow coat was red from the shoulder down.

"You bitch!" Mary screamed as she reloaded again. "Come after my husband, will you? You're dead meat, bitch" Mary fired again and again. The woman returned fire with her automatic weapon. She saw her husband making his way along the far railings of the path by the River. When he was as close as he could get to the murderer, he took aim and opened fire."

"Shoot her in the chest, not the head, Hubert!" Mary screamed yet again. "Her chest is a bigger target." Hubert kept firing until his Police gun was empty.

"Mary, there are more rounds in your bag. Throw me a box of them."

"My coat! Right!" She reached into her coat but found that both pockets had been ripped out. All she came out with was a few spent cartridges from her own sidearm. "Hubert, I can't! None!" she yelled as she held up an empty hand.

The woman opened fire again with her automatic rifle. Mary felt a sting on her hand and, pulling it down, found that two of her fingers were bleeding like a stuck pig. She heard more automatic firing and, looking up, saw that Hubert had both of his hands up. "Hubert, you know what to do now, don't you?"

As he nodded, the murderer laughed and yelled to Mary, "I'm sorry Mon Femme. He won't have time." Then she motioned with the machine gun toward the River. Hubert, his hands still up, backed toward the gap in the wall and the steps leading down to the Thames. He had to step over a number of bodies, and found that his footing was slippery because of all the blood. The woman turned to Mary. "Say goodbye to your husband, Mon Cherie. He was a very good husband but now, for no reason except for an order by my Generale and a large payment, this husband is dead."

She turned again to face Hubert. Mary opened fire again with her left hand. Her aim wasn't as good as with her right hand but she peppered the concrete all around the woman's feet. She heard Huburt scream once. Mary lifted her head again above the bonnet of the Taxi. She saw her husband spin around once then fall over the rail. As he fell she could hear him scream again.

"You fucking, fucking bitch! You murdered my husband."

"Then murder my General and we're even, okay you silly woman?" Jennifer retorted. "Now, all there's left for me to do is bid you Adieu!"

As Mary began running across the street, Police Cars pulled up. All she could do was watch as the woman in yellow climbed up on the railing and jumped.

"Call the Rescue Boats. Tell them we have a body in the River as well as a fugitive on the run. Tell anyone to see her that she's armed and dangerous," a Sargent ordered one of the Police Officers.

Mary fell into the arms of an EMT technician. Sobbing, all she could do was cry Hubert's name over and over again.

"Where's that husband of yours anyway," Gertrude said as she walked up with Simpsa. "The General's been wounded and can't pay the bill. I need Hubert to pay the bill."

Mary looked at her and grimaced. Her head was pounding, as were her fingers, heart and spirit. "Mum, he's dead. Jump into the River and get the wallet from his jacket. Then you can pay the bill."

As she was taken into the Ambulance, Mary would later swear that she saw her husband sitting beside her as well as the small mouse from the station. She knew they couldn't be real but she wasn't sure. Then the door opened again and the General was carried inside. He took a seat beside Mary. The door opened again and Gertrude and Simpsa were brought inside. They sat down, one on each side of her.

"Let's go!" the EMT specialist ordered to the Ambulance driver. As the large yellow, blue and white truck moved up the River toward the nearest hospital, Mary whispered, "Please, dear God. Let me sleep and then take me. I don't want to live without Hubert. Or make me insane. I feel insane already. I…"

Her head fell over and the technician rushed to her side. "Give me room, ladies," he ordered. Taking Mary's pulse and her blood pressure, he saw that both were highly irregular. "She needs oxygen and a tranquilizer right now! Driver, get us to the hospital as quick as you can. We're out of oxygen for some reason. I have some tranquilizers here and I'll give her an IV and a bullous bag full of them." As he lifted his new patient off the seat and put her on the gurney beside him, Mary opened her eyes a little and thought she saw an Angel that was also the station mouse.

"Be well, my Mary Sweet," the mouse whispered. "Your husband may be dead to you right now, but he'll be back. That's a mouse Heaven promise."

The EMT put a needle into her arm and set up the bag. When he turned a small grey device on the line, Mary could feel herself starting to relax. Then she was floating as high as any Mouse Heaven in the entire Universe. "Goodnight, Mister Mouse. Sweet Dreams."

In an instant, she saw nothing at all, only the whites of puffy clouds, rainbows and stars that twirled all around her.

CHAPTER 3

Mary Sweets Recovery from the Murder of Her Husband

When Mary woke up from the drugged sleep, she had trouble remembering where she was, why a number of needles were in her arms, or why a dark-faced Doctor hovered over her.

"Inspector Sweet? It's time to wake up. Come on, try to sit up in bed."

Mary tried to do that but when she did, the room began to spin again. "Who are you? Am I in Africa again?" she asked, remembering how she and Hubert had flown to Zambia on their honeymoon. "Where's my husband? Is he out swimming?"

The Doctor only smiled. "Don't worry about your husband, Inspector Sweet. He's in another room in the hospital."

In Mary's mind, she suddenly remembered the flash and bangs of gunfire and explosions. She recalled how that crazy woman with the small machine gun had killed her husband. "Oh, God. My Hubert! He's dead!"

Sobbing as she never had in her life, she leaned into the Doctor's arms. "Mrs Sweet, my name is Doctor Tonya Gale. I'm originally from Zambia and was a waitress at the hotel where you both stayed on your honeymoon. Well do I remember the large tip that you left me when you left our country. That tip was huge by our nation's standards back then. With it, I was able to apply to college and eventually went to medical school."

Mary focused on the beautiful woman's face and, when she did, remembered the teenager who had helped them out so many times. "And I remember you too," she said as she tried to dry her eyes. "We became so fond of you, you were like our daughter."

The Doctor, smiling, helped Mary to settle back into the bed. "Mrs Sweet, you've been through a horrible shock. For years, before I became an Emergency Room doctor, I was a psychiatric nurse. I know just how much people suffer when they've lost someone dear to them. For that reason, I'm asking you not to leave this hospital floor for at least two weeks. You need complete bedrest." Doctor Gale looked down at Mary's hands. "Mary, hold up your hands. What do you see?"

Mary held up her hands. Both of them were shaking. "Doctor, give me a glass of water, please. I'm thirsty."

The Doctor picked up the glass full of water from Mary's bedside locker and held it out to her patient. When Mary took it with both hands and tried to take a sip of water from it, she ended up pouring water all over herself. "Look what I've done. Without Hubert here, I'm useless."

"It's only water, Mary," the Doctor said. "That will dry in no time. If it doesn't, the nurse will change you into a brand-new nighty that your mother sent."

"Don't tell me. Gertrude's here?"

"She's in the waiting room with your maid. Simpsa, is that the woman's name?"

"I can't stand it! I want to get out of here right now!"

"Don't worry yourself," Doctor Gale said as she placed her hands on Mary's arms. "Unless I authorise it, no one is allowed in to see you. And those will only be special visitors that I know you'll want to see."

At that moment, Police Officer Bridgestone walked into the patient's private room with two large bouquets of flowers and a giant card. Giving them all to a nurse who had led him into the room, he took off his Uniform cap then reached out and took Mary's hand.

"Your entire Team wishes you a speedy recovery, Chief Inspector Sweet. I'm afraid we've not yet been able to find the person who murdered your husband. But Scotland Yard is working on that case. The King himself has sent you a special message of Royal Promotion. It's in the envelope with the Card signed by every person working in our Station."

The nurse gave Mary the card. When she had trouble opening it, the Doctor did it for her. "Why, it's so beautiful, Officer," she whispered as she read the notes of both condolence and get well. "Even the Station dog signed it. That's his paw print, isn't it?"

"So it is, Ma'am," he stated, then smiled.

"Officer, you called me 'Chief Inspector'. That's my husband's official title." When the Royal Message slipped out of the card, she read it. It was signed by the King himself and bore the official seal of his new office. "My husband is never coming back, is he?" she said with tears in her eyes. Picking up the Royal Message, she read it aloud. "I, King George III, hereby appoint Mary Sweet as London's Chief Inspector." He had signed it with a royal flourish in ink and pen.

"I'm the Chief Inspector of all the Police forces in London," she whispered in a mix of awe and grief. "The King himself has made it so." Then she looked up again at Officer Bridgestone and frowned. "Today's the day, isn't it, Inspector. Today is the day of the Royal Coronation."

"Madam, I'm not an Inspector. I'm a lowly Police Officer. I was never able to pass the written exams nor do I have the experience to reach a higher rank."

"Tough, Bridgestone. I need a man I can rely on. From this day forward and for the rest of your life, you are now the Inspector of our Station. In the event that I die, the King will appoint you as Chief Inspector."

"Then what are your orders, Madam?"

"Find that murderer now! And when you do, don't arrest her. Shoot to kill. She's a mad woman and I don't care what she said to me. That woman dressed in yellow will be at the Coronation, probably in the crowd. Working with that traitor General Gatwick, they'll do everything they can to execute the King and Queen of our United Kingdom and the Commonwealth of Great Britain!"

Doctor Gale had been standing in the corner talking to the nurse. Hearing Mary's voice rise, she walked over and stood tall in front of her. "Please calm yourself, Mrs Sweet. Getting yourself all worked up is not good for your mental or physical health."

"Fuck my health!" Mary roared and, swinging her legs out from beneath the hospital bedclothes, tried to stand up. When she started to fall back into bed, she grabbed the arm of her new Inspector. "Get my Inspector's uniform. I'm sure it's in the closet."

"Madam, we have your new Chief Inspector's uniform just outside the door," Inspector Bridgestone stated formally. "The Station tailor had your sizes so made up a new one. She's a very thoughtful woman because she used your husband's original Chief

Inspector's uniform which she'd kept in storage and tailored your coat out of that."

"A good woman, Inspector. As good as gold."

"Mary Sweet, you're not leaving the hospital," the Doctor stated with a firm voice. "If you do, I can't be held responsible nor can any of the staff that are now on duty."

"Doctor Gale, please understand," Mary stated kindly. "There are a number of would-be executioners stalking the King and Queen. If I don't go back on duty, those good people as well as the entire Royal family and many innocent people will be murdered by these sons of bitches. I'll write you a very special note stating the reasons why I'm forced to leave. When these bastards are caught, I promise that I'll come back here and check myself in for that rest you've ordered." Then she looked the new Inspector in the eye. "Inspector, as to my Mum and her idiot housekeeper. Now hear this! When we leave here they'll follow us no matter where we go. All they'll do is get in the way again. They were almost killed at that restaurant on the Thames. So here's what you'll do," Mary said smiling again. "Grab an Officer from our Station. Tell that man or woman to find Mum and Simpsa. Let them both know that I want them at the station and there, I'll give them both a special job to help us find the perpetrators of those who killed my husband. Put them in a police car and using the siren, get to the Station as fast as possible. When they've arrived, put both of them in a cell with a pen and paper. Tell them to write down everything they remember about the shootings at the restaurant including a complete description of everyone and everything they saw. But make sure someone locks the cell door or Mum and that Simpleton will get out and drive me crazy again. Do you understand, Inspector?"

"Completely, Madam. Or, Chief Inspector, would you prefer 'Sir'?"

"Madam, I guess. Hubert was Sir. So Madam is fine by this simple woman."

Shaking hands with the Doctor and Nurse, the new Chief Inspector and her Inspector marched from the hospital room. As they did, the tiny Mouse appeared on Mary's hospital bed. Looking up at the Doctor, the small rodent squeaked: "She's not simple by any means, is she Doctor Gale?"

The Doctor looked down at the Mouse and smiled. "No, she is definitely not simple. Why, Mister Mouse! I remember you! You were in the hotel years ago when I was a lowly maid. You arrived with the just married Mister and Mrs Sweet."

"Sure, and wasn't it me, Doctor. Just off the plane from Ireland and I didn't have a place to stay. So when I saw that very special couple, I hopped into their taxi completely unseen."

"Mister McMouse, you used to talk in my language, didn't you? Or was that some form of Rodent Talk?"

"No, Ma'am. It was a special combination of Irish, Scots and McMouse language. Sorry, now, but I have to run. I've been ordered by my country's Chief Inspector to protect Mary Sweet at all costs! You'll soon understand why she was forced to leave. I can't tell you yet because it's a secret and I alone know the entire story. But soon, the entire Commonwealth will understand the bravery and loyalty of one Chief Inspector Mary Sweet."

CHAPTER 4

The Coronation and the Foiled Plan of Royal Execution

When the Chief Inspector arrived at London Police Station, she climbed out of the car before the Police Car had come to a full stop. Marching through the crowds of people in Central London, her Station — which was just down the block from Westminster Cathedral — had throngs of police officers and detectives on the steps waiting for her.

"Three cheers for our new Chief Inspector!" someone in that crowd yelled, and as they all started to cheer, Mary stopped just in front of them.

"Don't cheer me, not ever," she yelled. "My new position was caused by the murder of my husband. Inside, all of you, for a special briefing. Captain, step forward." The Captain of the Station stood to attention in front of her. "I want teams of sharpshooters on top of every building and in every window along the route of the Royal Coronation Parade. Get the Prime Minister on the phone. I also need the Army to help us patrol the streets and alleys. There are so many people attending this Royal Coronation that we need at least one-thousand to two-thousand officers from across England as well as the Army to look for that bitch who was dressed in yellow as well as that treacherous General."

Saluting again, the Captain rushed inside. As Mary followed with Inspector Bridgestone, she looked down at her hands. 'They're still shaking,' she said to herself as she stumbled against a fellow Officer. 'And I'm still dizzy. Never mind. I'll get that rest as soon as we find and kill those that ordered and carried out Hubert's dastardly murder.'

Inside the station, they all assembled in the Conference Room. Mary was so small she had trouble seeing everyone so she climbed up on the top table. "Come to order! Come to order! Listen to what I have to say." As the room quieted, she couldn't help but remember that the last time she was at this very table her husband had been the one to brief the Team and issue orders. "Ladies and Gentlemen of the Station. I've had our Station artist create what I think looks like the Woman in Yellow." Then the lights dimmed and the room was as silent as a Church. The projector switched on and suddenly, a woman dressed all in Yellow appeared on the screen. "I think our primary suspect is from Russia because she talked with that kind of accent." Using a pointer, Mary motioned toward the large illustrated figure that illuminated the screen behind her. "She has a very thin face and long hair. I'm not sure of the colour. For all we know she was wearing a wig. She would seem to be a master of disguise. But you can't change your height. Look for women that are almost six feet tall and weigh approximately one hundred and fifty pounds. She had dark eyes but she could now be wearing contact lenses. For all we know, she could now be disguised as a man." Turning to the projectionist, Mary smiled at him. "Next slide, please."

Now the screen was filled with a picture of the General. "You all know who this man is. Some of you have seen him every day. He lives not far from here and has often been in the station. He is still a strong, determined man for his age but he has many, many weaknesses, one of the worst being his large ego. He won't be in any sort of disguise. He'll dress like a General." Turning back to her Team, she stood as tall as she could. "We are certain that my husband's murder was no accident. The culprits want to cause diversions which is why they killed him. It is my suspicion that by murdering the late Chief Inspector, and in the chaos that followed, they were able to smuggle in additional weapons as well as many more people who will work together to execute our King and Queen. We have piles of copies of both of these suspects. Take a handful as you leave. Place them wherever you think people will see them."

Then Mary Sweet stood to attention and saluted all of the Officers in the room. "The fate of England is in the balance. If the King and his Queen are killed the world will know about it. They'll know that we failed. They'll wonder if Britain is still a real power on this Earth. And if that happens, there's no telling what that Rat Vladimir Putin will do next. He'll try to destroy many other countries in the old Soviet Union to once again consolidate his grip in that part of the world. Do you all understand me?"

"Yes, Ma'am," an Officer whispered.

"I didn't hear you. Shout it!"

"YES, MA'AM," the room shouted.

"That's much better. Now, get out there and defend our Royal Family as best as you know how."

As the room cleared, the Inspector helped her climb down from the table. Taking Mary's hand, he felt the sweat in her palm. "Chief, you'd better rest for a few hours. Remember what the Doctor ordered you to do."

"Fuck that Doctor," Mary grumbled as she stood again on the floor. "Inspector, were you able to contact the Prime Minister?"

"Yes, Ma'am. I did. He said that he'll send not only the Army to London but also many troops from the Royal Marines. Aircraft and helicopters from all the branches of our services will fly over the Royal Parade route, just as planned. But he's ordered the officers of those flying units to bring along infrared binoculars and, for the choppers, high powered rifles. The kind that sharpshooters use."

"Good," Mary said as they moved to the door. "And Mum and that Simpsa? Are they in a cell?"

"Just as you ordered. They're busy writing that report. I guess it will take at least a full day or maybe two to finish it."

"Good again!" Mary exclaimed as she walked out of the Conference room and into an empty hallway. "Tell Mum that I'll visit her as soon as I can."

"There's no need, Chief."

"Why's that?"

"She's now so busy, and think she's so important to this mission, that she told me to tell you to stay away from that secure hotel room until she and her housemaid were finished writing the report."

"Oh, just perfect! Peace and quiet at last!" Mary said smiling, and then remembered the purpose of her Royal task. "Inspector Bridgestone, what's your first name?"

"Bernard, Ma'am. But people call me Bernie for short."

"Okay, Bernie. Call me Mary when we're not near our other Officers. That will let us get to know each other better and that's critically important. We must learn to think like each other. Got it?"

"Got it, Sir. I mean Mary," he said and, holding the front door open, followed Chief Inspector Sweet out onto the crowded steps.

Mary scanned the crowds, her eyes narrowing as the sun swept the city. "They're all in that mass of visitors somewhere," Mary said to Bernie. "Not just that bitch of a woman and the General. There are other men and women waiting somewhere to murder our King and Queen."

With that, she started to cry again. "Oh, Bernie. What am I going to do now? My husband should be here. I'll be a failure, I'm sure of it. I'll be the one who will be responsible for the killing of…"

"Don't cry and dry your tears, Mary," Bernie replied as he handed her a white handkerchief. "Take this and keep it. I have a few more in my pockets."

Taking the white cloth, Mary dried her eyes and blew her nose. "That's so kind of you, Bernie. That's exactly what Hubert always did when I cried or needed to blow my nose."

"He was a good man and always will be," Bernie replied. "Do you know, Mary? You look somewhat like my ex-wife. She's dead now, but for many years we were so very happy."

Putting the handkerchief into her new Chief Inspector's jacket pocket, Mary smiled up at him. "We'll speak more of these things another time, after we catch those foolish people. Come on, Bernie. Let's stroll up the street.

As the pair began walking through the crowds, Detective McMouse climbed up onto Bernie's shoulder. From there, he scanned the crowd with intense black eyes. 'You wait, Mary and Bernie," McMouse said to himself. 'I'll be the one to see them both! And when I do, I'll tear at their eyes and faces and you can arrest them. For you see, I had many members of my family including my ancient papa and mama as well as many nieces and nephews outside the restaurant when that Hubert man was killed. They know exactly who they are, particularly that woman and other members of the General's gang. Our family members live in their many cellars, after all.'

"They're here, right here!" McMouse squeaked as it waggled its long whiskers. "With the courage and amazing intelligence of Mary Sweet and this Bernie human man, we'll not only catch one of the perpetrators, we'll catch the entire Gang!"

As Mary and Bernie attempted to walk across the crowded street, McMouse crawled from Bernie's shoulders to the top of his Inspector's cap. There, clinging onto the Official Bag, that little Mouse scanned the street in front of Westminster Abbey, as well as the Royal Courtyard. 'No sign of anyone in yellow!' the Detective mouse thought to himself. 'If we don't find those thugs, we could all be as dead as I would be if caught by a giant cat!'

At that moment, a Ginger Cat appeared, walking on the street at Bernie's feet. "Cat, do you see anything yellow?" McMouse squeaked loudly to the cat. "If we don't catch those murderers, many cats as well as mice and human beings will die in the terrible onslaught as they try to kill our King and Queen!"

The cat looked up at the mouse and twitched its short whiskers. "Not a damned thing!" the Ginger Cat meowed. "I am Chief Inspector Claws Catnip. I've been assigned to this area as part of our General Investigation to find the murdering cat-slayers that wrought havoc to my family of kittens when those explosions went off in our favourite French restaurant."

"You too, Inspector Catnip?" the tiny mouse sighed. "I lost many children and grandchildren that day but fortunately some survived. If you see anything can you and any troops that you have roar like a lion? Then I'll squeak to Bernie and tell him what messages you send to me."

Chief Inspector Catnip saluted the mouse with his right paw. Then she began running toward the steps of the Abbey. "Here!" the cat roared. "I have a man or a woman in my sight. Whatever sex that is, it's wearing all yellow! This time, this human pig is wearing a mask to make it look like a Royal Soldier. Do you see that human person up there on that giant white clip-clopping beast? That must be the person who murdered so many cats, mice and human beings."

McMouse took out a tiny pair of binoculars from its uniform coat. Scanning the crowd, he finally saw what looked like a tall man dressed in a Royal Uniform, wearing a yellow rose upon its lapel. Looking closely at the eyes, the mouse saw a pair of deep blue eyes and a narrow face beneath the Uniform cap.

"That's no Royal Officer," the Detective whispered to itself. "That's the women who was dressed in yellow that shot Chief Inspector Sweet and unleashed that rocket attack! We must stop her before more innocent bystanders are killed and injured."

Crawling down to Bernie's shoulder, McMouse began to squeak as loud as it could. But all that Bernie could hear was a constant chatter in his ear.

"Inspector Bridgestone. See that line of white horses over there? And see that Royal Soldier wearing a yellow rose? That's no soldier. That's the woman who killed the former Chief Inspector Sweet!"

Over and over again, that wee little mouse chattered the same message. But all the Inspector did was try to brush that infernal noise off his shoulder. "Mary, what's that I have on my shoulder? The damned noise is driving me bonkers! Is it a giant horsefly?"

Mary looked up at the Inspector and as she did, McMouse jumped off the Inspector's shoulder and onto the Chief Inspector's cap that Mrs Sweet wore. "Mary, my dear Chief Inspector. Please listen to what I tell you. Use your imagination to understand my squeaks and squeals." The Detective cleared its tiny throat and began again to tell Mary his important message. "Mary, see that tall Royal Officer sitting on that white horse? See how the horse is starting to trot in time with the Royal Marching Band? That means the King and his Queen are coming soon sitting in their Royal Pumpkin Carriage. That's the murderer! See the yellow rose she wears in her Royal Uniform? Beware of this imposter and assassin. Soon, she'll use that large telephone she has in her breast pocket to call the General and then, why then. Then, oh Mary! Do something! Tell your Team as well as the sharpshooters to kill that woman before she kills many other people once again."

Mary only shook her head at the squealing noise that seemed to come from the top of her head. Looking down at her hands, she could see that they both shook again. Once more, she heard that confounding squealing noise on top of her head. The squeals grew louder and louder, almost as loud as a trumpet in both of her ears. Finally, she took off her cap and looked at it.

"Why, I know you, don't I?" she said to the tiny mouse. "You came to visit me in the hospital but I wasn't well enough to understand you."

"No you couldn't but the Doctor could. She was the one who told you to rest and you promised to do that only when you were finished saving the life of the Royal Family."

"Mouse? You can talk?" Mary whispered as she and her Inspector walked closer to the line of soldiers all on horseback. "I could hear you squeal but now I understand you! Or am I truly mad. Mice can't talk English."

"I beg to differ, Ma'am," the mouse said as he saluted. "Chief Inspector, I'm out of uniform. My uniform was destroyed when that dastardly women tried to blow up our family's favourite restaurant. But yes, I can talk in English if I try hard enough. Most of the time, I choose only to squeal or squeak. Ma'am, did you understand the important message I said to you and the Inspector over and over again?"

"I did," Mary stated then swung back to look at Inspector Bridgestone. "Inspector, do you see that Royal Officer on her white horse? Arrest her right now! That's the same woman in yellow who killed Hubert!"

Bernie looked over the crowd and saw that the white horse with the disguised perpetrator was moving past them. Then he saw a female Bobby on duty that was jogging close to the horse to keep the crowd away. "You! Officer! Arrest that woman!"

When Jennifer Markova heard the order, she reached into the bag that she was carrying and brought out a handgun. Aiming it over the crowd toward the Chief Inspector and Inspector, she pulled the trigger. Pulling Mary to the ground, the masses of people began to scream and run toward the River Thames. "It's just like the day she murdered your husband!" the Inspector shouted to his boss. "Stay here and I'll kill that woman." Getting out the radio from his jacket pocket, he ordered the sharpshooters to kill that woman. "Kill her before it's too late! In all likelihood she has a number of rocket propelled grenades in that bag she's carrying. Aim for her head. And that's an order!"

As arms fire began from the many roofs around Westminster Cathedral, the woman with the yellow rose fired again and again. Each time she did, the crowd screamed and, running right by Mary and Bernie, sought refuge wherever they could.

"Bernie, get off of me," Mary shouted. "I have a revolver in my jacket pocket."

When Mary pulled herself to her feet, a bullet whizzed over her head. Spinning around, she saw a man dressed all in yellow get hit in the throat. "That man's in yellow! He's one of the gang of perpetrators that are trying to kill the King! But why is…?"

Looking again at the woman dressed as a Royal Officer, Mary watched as the woman took careful aim again. When she pulled the trigger, Mary saw a woman dressed in a yellow hat with a gun in her hand fall to the ground. "Bernie, that woman in yellow was trying to kill both of us," Mary shouted over the crowd. "Get on your radio. Tell your Team to arrest anyone dressed in yellow or wearing anything yellow on them."

"But many people are wearing yellow today," Bernie shouted back. "Yellow is one of the King's favourite colours. If you arrest them all, there will be many complaints about you to the King."

"To hell with the complaints. Arrest them all before it's too late."

More firing took place as the woman with the yellow rose on her lapel dismounted. Marching tall through what remained of the crowd, she stepped up to Chief Inspector Sweet and saluted. "Chief Inspector, my name is Jennifer Markova. And yes, I'm the bitch that murdered your husband. If I could take that back, I would. You must understand that the man you call General Gusto Gatwick isn't a General at all. I was held for ransom by a gang of thugs which brought my husband to him. Then a man dressed in a dark blue suit and a trench coat that talked with an English accent murdered him." As Mary watched helplessly, Jennifer started to cry uncontrollably. "How wrong I was to believe the General. I was told that your husband, Chief Inspector Sweet, murdered my Pavel! But I was wrong. So very, very wrong. Oh, Mary Sweet, how can you ever forgive me?"

"Forgive you?" Mary seethed. "I can never forgive you. You murdered my Hubert, the love of my life. How could I ever…"

"But don't you see? Pavel was and is the love of my life. And that General Scum is our enemy. Don't you see how much we have in common?" Reaching into her jacket pocket, Jennifer pulled out a business card. "Mary, I am out of uniform yet again. I worked for many years as a spy for the Mossad, the Israelis special forces. Then, they asked me to serve with Interpol which is where I met my husband. We were assigned to work in the Crimea to track down a gang of murderers who were made by that conman Putin to go first to Africa and next to the Crimea. Wagner, that's what they were called. And when I was held captive and put up for ransom, that's when one of Wagner's men shot my husband. But, as it turns out, those goons were also in the employment of that fake Scumbag General."

Mary took the card and as she did, they all heard an explosion. Then another one and another one. "Get down, people!" Mary shouted to the few bystanders that were still near her. "Get into a building! Right now!" She glared first at Jennifer then at her Inspector. "They're after the King now! Have the Team surround the Royal Carriage. McMouse, where are you?"

The small mouse looked out from Mary's handbag. "In here, Chief Inspector. Those loud bangs frighten me."

"Your job is to get any mice or cats that you find to keep a close look out for anyone dressed in yellow. Too, we must find that fake General Gatwick. He's the man giving the orders to kill the King and Queen!"

The mouse saluted and scampered off as the Inspector and Jennifer began running toward the Royal Carriage. Now in sight, Mary watched as the Team from her Station surrounded it. Some had automatic weapons and handguns. Drawing them, they pointed them up in the air. Soldiers from the Royal Marines also formed a barrier around the Royal Carriage. Overheard, Mary could hear the scream of jets. "Just as promised," she said to no one. "I'm going to go to the Tower. There, from the top of it, I can get a good view of what's happening below and keep a lookout for the General and anyone dressed in yellow."

Jogging past Westminster Abbey, she made her way toward the Thames. Spotting a London Taxi, she put out a hand and the cab pulled over. Climbing in, Mary ordered, "The Tower of London, right now, man!" The Taxi driver looked at her Chief Inspector's uniform and did as he was bid. Climbing into the back of the cab, she clung to her seat as he picked up speed.

"Ma'am, why the London Tower?" he asked her over the speaker. "The King's back near the Abbey. The Tower…why, t'isn't nowhere near the scene of all that violence."

"Driver, just get me there as soon as you can! From there, I can scan all of London, most of it anyway. I have no idea, nor does anyone, where the man who is ordering the attack on the King and Queen is right now."

"Scan it with your eyes?" the driver asked. "That takes some real good eyesight. Ma'am, why not take the telescope that I have in this car's boot? A passenger left it behind."

"Thank you, sir. That's exactly what I'll do."

When they arrived at the Tower, Mary jogged up the steps. At the door, she flashed her badge to a Tower Guard who opened the tall black gate. Inside, Mary walked alone down a hallway made famous by King Henry VIII. "Good Lord, but it's dark in here," Mary said in a whisper which echoed against the sixteenth century stone walls and ceiling. "If I'm not too lucky, I could have my head chopped off like Anne Boleyn."

"Anne Boleyn? You mean the wife that I had executed for cheating on me?" someone else whispered from close by. Turning around, Mary confronted a man dressed like a long-ago King.

"Why, your Majesty!" Mary said as she curtsied. "I'm here to save the new King and Queen of…"

"England? Yes, a new monarch just in time to save my old Kingdom." The ghost of the old King bowed to Mary. "Mary Sweet, I was told that you were coming. A young ancestor of mine has been praising your name for just over a year. Her name is

Elizabeth. She is the Second Elizabeth that was Queen of this Realm. Do you know her?"

"No, Sire. I have never had the pleasure of meeting her," Mary whispered. Feeling faint again, she knew she had to sit down but realized that if she sat in front of this King, he would have her beheaded. "I'm sorry, my Liege, but I'm feeling faint."

"Are you, my dear? Then take my arm and let me sit you on some sort of stool." Leading her into the darkness, Mary finally saw some light. That light twinkled in the shadows and she realized that they were walking past the display case for the Royal Jewels. "My crown is in there, I think," the King said. "As are my Royal gloves and a sceptre or two. Even my old armour is around here somewhere. It gets lonely in this place of hiding, and lonelier at night. But never mind. Most nights, one of my wives stop by with dishes of my favourite foods and to spend the night."

'What a scumbag!' Mary thought to herself. 'That King killed many of his wives and children. He always thought that someone was going to betray and murder him.'

"But I was wrong, wasn't I?" the King said kindly. "Yes, Mary, I can read your mind. Many of the people you will see in the near future are ghosts from the not-so-distant past. We are all here to help you not harm you. My lady, are you feeling a bit better now?"

Mary found herself sitting on a stool in what looked like an old jail cell. "This is where Anne, your wife slept, before she was executed, isn't it, King Henry?"

"Yes, and if I could take that murder back that I caused, I would have been a very different man and King. You see, Mary Sweet, I loved that Queen like no other Queen I had before or since. At this point, I have dozens of Queens but I never beheaded any of the new ones. I was mad to have ordered the slaying of such a beautiful Queen Anne Bolyn."

The King sat down beside her and took her hand. "Someday, you will have back your new King Hubert. That is a promise I have the power to bestow on you. You shall one day be the new Queen of what my subjects now call Great Britain and the New Commonwealth. Or the Queen of France. But, Mary," the King said, "Heed my warning. Believe no one except those you come to trust. Soon, you will not only see more ghosts but also people whom the authorities call Insane. Then, they will also call you insane and lock you in something like this Tower for what will appear to you as the rest of your days. But I, with many other subjects, will then free you to fight on in your capacity as the Chief Inspector, then the Prime Minister and then a Royal Queen."

As Mary watched, the ghost disappeared. "Who in their right mind thinks they can see a dead King?" Mary whispered into the dark cell room. "I wonder who else I will see?"

As she looked, Mary beheld a very bright right coming from down the hallway. Rising, she ventured out of Anne Bolyn's ancient jail cell and crept back toward the Royal Jewels. A figure dressed in Royal Robes and wearing a silver Tiara smiled at her as Mary curtsied then knelt on the cold stone floor.

"My Majesty, I am honoured at your presence before me."

"Rise, my child. I am what you think I am. I am Queen Elizabeth the Second. By Royal Decree, you have been brought to me this day. You have already saved my son. Now you shall save what remains of our Commonwealth and France."

"Your Majesty? I don't understand."

"Rise, Princess Mary Sweet. Upon your head I place the Royal Tiara that Princess Diana wore when she married my Charles." The Queen placed the Tiara on her head. "Now I want you to break the glass that protects the Royal Jewels. Soon, there will be thieves in her including a disloyal would-be General. Break it so my Royal Tower Guards come to you."

Mary looked around and saw nothing to break the glass with. Then the Queen gave her the Royal Sceptre. With that, Mary pounded on the glass with all of her strength. When the glass finally shattered, an alarm began to sound. Lights came on throughout the Tower as Mary heard the footfalls of the new King's Tower Guards running toward her.

"And look what we have here?" a squat Guard said to her as he snatched the Tiara off of Mary's head. "Would ye be a stinking little rat, would ye be? Or maybe some sort of vermin?"

"Neither, Guard," Mary stated with a voice like ice. "Give that Tiara back to me. The Queen herself gave it to me."

"The Queen? Which Queen?" the Guard said as other Royal Guards ran up. "Would that be a new Queen or an old one? Maybe the ghost of Anne Bolyn?"

The Guards started laughing as Mary began to seethe again. "Queen Elizabeth the Second. By Royal Order she's making me the next Queen of all of the United Kingdom and the Commonwealth."

"Oh, is she now?" a tall Royal Guard smirked. "And I suppose you'll be the one to order, 'Off with their heads!'"

As the two Guards laughed, a group of Police Officers ran up. In the lead was Inspector Bridgestone. Huddling with the Royal Tower Guards, Bridgestone looked back at Mary with a frown on his face. Finished talking to the Guards, he walked up to Mary.

"Chief Inspector, I've just received an order from the King Himself. You're to come with me back to the Hospital where the Doctor will meet you, the King and the Queen. Due to the un-Holy mess the General caused, the Coronation has been delayed. The King has ordered you to have that rest you promised your new doctor. Remember? The one who told you to take medication due to the stresses you've been under." Bernie looked around at the brightly lit Tower hallway and at the shattered glass that protected the Crown Jewels. Bending over, he picked up a sparkling Sceptre.

Its jewels glittered in the light. "Am I right in understanding that the old Queen gave you this to break the glass?"

All that Mary could do was nod her head. Then she heard someone whisper. Looking down the hallway, she could see a tall figure of a man walking toward her. "My Lord in Heaven. It can't be!" she uttered.

Bernie looked over his shoulder. "Can't be who, Mary."

"It's Hubert! He's coming toward us."

"Of course it is, Mary," Bernie replied as he took her by the arm. "Let's get you back to the hospital. Then you can explain everything to me."

When Mary, Bernie, the Tower Guards and the Police left, the lights went dim again. Hubert stood beside the shattered glass and picked up the Tiara. As he examined it, Queen Elizabeth and King Henry appeared next to him.

"That woman is a very special woman," the King said. "She'll be the next Queen of England if I have anything to say about it."

"And so she will be," the Queen replied. "By Royal Order, we have made it so."

"Does that include me?" Hubert asked as he smiled. "Mary has always been my queen ever since the first day I met her."

"And you fell right in love with her," the King said, "just as I did with my Queen Anne Bolyn."

There was a flash of light and next to the Queen stood Prince Phillip, the Royal Consort. "My Lady and gentlemen. You well know who I am. I fell in love with my bride the first time my eyes fell upon her. No one could sunder our marriage vows, not even death. My dear," he asked the Queen. "Shall we?"

Giving her his arm, they all walked up the steps of the Tower and onto the roof. From there, they looked down at an ambulance and a group of Police Cars as they drove back down the Thames. "That Mary Sweet. What a wonderful wife," Hubert said to the Royal gathering. "I'm no King nor am I prince. But I feel like a prince among all of humankind when I'm with her."

"Then by Royal Command, I order you, Hubert Sweet, to be with your wife Mary Sweet for the rest of Eternity," the Queen stated sternly. "And by Royal Decree I make you her Royal Protector. You shall protect her from harm for the rest of Eternity. My will be done." With that, that entire assembly disappeared into thin air. All that were left on the roof was a crow looking for insects or mice.

"Royal, shmoil," the crow said to no one. "Nothing else on this roof yet to feed even one Royal Crow. Guess I'll have to go somewhere else to find my vittles. Maybe a mouse or something else." Looking down the River Thames, the crow could see some blue ambulance and police lights flash on and off. "That Mary Sweet one. She sure is a sweetie. She'll do just fine, I'm a-thinking." Then, the crow flapped its wings and as it flew over the Thames, following Mary's ambulance, it thought it saw a little mouse clinging to the roof of a Police car. "That damned Detective McMouse. Persistent little guy. Not so many days ago, I tried to eat 'em. But he banged my head with an acorn nut or somethin' strong and man did I get a headache."

Then, just like the Royal Assemblage on the Tower roof, the Crow disappeared. The sun began to creep low into the west as, in the hospital, Doctor Tonya Gale once again put her patient to bed. "Not one person is to come in this room until I give her a comprehensive mental examination, do you hear me Inspector Bridgestone?"

"That's a promise, Ma'am," Bernie said as he took off his cap. "Any idea of the prognosis?"

"From what you tell me, Inspector, Psychosis and perhaps some Schizophrenia. From her medical history, I see that both illnesses run in her family. That, and Early Onset Alzheimer's. Any one of these grave illnesses could cause what you told me she said and saw."

The Inspector scratched his head. Removing a handkerchief, he gave it to the Doctor. "Please give this to Mary. Tell her I'll visit her as soon as she can see someone. And Doctor, if she has to go to the Mental Asylum, let me know and we'll give her a guard of honour all the way to that London Psychiatric Ward."

"Done, Inspector. Done. Now if you'll excuse me, I have to see the patient."

When the Inspector had gone, Doctor Gale opened a door and found Mary already asleep in her new bed. Looking around the quiet room, she could see nothing else but her patient and hospital furniture, not even the little mouse that she had talked to only the other day. "I wonder where that mouse is? The one I could understand? I guess he also heard my orders. No visitors until my little Mary has had some welcome rest."

Outside, it had begun to rain. Detective McMouse, now dressed in his official uniform, wore a deep blue trench coat against the rain, hail and wind. Looking up at a window high in the hospital building, he smiled to himself. "I can hear you Doctor, even from here," he said in English. "I'm sure you can hear me too. Protect our Mary Sweet. Nothing will disturb her tonight. Not a wee little thing. We've set up all sorts of patrols around the hospital composed of mice, cats and human beings. That General rat will not touch one hair on my Mary's head. Not a single one."

Crouching beneath a tree, the mouse began to shiver. "Cold is a small price to pay for having the honour of guarding this Chief Inspector. Soon, I'll be asleep anyway."

And for once, the mouse was right. As the full Moon rose in the East, all that his mouse relatives could hear was gentle snoring. A woman mouse hopped up and covered him with some old leaves and twigs. "That human Mary, the English Chief Inspector, needs sleep and so does my mouse Detective," Mrs McMouse said to no one. "He's not fit to do much of anything except guard that fine woman. It seems we never have time to spend with each other or to make more little mice to replace those that we've lost." Gently, she kissed him on his furry cheek as tears fell from her eyes. "Goodnight, my husband. And sweet dreams. I'll see you on tomorrow. I'll bring you a fine breakfast and maybe then, you'll have time to sleep with me."

Then she too was gone back to bed in her little nest next to the Thames. And by the morning, when the sun had risen, and McMouse was awaken, he knew that it would be another fine day. A perfect one to escort his Mary Sweet to the London Insane Asylum.

CHAPTER 5

The London Asylum for the Insane and How Mary Learns to Love It

Mary, do you remember me? It's Doctor Gale from the London Hospital."

The doctor looked down on her patient. The one she had done her best to protect but who wasn't her patient anymore. Mary sat on a chair staring blankly into space. Across a small table from her, the Ward Psychiatrist, Doctor Cheryl Watts, tapped a pen on the wooden surface in an attempt to get her new psychiatric inmate's attention.

"Mary Sweet, can you hear me? Mrs Sweet?"

The Psychiatrist looked up at the doctor. "I know she's suffering from stress and overwork and some PTSD, Tonya. But she's in no shape right now to take a psychiatric examination."

"Let me try something, Cheryl," Tonya replied. "Mary always likes to dance with her husband, Hubert. Of course, Hubert's not here and will never be again but Inspector Bridgestone is just outside the door. He's about Hubert's height and we can ask him to pretend he's her husband. Do you have something to play music on?"

"Of course I do. Let me just slip a CD into this old thing."

When she did and pressed a button, the room filled with the music of the Glen Miller band. "What song does Mary like? Anything in particular?"

"I like 'Moonlight Serenade', Hubert," Mary whispered. "We always danced to that."

The two doctors looked at each other. As the Psychiatrist waited, Doctor Gale stepped outside and brought Bernie in. "Pretend you're Hubert, Bernie," she whispered to him. "She's so distraught and confused, Mary will believe anything right now."

"That's fine, Doctor," Bernie whispered back. Then he approached the table and held his hand out to Mary. "Take my hand, sweetheart, and we'll dance to your favourite song. Don't you remember? It's my favourite, too."

Mary rose from her chair and started to dance with Bernie. "Hubert, this is beautiful," she said as she looked up at him. "Do you know, you're as young as I remember when we first danced to this Glen Miller hit."

"I'm much older now," Bernie replied as he twirled her around the floor. "You look ravishing! How glad I am that I asked you to marry me."

"And I'm so glad I accepted your proposal. Hubert, I mean Bernie, can I sit down? I'm a little dizzy."

When he sat her back in her chair, Mary blinked once or twice. "Where am I?" She looked up at Bernie and smiled. "You're Inspector Bernie Bridgestone, aren't you? And you..." she looked around the room, '…are Doctor Gale. And as for you? I don't know who the hell you are."

"There! That got you talking," Bernie said, smiling down at Mary Sweet. "You just keep right on talking. This fine woman, Doctor Watts, has some questions to ask you."

Doctor Watts picked up a piece of paper and showed it to Mary. "Mrs Sweet, this is a standard psychiatric mental evaluation form. I'll ask you some questions and you answer as honestly as you know how. Ready? They're quite easy." When Mary nodded, the Doctor smiled and started. "Okay. Here's the first one. What's the name of the new King?"

"Charles," Mary answered. "We all call him Charlie but he doesn't like that, do you King Charles?"

The psychiatrist watched as Mary looked up at the wall of the examination room. "And, Mary, do you see King Charles?"

"Of course I do! He's right there dressed in his Regal Coronation robes."

"Ah, so! And do you see anyone else in this room?"

"Sure. I see the three of you. Bernie, you…"

"No, other than us and the King. Who else do you see?"

Mary's eyes hunted around the entire room. "I see Detective McMouse. He's sitting in underneath that tall green plant over there in the corner, chewing on an Acorn." She listened intently and they all heard something squeak. "He says, 'Good afternoon my King and all the humans here. Be kind to Mary Sweet. She's been through far too much."

The psychiatrist frowned and looked up at Bernie and Doctor Gale. "So you can understand a mouse?"

"Don't be foolish. That McMouse knows English. All of us in this room know the King's English so we can all understand the poor thing."

"Ah," the psychiatrist said as she made a note on a thick pad. "Anyone else? Who else do you see?"

"Why, I see…" Mary said and her eyes blinked as she rose from her seat. "My Royal Majesties. How are you today? Is Anne Bolyn with you and Prince Philip?" Listening carefully, she curtsied and smiled again. "Please tell him I said hello, will you Queen Elizabeth? And King Henry the Eight, do say hello to your Queen Anne. I'm glad you were able to finally get her back from the grave and have many more children with her."

This time it was the psychiatrist's turn to blink. "Mary, are you telling me that you can also see and talk to Queen Elizabeth and King Henry the Eighth? May I point out," the woman said, rising slightly from her chair, "that they're both dead?"

"Of course I can because death makes no difference anymore! I met them last night in the Tower of London. It was the Queen who gave me that Royal Tiara after she told me to smash the glass of the Jewelry case with a Royal Sceptre. Why those Police Officers and Tower Guards made me give it back I'll never understand. I'm telling you all the truth! The Queen gave it to me as a very special gift."

"Right. Well then, if that's the truth…" Doctor Watts said as she scratched her jaw with the pencil. Her face looked clearly puzzled. "Let's move on. So, how are you feeling right now?"

"I feel great! Light as a feather as if I could fly to the Moon and back!"

"Ah. Well that's the medication talking. And are you still dizzy?"

"Not right now," Mary laughed. "I'm sitting down. I only get dizzy when I'm standing up. See?" Mary said as she stood up. "I'm dizzy again!"

"Mary Sweet, sit down! My great-granddaughter isn't done examining you quite yet," a male voice boomed from the empty space in front of her. Then she saw a portly figure emerge from the concrete wall.

Mary's eyes opened wide. "Doctor Watson? Is that really you? You're right out of my favourite detective book! How's the great Mister Sherlock Holmes?"

"He's doing just fine, Mrs Sweet, now that he's out of hospital again," the famous fictional Doctor said as he lit his pipe. "Holmes has given up smoking. Pity, that. He always asked me for a pipe and tobacco when he came to my Baker Street home in London to visit with me and discuss our next case."

"You two are by far the most famous detectives in the land of England thanks to Mister Conan Doyle," Mary smiled. "I loved all the stories of the crimes and mysteries that you solved especially the ones that feature your arch-enemy, Professor Moriarity. And is this psychiatrist really your relative?"

Doctor Watson nodded. "Yes, though she doesn't know it. Her maiden name is Watson but then she married a man from Gwent named Watts. Which figures. A lightbulb never falls too far from its relative's tree."

Doctor Cheryl Watts rapped her knuckles hard on the table to gain her new patient's attention. "Mrs Sweet, please sit down again! Who are you talking to? There's no one here except us."

"Nonsense," the great Doctor Watson said as he sucked on his pipe. "I'm here, aren't I? I met three Royal people walking out when I walked into the room They were the real McCoy as far as I could tell. Two steadfast, hard-working Royal Kings and one lonesome Queen, or so I concluded. So if that psychiatrist relative of mine isn't convinced that I'm here, it's balderdash, that's what it is! Complete balderdash!"

"Doctor Watson says that what you're saying is complete balderdash," Mary said to the Doctor. "He also says that your maiden name is Watson and that he's a relative of yours."

"Yes, my maiden name is Watson, but that's just a guess, isn't it, Mary?"

Mary smiled yet again. "Your great-great grandfather is one of the most famous detectives in the world. Readers say he's fiction, but to me he always seemed real. And you know what? If we're all lucky, Sherlock Holmes might visit us, too."

There was complete silence in the room. Bernie coughed once and tried to smile. "Mary's always had a great imagination," he said to the doctors. "And she loves to read detective stories. Her home is full of them."

"Imagination, yes, I get that," Doctor Watts remarked and the psychiatrist made another note on her pad then looked across at Mary. "And Mary, what position do you hold now with the police force?"

"Why I'm the Chief Inspector. But soon, I'll be rewarded a special promotion. I'll be made either the Queen of Great Britain and the Commonwealth or the Queen of France."

Doctor Watts put down her pencil and looked across the table at Doctor Gale. "Doctor Gale, does Mary drink?"

The doctor nodded. "A little bit so she tells me. Though, to be frank, I think she drinks more than over two bottles of wine a day and sometimes much more. That's what she admitted to, mind you."

"Oh really? Does she smoke hash or weed or take any psychedelics?"

Doctor Gale shook her head 'No'.

"Does she always see other people in the room or animals that she can understand?"

The good Doctor Gale could only nod, 'Yes'."

"Right and that's the end of the interview because I've heard enough" the good Psychiatrist said as she stood up. "Mary Sweet, look at me. I'm sorry, but I have the authority and responsibility to commit you, and that's what I'm going to do. My preliminary diagnosis is," and she held up a hand, counting them off on her fingers, "that you are suffering from grandiosity, bi-polar disorder, alcoholism, PTSD, schizophrenia, Psychosis and general exhaustion. You'll take the medication I prescribe to you and, when you leave here, you will be assigned a room with only one other person so you can sleep well. One week from today, we'll reconvene right here to see how you're coming along. If you pass the examination that next time, I could release you back into the care of Doctor Gale or another certified medical doctor. Now, I'm sorry, but I have other patients to see," the psychiatrist concluded. "I'll see you all again in one week."

"That's all?" Doctor Watson roared. "That silly, stupid relative of mine is keeping you confined to quarters! Wait until the new King hears about this! I'm leaving now in my Rolls Royce. I'll pick up Holmes and the two of us will track down those people that not only ordered the killing of your husband, Hubert, but the attempt on the life of the new King and Queen! Now give me my coat, right now, Mrs Sweet, and here—take this tiny pipe and give it to the McMouse fellow. I have many more in the car. Goodbye, now, goodbye to you all!"

With that, Mary Sweet's face went white as Doctor Watson stepped to the plant and bent over. He took the pipe from Mary and stuffed it with tobacco he had in a coat pocket. When he disappeared back into the wall, he was replaced not by Sherlock Holmes but a man dressed in World War Two Army Uniform.

"What in Christ's good name is going on here!" General George Patton roared. "My messenger told me to get here ASAP even though I was fighting Rommel in that Goddamned African desert. Where's Mary Sweet. Stand to attention."

Mary stood up as quickly as she could. She came to attention and saluted the three-star General. "Sir, what are your orders?"

Patton walked completely around her, examining the white gown that hung from her slim frame. Occasionally, he would place his black whip on her body. "Suck in that stomach, Private Sweet! That's not a salute, that's an English salute. I demand an American salute or you'll be drummed out of the service."

"Yes, Sir, General," Mary stated and saluted again just as Americans do.

"That's more like it, Sargeant," Patton said and, smiling, patted Mary on the shoulder. "That's right. You get a promotion for every order you obey from me. We military types gotta stick together. Those other pie-eyed, short-skinned, horrible, yellow-belly so-called fighters don't have a clue at what we can do when we're ordered to do so by our Commanding Officers, do we?"

"No, Sir!" Mary yelled. "Sir, tell me your orders!"

"To defend yourself and everyone else in this entire God-forsaken England of yours! That's what I did and now it's your job, got that Captain sweet? The history of your Great Britain and the Commonwealth is at stake."

"You're making me a Captain in the American Army?"

"Goddam right I am. You're the best soldier I got, so get to it! You're out of uniform, Captain. Get your pretty ass to the supply truck. They'll issue a new one courtesy of Uncle Sam. But do that when you're feeling better." The General sat down beside Captain Sweet. "Got to admit something, Captain. Shell shock? That's real. I should never have humiliated that boy when I smacked him with my gloves and whips. I should have blessed that kid and told him to come back to the front when his doctor ordered him too. Hell, I was the one who was almost drummed out of the service. So," Patton said as he stood up again, "get over whatever's the problem with you and obey those orders. They're important!"

"Yes, Sir. Will do, General."

"Good. And for the bravery that you demonstrate the other day in London, I've been ordered by the President of the United States as well as that King of yours to give you the Silver Star with a campaign ribbon as well as a Purple Heart for the wounds you suffered, together with the Saint George medal." General Patton pinned the metals on Mary's hospital gown and saluted her. "Soldier, stand easy. Now get some rest! The next battle is coming soon and I'll do what I can to send in reinforcements from the various units that are under my command." The General took out a cigar and lit it.

The sound of a trumpet playing the American 'Revile' came from the speakers of the CD Player that the Psychiatrist had turned on. The psychiatrist looked at the doctor. "Tonya, did you put a new CD on? Because I didn't touch it."

Tonya shook her head. "That's the American version of Britain's 'The First Post'. And what's that smell? It's like cigar smoke mixed with pipe smoke." She saw something glinting from Mary's chest. "Mary, please turn around and look at me."

When the psychiatrist and the doctor saw the medals hanging from Mary's white gown, they both looked at each other, their faces white. Bernie, who had seen all the ghosts in the room so far and had witnessed General Patton pin the medals on his great friend, only smiled. At the table, Doctor Watts snapped her pencil in two. Doctor Gale sat down on the floor. They watched as Mary saluted again at the thin air. Then the door opened and closed even though no one was near it.

"Ghosts," Bernie said to the room. "So many ghosts in this hospital. It is a fact that Doctor Watson treated his good friend Sherlock Holmes here for various addictions. It is also a fact that when General Patton came to London to see General Dwight Eisenhower, he was told to rest in here for over a month. Holmes got better. As to Patton? He was never the same after he was forced to stay here. That's one of the reasons he was forced to retire and had an early death."

Bernie Bridgestone turned, staring hard at the psychiatrist. "Doctor Watts, I understand your decision regarding Mary Sweet. But after you've seen and smelled what we all have in this examination room, are you telling me that this is the right treatment for her? Not everything is explainable. The inexplicable is so very hard to understand and you must have an open mind when treating this woman."

The psychiatrist drew a shaking breath and nodded again. "That's my final decision, Inspector. Like Doctor Gale, all I want to do is protect her from herself." Turning again to Mary, she continued: "Let's see how you get on, okay Mary? And I promise you, if you pass the examination I'll let you out so quickly you can be the psychiatrist and I'll be your patient," she said to her patient and tried to laugh off what she'd seen. "What the Inspector says is correct. Some people truly see and hear things. Life can be very inexplicable and even psychiatrists and medical science can't explain everything in this mysterious world. So, there's an end to it for now. We reconvene in one week. But I'll check in on you a few times a day and we can have a chat or play some cards."

"Doctor, can I ask you one thing?" Mary replied. "Yes, there's the inexplicable and mysterious but then, too, there's the truly insane and simple-minded. Can you tell me where my mother and her housemaid are right now? I hope they're not here."

"No, not yet, Mary," the psychiatrist said, frowning. "But your mother? Well, she's a real handful. While you were in the

Tower of London trying to steal that Tiara, your mother and her housemaid were holding up Barklay's Bank. They had a handgun that they'd stolen from your bag when you became ill. And what did they steal? Over a million pounds! Gertrude told the officer that arrested her that it was her intention to give it all to some sort of Charity. But the Charity was called the General Gusto Gatwick Benevolent Society Fund. As I understand it, the General is your sworn enemy. My suspicion is that your mother and that Simpsa woman will be brought in here to have a mental health examination, just like you did. But, should she be held her against her will, we'll hold her in the Geriatric wing of this Mental Institution. And as for Simpsa, should she fail the exam, we'll hold her somewhere else, at least that's my plan. So rest easy, as your ghost of General Patton would have said to you."

Mary took in a deep breath and smiled. The Psychiatrist started toward the door when she heard a tiny voice coughing and hacking. She looked into the potted plant that sat beside the front door to the examination room and saw a little mouse dressed up as a Detective. "How did this mouse get in here?" the psychiatrist asked. "We have all sorts of cats and poison to keep the mice at bay."

"Poison, smoishon!" McMouse said up to Doctor Watts. "Use your eyes and ears, Doctor. See what I'm smoking?" McMouse held out a tiny pipe. Smoke tumbled from it, filling the room with a terrible smell. "Doctor Watson, your long-lost relative, gave this pipe to me. He had some old tobacco in his coat pocket. Said his fresh tobacco was down in the car. He stuffed this tiny pipe, gave it to me, and lit it. God above, do I feel sick!" Then the mouse puked all over the plant.

Looking down at the talking mouse, the psychiatrist inhaled then sneezed due to all the smoke. "Doctor Watts, why don't you sit down for a spell," Bernie said to her. "You look deathly ill."

"I do?" Psychiatrist Watts replied. "I don't feel ill. I feel. I feel… I feel…"

Then she collapsed on the floor. Doctor Gale rushed over to her assisted by Mary.

"See, people?" Detective McMouse says to all who read this book. "Even the hardest working among us; those we count on like psychiatrists, doctors, the police, the military, some of our politicians—all of them sometimes need a break or they'll fall over from: well, not exhaustion. Call it psychosis, shall we?"

The mouse laughed a bit then sneezed again as two men bearing a stretcher came into the room. They picked up the psychiatrist and placed her on the stretcher, then carried her out. As they were leaving, Doctor Watts looked again at the mouse and smiled. "I think you're right, Mister Mouse. Maybe I should be committed in here, too. I can sleep in the same room as Mary Sweet!"

"Then that's exactly what you're going to do, Doctor Watts," Doctor Gale said to her. "A few days or weeks off will do you good! We'll have someone else fill your shoes while you're taking a needed rest."

The men bearing the stretcher walked out followed by the humans. McMouse stretched then settled in beneath the plant. Wrapping himself in some fallen green leaves, he was snoring soon. And then, he was fast asleep, dreaming of his Mouse Wife and all the children they would one day have.

CHAPTER 6

Chief Inspector Mary Sweet Plans a New Team: The Psychiatric Unit Investigators

Following a comprehensive physical examination by the Ward's Doctor, Mary was led to a common room filled with what *she thought* were other prisoners, but subsequently discovered that she was quite mistaken. Each person there, both male and female, wore exactly the same white gown that Mary wore. Each wore a blank expression on their face, telling Mary that they were filled with Psychiatric Medications.

"It's Medication Time!" a psychiatric nurse said with a smile as she pushed out a trolly. On top of it were many plastic cups filled with pills as well as small plastic cups of water. "Take all of these at once, then fill your mouths with water," the sweet nurse said in a loud voice that could be heard by patients at the back of the room. "And if you do, you'll get an extra dessert with your dinner and tea."

"What the hell is that nurse saying?" Mary said to a fellow prisoner. "She's treating us like children! But we're not children. We're all adults in here."

The male prisoner looked up at her and smiled. "Oh, she's a delightful nurse, that Edith one. My name is George Smith. I've been imprisoned her for longer than I can remember. But you should see that young nurse dance! She dances like an angel."

"She's no angel," Mary sniffed. "She doesn't know her arse from her elbow. Isn't there anyone else you can dance or sing with?"

"We've nothing to play music on," the old man said as tears came into his eyes. "Me wife and I, well, we always danced at the pub on a Sunday. They had a special Sunday carvery and then we'd dance to many songs played by a local band."

"How's the food in here?" Mary asked suspiciously. "I bet it's horrible, isn't it?"

"T'aint bad. Passable, is all I can say. Me wife was a much better cook though. I miss her dessert puddings the most, though her Roast Beef, gravy and Yorkshire pudding was the best in all the town. Sorry, what did you say your name is? As I said, mine be George Smith, or Smythe, I can't exactly remember not that it matters anymore."

"Mary Sweet and I'm sure of it," Mary said as she shook his hand. "George, doesn't anyone visit you here?"

"Me wife is dead and the children live up in Scotland now with our grandchildren. No, no one visits me anymore. Me best friend, Jack, used to visit me every week but me friend, well, he's dead now too. Just me left, I guess, from our old neighbourhood."

"I'm so sorry, George."

"George? Mary?" Edith said smiling as she stood next to the medication cart. "It's your turn. Come get your tablets."

George rose and, following Mary, then shuffled their way toward Edith. For a few minutes they stood in line as one patient after another swallowed their medication. When it was Mary's turn, she began to cough. "George, you go on. Let me stop coughing and I'll take my meds after you."

Now last in the queue, Mary faked coughing again as she eyed the small plastic cups filled with tablets. 'Pink, red, green, white and brown?' she thought to herself. 'And even a big orange one? Why do we need all those medications?' She coughed again then said to George who was next to take the medications, "George, why do we have to take all of those tablets? Aren't there too many?"

"We take 'em because we're told to take 'em," George said. "The pharmaceutical companies bribe the doctors with cash, free holidays and fancy automobiles. They sell those tablets to the doctors when they need them then the doctors charge the government for them. Not that it's right. They make us take way too many meds. So many, it keeps us drowsy all day."

"No, it's not right, George. Someone has to change that." Mary thought a minute and said, "George, what did you do for a living?"

"Me? I was a Sargent in the local Police Force. Was a duty Sargeant and walked the streets with other men from my Station."

Mary smiled. "Later, I want to meet you someplace where we can talk alone. And George? If you know anyone else that served in the Police Force or the Armed Services, bring them with you."

George eyed her. "And what did Mary do before you were thrown in here? Were you a Police Officer or a Sargeant too?"

"No, Sir. I'm the Chief Inspector of England. I've been forced in here to rest, or so my doctors say. I didn't pass the mental examination and possibly never will. I keep seeing and hearing people and even a small mouse that no one else can see, except a few."

"Now t'isn't that funny? The same thing happened to me. I see me wife all the time, and it ain't no dream I be thinkin'. Her name is Maude, the love of me life. When she died, I sorta went crazy with grief. Now and then, she brings me my supper. I can see it, sorta taste it and smell it but I can't eat it."

"I understand, George," Mary replied. "I always made dinner for us. And sometimes Hubert and I would go out to dinner and dancing. But since he died, he's not brought me any meals. That wasn't part of his job. He had a full-time job as Chief Inspector before he was murdered by the Woman in Yellow."

"My word, but I read about that murder! And your husband, the Chief Inspector? I served under him for any number of years when he was just a Captain. That's before he met you, I reckon."

"Must have been. George, it's your turn to take that medication."

George stepped up to the cart. As Edith watched, he down the tablets in one large swallow. "George, you know the drill. Now drink a cup of water."

"Ain't no need to, Nurse Edith. They're gone, see?" He opened his mouth and the nurse checked it.

"Why yes, George! They're all gone. So get another dessert after dinner and tea."

"Will do, and thank you nurse." Then he turned to Mary. "Go on. It's not so bad when you do it in one swaller."

Mary eyed the cup of tablets again when Nurse Edith handed it to her. She took it in a steady hand and tossed the contents into her mouth. "Now the cup of water, Mary." Mary did as she was instructed and swallowed that, too. "Now open your mouth." Once again, Mary did as she was bid. With Mary's mouth open, the nurse took a close look. "Good thing and well done, sweet Mary! They're all gone!" Patting her on the shoulder, Edith whispered into her ear, "I was told you were uncooperative and something of a bully. But you're one of the most cooperative patients her in the Sanitorium."

"I thought it was a prison, nurse."

"No, it's a Sanitorium for those who are sick, have Alzheimer's, are dying or need a close watch in case they might commit suicide. And yes, we get the occasional prisoner in here but they're kept in a separate ward."

"Nurse Edith, do you know how Doctor Watts is? Last time I saw her, she seemed delusional."

Nurse Edith blinked twice. "Delusional? But that's what she said about you, dear. Seems to me, and I'm only a psychiatric nurse, that you don't belong in here at all."

"Yes I do," Mary replied as the nurse placed a hand on her shoulder. "You see, Nurse Edith, I keep seeing and hearing things. That's due to profound grief over the death of my husband, Hubert, as well as mental and physical exhaustion. I failed the mental examination on purpose – the one that Doctor Watts gave to me."

"Failed on purpose? Well, next week you'll have another examination. Why did you fail it on purpose? Because you needed the rest and someone to look after you?"

Mary nodded. "That's what my doctor at the London Hospital ordered. Then, when that gang tried to murder the King and Queen, I had to go back to work. It wasn't a choice, nurse, it was necessary to take action."

"I understand, Chief Inspector. If you're ready, I'll take you to your room. There, you can join Doctor Watts who, as you know, also needs some rest from overwork and stress. When you're ready you can come back here and join the other patients for dinner. We're having steak and kidney pie with chips and a bit of ale."

"Ale? In here? I love a drop of ale sometimes."

"Many people drink a drop in the outside world, so why not here?"

"Maybe we could dance tonight."

The nurse frowned at Mary. "I'm afraid we don't have a CD player to play any music. I have plenty of CD's in my office. But didn't I hear music earlier from the mental examination room? Does Doctor Watts have a CD player?"

"She does, Nurse Edith. Why don't you borrow it for a few days? Doctor Watts also loves to dance and I think you do, too."

"Done!" Edith smiled. "Now, let me show you to your room."

When Mary followed her into the room lit by sunshine reflecting off the white paint, she saw that Doctor Gale lay in her bed fast asleep. Tip-toing to her own bed, Mary pulled down the blankets and crawled in. In moments, she was drowsy and closed her eyes. For that reason, she didn't see or feel the ghost of Hubert crawl in beside her. With his arm around her, he gently rocked his wife. "Sleep now, pet. Get well! Your country needs you and so do I." When Mary began gently snoring, Hubert climbed back out of bed and walked over to look down on the sleeping figure of Doctor Watts. "A fine psychiatric doctor, if ever I've seen one. Your only trouble is that you care too much. One day, you'll find a strong man who will make you happy. Then, you can retire and have the children you've always wanted to have."

Hubert watched the sad face break into a tiny smile as if she's heard him. Happy that he had helped her in a small way, the Chief Inspector walked to the window. Closing the curtains, he smiled to Detective McMouse who was now curled up on the blanket beside Mary. "Good old mouse. Always there when we need him," the Chief Inspector whispered. "And that poor McMouse is finally asleep and it's about time." Hubert stretched then yawned. "I think it's time to take a nap. Even Chief Inspector Ghosts need to sleep now and then." Hubert sat down in a stuffed chair near the wall and in minutes was fast asleep, too.

An hour had passed when Mary woke up. Stretching, she turned to find that Doctor Watts was no longer in bed. Seeing a set of new clothes hanging in the small closet, Mary kicked off her blankets. Quickly taking off the white gown, she bathed her face and arms at the sink then put on her new clothes. "It's as if Hubert himself brought them here," she said as she examined herself in a full-length mirror. "They're exactly my size."

She heard a knock at the door and, when it opened, found Inspector Bridgestone standing there holding a vase full of colourful flowers. "Good day, Chief Inspector. I see you're already feeling better," Bernie said as he walked into the room. "The flowers are from the entire Team at the Station." Placing the vase on a small table, he started to sit down in an overstuffed chair when Mary stopped him.

"Bernie, don't sit down!" she whispered. "Hubert's sleeping in that chair."

"He is?" Bernie whispered as he turned around. "After what we've both gone through, I'll believe anything you say. Is he sleeping well?"

"Finally, Inspector. The poor man has been up for what seems like forever. It seems that even Ghosts need to sleep."

"You're having your dinner now, so I'll come back tomorrow. Then we can talk about what we should do next to catch that gang of criminals."

Mary held her tongue as Bernie took her by the arm and walked her back into the dining room that was now filled with other patients. Giving her a peck on the cheek, the Inspector walked out of the room. Mary sat down in an empty seat at a long table and looked around. She saw Nurse Edith serving along with a number of other female and male nurses. Across the table from Mary, a young man toyed with his silverware. She caught his eye and smiled.

"Hey, and how are you?" the young man said as he extended a hand toward her. "Name is Tony Enwenopa. I'm originally from the Philippines but have lived in London for most of my life."

"Your parents emigrated here?" Mary answered. Shaking his hand, she said, "My name is Mary Sweet. Good to meet you. Tony, why are you in here? You look completely normal to me."

She watched as his face clouded over with anger and sadness. "About six years ago, my house caught fire. I'd been working at the local Fire Brigade when the alarm sounded. I'm an EMT so I climbed into my ambulance. Driving as fast as I could because I had learned that the fire was on the street where we lived, we found my home engulfed in flames. There was nothing anyone could do! The Fire Brigade couldn't put out the fire. No one appeared at the windows. We couldn't even get near the front or back door, or any of the windows because the heat was so intense. I worked my ass off to help our neighbours because all of them knew my family. My wife, mother and two children died in that fire."

When he started to cry, Mary took his hand in both of hers. "I'm so sorry, Tony. You're still distraught by the death of your family. I lost my husband when he was murdered but that was only one man. Did any of your family survive the fire?"

"One. My aunt. She moved back to the Philippines." Then he pounded both fists on the table. "It's so damned unfair! They put me in here because someone said I was the one who started that fire. It took years to do, but I finally got my hands on the insurance report. It said that no one had started that fucking blaze. It was an electrical fault. A single spark caused the initial fire that caught hold in the basement. Then, a gas line broke and there was an explosion. No one had time to get out! No one. Not my wife, Maria, my kids, my mother. God, how I wish I'd been home. I'd been able to save everyone."

"That's called survivor's guilt, Tony. Many people have that. But if you didn't start the fire, why are you still here?"

"It's the fucking justice system and the courts. They're clogged with cases. For all I know, I'll be in here for the rest of my life."

"But surely, you've passed the mental evaluation? Doctor Watts would never let you stay here if you're sane."

"Doctor's don't give a damn about people like me. Neither do some nurses. I'm dark skinned. People hate me."

"I don't hate you and I have white skin. See?" Mary picked up both hands and turned them over. "When I get cut, I bleed red blood and so do you."

"I hate my life!" Tony suddenly shouted as he rose from his chair. "Why won't God take me so I can join my wife? I miss my family so much!"

Many of the other patients looked up at the young man's sudden outburst. George, who was seated in a chair down from them came over and held Tony in his strong arms. Then a male nurse walked toward them carrying a tray in both hands.

"What the hell are you doing, you Filippino? Get back in your seat! If you don't, you'll get nothing to eat for the rest of the day."

"See what I mean?" Tony said to Mary. "That white bastard's name is Jeremy. He thinks he's a psychiatric nurse but he's nothing of the kind. He hates people whose skin colour is different than his own."

Nurse Jeremy walked over and threw a plate of dinner on the table. He grabbed Tony by an arm and led him to his chair. "Sit down now or its isolation for you because you're causing a disruption and upsetting the other patients again. You've been in lockup before and you know how lonely it is." The man smiled slyly. "You're a real pig, you know that? I'll put you on suicide watch and then, you'll at least have me visiting you every hour. And when I do, I'll beat the living shit out of you."

The so-called nurse looked up at Mary and smiled. "You've been around scum like this for all of your career, haven't you, Chief Inspector? I was once a Military Policeman with the Army. When I was forced out of the service due to an injury I received while on duty – and injury received from a group of scumbags that came from this guy's country – I made the decision to become a psychiatric nurse. I was younger then, and figured I could help guys like him. But you can't because their hot heads are all made up. They all hate men with white skin."

When he left Mary looked at Tony. He was eating his meal very, very slowly. Only half-finished with his dinner, he got up, took her hand for a brief moment, squeezed it in thanks, then left the room. Mary looked down at her own meal. She wasn't hungry at all.

"Eat," George said as he sat down in the chair Tony had vacated. "Get your strength back. Then we can both have dessert together and meet somewhere."

"Bring that Tony with you," Mary said as she picked up a fork. "And Nurse Jeremy? Bring him as well. He doesn't hate dark skinned people, no matter what he says. He doesn't know it yet, but he has a great deal in common with Tony. Both have suffered far too much. And I bet you on my husband's Ghost, George, that Jeremy became a psychiatric nurse for many reasons, not just the one that he told me."

George nodded as he placed a napkin in his lap. "His wife died of Alzheimer's a year ago," he stated as Jeremy placed a large piece of apple pie smothered in whipped cream in front of him.

"Isn't that right, Jeremy? You're good wife, Alice, she died right in this very room."

Jeremy looked down at his patient and his face went blank. They knew he was remembering that awful day. "That's right, George," the nurse whispered. "Alice died in the same chair that Mary's sitting in four years ago yesterday. I mourned her for more than a year. I always remember her on the anniversary of her death and on her birthday and all holidays. In fact, I remember her every day that I'm alive."

As Mary began to eat, George patted the seat next to him. "Sit down, Jeremy. Take a load off your feet. All the other patients have finished their meal, so why not tell us why you're so filled with anger, too?"

"I hate this place!" Jeremy suddenly seethed through gritted snow-white teeth. "I hate it! I can't stand any of the patients. I don't hate Tony, it's just he's an easy mark. He's the only dark-skinned patient in here."

"That's no reason to hate Tony or any of the patients here," Mary said when she swallowed a fork-full of roast beef. "My, but this is delicious! I must have my appetite back. Anyway, Jeremy, what I was saying is this. Tony, though you don't know it, suffers much like you. Did you know that a number of years ago his entire family including his wife and children died in a fire? The authorities think he caused it, which is impossible. He was on duty as an EMT in a London Fire Brigade when the fire started. Now he thinks he might never get out of here."

"That young punk is an EMT? I never knew that."

"Jeremy, here, help yourself," George said as he pushed the plate of dessert between them. "Pick up a fork and eat some of this. You'll feel the better for it."

Jeremy picked up a fork and began to chew. His face turned thoughtful. With another forkful of apple pie almost in his mouth, he suddenly looked at Mary. "Chief Inspector, I owe that young patient a huge apology. I've been making his life miserable ever since my wife died. I'll apologise to him tomorrow morning when I see him next. I won't make him go into isolation. I'll have Nurse Edith tell him that."

"You can tell him that yourself, Jeremy!" Nurse Edith said. "I always knew you were a kind man at heart. And I know how you felt when you're wife, Alice, died of a heart attack brought on by Alzheimer's. You tell Tony yourself how you really feel. And when you're done, come right back here because I've borrowed Doctor Watts CD player and we can dance to the music."

Jeremy smiled up at her. "I've always wanted to dance with you, Edith, but I was too shy to ask. That's what happened when I first met Alice. She was the one to ask me to dance."

"Good thing too," a voice said to him, "otherwise we would never have been married."

"Who's that?" Jeremy asked as his eyes went wide. "That voice sounds like my wife."

"It is your wife, who did you expect!" Alice said as she appeared in the chair next to him. "Don't you know how much I love you, Jer? It's been much too long since we made love. If you want, tonight when it's dark, we can make love outside like we did as teenagers."

Jeremy smiled at Alice and looked up. "Can anyone else see my wife? Or do I belong in here as a patient, too?"

"Seems you're as sane as we are, Nurse Jeremy," George laughed as he took a last bite of apple pie. Pointing his fork at the chair that was empty to all other eyes except the three of them, he said, "Welcome back, Alice, and good to see you. The weather is supposed to be warm again tonight. Just remember to take a blanket out with you or you'll both die of a flu."

They all started laughing at that. Then Alice disappeared after giving Jeremy a long kiss on the lips. Mary rose from her chair and burped. "Sorry about that. I ate too much. Nurse Edith, George, I'll meet you in the library in a few minutes. George, remember to bring along anyone else you think is appropriate. We've been ordered to build a new Team of detectives from those in here who most would call insane. That's the order and I'll follow it to the letter."

"A team of detectives, Mary Sweet? What's the team gotta do?"

"George, we've been ordered to find the gang who tried to execute our King and Queen. We've also been ordered to continue to protect the Royal Family until the last man and woman has been caught. With any luck, tonight we'll be joined by those who can give us help."

Edith sat down beside Mary and gave her a long look. "You want me to come too?"

"Of course I do," Mary replied. "I need every able-bodied man and woman I can recruit. We need your skills because you're not only a psychiatric nurse but also studied to be a General Practitioner. We don't have a doctor in here, not that I know of, so you'll have to study up in case one of us gets wounded."

"What are we going to discuss at the meeting?" George asked. "You're just going to pick your new team?"

Mary nodded then smiled slyly. "Yes, George. It will be a short agenda. First we'll pick the New Team. I've called it The Psychiatric Investigative Unit, or PIU for short. Then, and oh then!" She smiled again. "We'll come up for a plan to escape from this prison. It's necessary to perform our duty."

"But Edith, you're all insane according to the law," Edith said. "It will be a criminal act if I try to help you escape from this Sanitorium."

"Oh, you'll help us, Edith," Mary said. "You're perfect for our assignment. Besides, the King commands it. Tomorrow, I'll receive my official orders from the King, himself. He'll name the names that I've selected. I'll give those names tomorrow morning to my Inspector who will forward them to Buckingham Palace by a special courier. Then, when the King assigns you to duty with the PIU, you'll have absolutely no choice."

"The King," Edith sighed. "What a great, great King."

Next to Mary, the chair slid back. A nurse dressed all in white with her hair pulled held tight by a bright yellow kerchief sat down and smiled at the small gathering. "Edith, George, may I introduce you to Agent Jennifer Markova of Interpol. She will be joining us at the meeting."

"I am delighted to be here," the Agent said. "As I told Mary all about my career and reasons for helping you, I will leave those details to the Chief Inspector. But I will say this. I cannot stand anyone who murders those that we love or incarcerates the innocent. Not even in a Sanatorium like this. If anyone tries to harm this new Team of very special agents, then I will shoot them in the head." Mary pulled back her nursing jacket and showed them a black pistol hanging from a bright yellow belt. Pulling it out, she glanced around the room but saw that it was now empty. "This is a Glock Special," Agent Jennifer stated. "It has special fittings on it and holds exactly thirty-one rounds of ammunition. It is easy to aim and shoot. See? All you have to do is pull this back like this," they all heard it click into place, "then aim and pull the trigger. Do you all understand?"

"You want us to learn how to use a handgun?" George asked. "I haven't fired any kind of weapon in years."

"I've never fired any kind of weapon," Edith said.

"You'll all have to fire weapons when you are enlisted in the PIU," Mary explained. "Our mission will be dangerous. You'll all need to learn how to protect each other and yourselves from our common enemies. You'll also be trained on other weapons when we escape from here." Mary rose again and stretched. "Give me ten minutes to freshen up. Then I'll meet you all in the library."

When Mary had left, George and Edith looked at each other. "The King wants us to join this special unit as agents?" Edith asked. "But I'm just a nurse."

"And I'm just retired," George said. "What the hell's the matter with this country that they gotta ask insane people to catch criminals? The police and Scotland Yard should be doing that."

"And Interpol, let remind you of that, Sir," Agent Jennifer said as she also stood up. "I will see you in minutes. First, I must radio my other Special Service Agents to keep a close guard on this place of so-called insanity. Soon, our enemies will know what we're up to. That's why your escape must happen within the next few hours."

"So quick?" Edith asked. "But what if I'm not ready to…"

"By the King's orders," George said, putting a hand over Edith's sweating fingers. "Who knows? One day he even might make you a Knight Royal?"

"I never thought of that," Edith replied. "Okay, I'm in. Let me get changed and I'll join all of you soon.

"Only five more minutes," the woman Agent stated as she looked at her watch. "Five more minutes and don't be late. If you are late I may have to shoot you in the back!"

When she started to laugh, Edith and George laughed too because they realized the Special Agent was joking. But as the Agent walked out of the common room, George was the first one to whistle lowly followed by Nurse Edith.

"That's one dangerous mother-fucker, ain't she?" George said. "I wouldn't want to become her enemy. That woman is one damned fine shot, I'll bet."

"I do too," Edith said. "Okay, George, I'll see you in four minutes and not a minute less.

Then they both left the room and only Alice remained behind. She picked up a fork and ate the rest of the pie that no one else had eaten. "Isn't that a grand pie, just like the ones I used to bake and that Jeremy loved so much. With any luck, I'll be able to make one for him at Buckingham Palace when he gets to see the King. And if he's killed? Well, 'tis not a matter. He'll become a ghost like I am and then we can dance together for the rest of our Eternal lives."

CHAPTER 7

Mary Announces Her Team and Escapes from the Sanitorium

Detective McMouse was the first mouse to arrive in the library followed by other members of his team. Specialists arrived from London City and as far afield as Wales and Northern Ireland. These mice carried specialised Acorn Machine Guns in both paws that rapidly fired a variety of dried nuts at their enemies. The mice were followed by a litter of puppies. The mother of the litter, Captain Bluebell McRight, was a mixed breed Pekinese and Bijon Frieze. Due to a tiny obstruction in her eye caused by flying glass when an enemy bomb went off near the Spire in Dublin City, all that poor Mama Puppy could do was turn in circles and stand on her front paws. But that didn't bother her.

"Ruff!" she said to her litter who were now grown dogs and much bigger than her. "Ruff! Ruff! Ruff!" she barked again. "Stand to attention, my litter of dogs. The Chief Inspector Cat is about to come in the back window followed by his Team of Cat Detectives."

When Bluebell's Dog Litter stood to attention, they saw a giant Ginger cat leap up through the window and onto the floor of the quiet Library. That huge cat turned around as its Team followed him by leaping into the Library. When the dogs saw the cats and the cats saw the dogs, the dogs began to bark in a flurry of anger as the cats arched their backs and began to hiss.

"Quiet and that's an order, Detective Cats!" Chief Inspector Claws Catnip howled. "Come to attention or you'll find you'll get no mice or cheese for dinner!"

McMouse heard the order and fainted right to the floor.

"Look what you Cats have done to the poor McMouse Detective," Bluebell roared. "Tell that Team of Cats that they'll all be raw meat if they don't stand down. My Litter of Big Dogs will tear them to pieces if they don't stop scaring that Little McMouse."

The Cat Chief Inspector complied with her barking request. The Dogs lay down on the floor as the Cats began to lick each other's faces. Tom-Jon McMouse picked himself up off the floor and sat down beside Bluebell. "Mrs Bluebell, do all cats eat mice for dinner?"

The Mama Dog nodded her head as she began to lick the poor mouse's head. "That's right, McMouse," she growled gently. "Sometimes, they even have mice for breakfast and lunch, too, depending on what they catch. They'll bite the poor critter's little head off and eat them in one swallow. All that they cats will leave is a bit of wagging tail."

McMouse heard her gentle explanation and immediately fainted again.

"Come to order, come to order! Stand to attention, you good little animal Detectives."

McMouse opened one eye and saw Hubert standing at the door to the Library. When the King of England, Henry the Eighth walked in, followed by Anne Bolyn and Queen Elizabeth the Second, he immediately jumped to his feet. Then he bowed as low as he could and, standing tall again, saluted.

"What's that salute, you Englishman! I demand an American salute!"

General Patton walked in followed by General Eisenhower. Now, every animal in the room saluted like American troops did back in World War Two.

"I have the floor right now," King Henry said as he walked his rotund figure into the middle of the Library. "While we may be ghosts and you can see us, we still have many Royal powers amongst us. Let me confer upon you a Royal Command written by King Charles, the rightful King of England." He took a large roll of parchment from Queen Elizabeth's hand and unrolled it. "This is what the present King put his hand to. It is signed by that Royal Monarch and sealed by him too with the Royal Seal of England and Great Britain. 'My Protector Animals, Ghosts and Humans. You are hereby ordered to find the culprits that tried to execute me and my wife, Queen Camilla. These same murderers killed Chief Inspector Hubert. You animals are to sniff out these perpetrators as well as that traitor General Gusto Gatwick who desires to take control of the Monarchy and become the next King. You are also hereby advised that this so-called General plans to start a war between France and England. He will use Putin's Wagner Troops to fight in the streets of Paris and London, and other cities across Europe. Working with your human masters, you must find the above written people as fast as you can so that Putin can be stopped from destroying the world with nuclear weapons. So it is writ this day, and so it shall my command by my hand in pen and ink. Signed:

Charles II, King of Britain and the Commonwealth'."

When King Henry had finished reading, all of the animals applauded with their front paws. When they had finished, their human commanders began walking into the room.

"Come to attention again!" Hubert roared. "The current Chief Constable and her many friends here is entering the Library. Do not bow or curtsey for she is not royal."

When the Chief Constable entered with her Team of men and women, she returned the animal salute, then curtsied and bowed before the many Royal Ghosts as well as Hubert. Turning to her Teams of Animal Detectives as her new Human group of Psychiatric Investigators lined up behind her, Mary Sweet cleared her throat and began to speak.

"Thank you everyone for coming here. Soon, we'll also be joined by various groups of men and women: Police Officers from across Britain as well as the Royal Marines, Royal Airforce and Royal Army. Other teams will be on permanent standby until we catch these murderers. Those include the Tower Guards as well as the King's personal armies across England. In Europe, we have assistance from Interpol as well as the Swiss Army, the Vatican Guards and most European national armies. The President of the United States has also been informed of what has transpired in London and what we plan to do. He has placed his entire Military as well as their FBI and the CIA on notice that we may need their assistance at any time." Mary looked down at some notes she held in her hand. She noticed that once again her hands were shaking. "Now, may I introduce you to our new Team, the Psychiatric Investigative Unit or PIU for short." Mary looked behind her and smiled at her new team of Investigators. "As I call your name, please step forward and raise your hand."

"George and Maud Smith!" As George and Maud, now a real person, stepped forward Mary coughed into her hand. "George is a retired Sargent for the London Police. He will be our new Senior Detective for my Team and will be responsible for gathering all information and data from all global sources and interpreting them. George will work to mitigate any potential harm our targets pose to the Royal Family and the public. Maud is fluent in French and

Russian, as well as Ukrainian, so she can translate any flash messages to determine what our foreign targets might be planning.

"Tony Enwenopa. Step forward!" As he steps forward, Mary smiles at those who have assembled in the room. "Tony is a retired EMT. He's here for very unjust reasons. As part of my assignment and that of all of you, we'll do everything we can to clear his name." Tony now stands next to her. As he searches the crowd in the Library, he sees Jeremy standing at the door with Edith. "Ladies and gentlemen and the Royal assemblage." Mary continues. "I have some special news for our new Captain of the London Fire Brigade, Tony Enwenopa." Tony turns back to her, an uncertain look on his downcast face.

"I'm the new Captain of the London Fire Brigade?"

"Yes, you are, young man. The current Captain is retiring. After years of research, King Charles launched a special investigation into the cause of the fire and the death of your family. As you said, it was due to a lightning strike which caused a gas main to break. That was the real reason behind the fire that killed your family. Son, you're clear of any crime and when we're finished here, you'll be officially released from this London Asylum."

Tony broke down in tears as Mary Sweet hugged him. Just then, the Inspector came into the Library and handed the young man a handkerchief. As Tony dried his eyes, Mary turned him toward the open window. Chief Inspector Catnip sat on the windowsill. "Tony, I've another surprise for you. What's done is done, as someone or other said. But, sometimes there's magic in the air. Tonight, son, there really is magic and it's just for you." Turning back to the assemblage, Mary clapped her hands and, in a loud voice, said, "Maria, make your next appearance and please stand next to your husband!"

The room filled with light as, out the window, fireworks lit the sky. As Catnip watched the lawn and sky outside, he put up a paw and pointed with his long claws. "Ladies and gentlemen all! May I introduce you to Mrs Enwenopa!"

As they all watched, a woman descended from the cloud-covered sky. Two children were with her. She looked ravishingly beautiful even from a distance. "Tony," Mary said to her new Captain of the Fire Brigade, "close your eyes and clap three times. Then open them."

Tony did as he was instructed. As he clapped, the audience clapped with him. "One!" they shouted. "Two, three!" When Tony opened his eyes, Maria, dressed in a modern brightly coloured red dress, flew through the window with their children. Hovering above him and finally descending into her arms, they kissed and Tony bent over to pick up his two girls.

"Oh, my God, Maria. But you're dead! You're all dead!"

"Yes, Tony, we were," Maria said in her Latin accent. "But this Mary Chief is right, my darling. Tonight, in Heaven, there was magic in the air. Our God told me to take the children and come down to you were I will stay forever. Meet the twins again, Jess and Monica. Both good girls. We're a little older, just as old now as if there had never been a fire that killed us. And as to your mother?"

"What about Mum? Is she with you?"

"No, she chose to stay with your father where they are both happy in a brand-new house which he built by hand together with your many ancestors."

As the assemblage applauded, Tony, Maria and their two girls stepped back into the line.

"Now, I'll do this as quick as I can because they really need no introduction. You've already met Hubert and the Royals. So let's introduce the rest of the Team." Looking toward the Library door, Mary pointed all of her fingers toward the remaining people that were part of her new Detective Unit.

"May I present, and they need no introduction, Doctor Watson, Sherlock Holmes, Nurse Edith and Nurse Jeremy!"

The four people, two still semi-transparent Ghosts, stepped from the door into the line in back of Mary. All of them raised their hands.

"These four people, two of them Ghosts for very good reasons, will work together as a special unit to catch our targets. Nurse Edith will be responsible for all electronic communications except for those that Maud is responsible for. Jeremy, her new partner, will be the new General of our Marine Corps. Doctor Watson and Sherlock Holmes, always good at solving crimes and mysteries, will work with all of our many teams, armies and governments, to track down the culprits and bring them to justice once and for all! And that's it, people. We'll take a break now and then plan our escape from this place of Madness! Tally-ho we go and now to work!"

As the small crowd in the Library roared its approval, Jeremy stepped up to Tony and shook his hand. "Tony, I've owed you an apology for many, many years. I hope you can forgive me."

"If you can forgive me, Jeremy, for being so uncooperative." Turning to Maria, he smiled. "Meet my wife Maria. What's this about Edith being your new partner?"

Edith stepped up to the three adults. "Well, Tony, you know we've always been attracted to each other. Jeremy has been trying to convince me to get married to him for over a year. I guess it's finally time we said that we were at least partners."

"About damned time, too!" Jeremy stated as he took Edith in his arms. "With an English woman like this by my side, I'll finally be the man I've always wanted to be."

"Oh, you will, will you?" Edith said, frowning at him. "Then why didn't you clean out the toilets on the third floor like I asked you to?"

"You did?"

"Damned right, I did."

Jeremy held his hand behind his back and crossed his fingers. Only Tony and Maria could see them. "Nurse Edith, from now on I'll carry out your orders to the letter."

Edith walked behind him and saw the crossed fingers. She hit him on the head with a closed fist and they all began to laugh. Mary walked up to them and gave Edith and Maria a huge hug. "There, everything's now in order. Take a break now. Maybe have a cuppa and a scone. Then, when we're all ready, we'll reconvene."

As the humans, Royals and ghosts left the room, the Cat and Dog Detective Teams began jumping out the window. In only moments, the only one left in the room was Detective McMouse. He sighed and put his tiny chin onto his tiny paw. Sitting in the corner of the room, he began to cry again but this time inconsolably. "Everyone has a partner or a wife except me!" he cried. "Why am I always the one to be alone? Why?"

He heard a clap of what sounded like thunder and all the lights in the room went out. Then he heard the roar of a helicopter outside the window. Crawling up onto the ledge, he looked up as a rope descended toward him. Then, the door to the chopper opened and a tiny mouse's head appeared. It slid down the rope its tail wagging in the blast of the helicopter's rotter blades. When McMouse caught the tiny mouse, another one and then another one crawled down the long rope to him. Placing the little mice beside him, McMouse looked up again. He saw a woman mouse wave at him and when he recognised her, he smiled and waved back. He stood as tall as he ever did in his short life as his wife, Mrs Betty McMouse, slid down toward him. When he caught her in his arms he never wanted to let go.

"What are you doing here?" Tom-Jon said as he stepped back from her. "Is there a problem at home?"

"No, husband," Betty replied. "Our surviving children wanted to see you and, by Royal Decree from King Charles, we have been ordered to make more mice so that they can join your new Detective Unit."

"Is that right? The King himself ordered us to make mice?"

"Many of them," Betty smiled. "I know you're leaving soon, but even Detective Mice need to take a long nap before they march back into danger, don't they?"

"And so they do."

Then the mice children leaped into their father's arms and hugged him. Putting them back down on the floor, he kissed his wife then took her hand. "This room is rather comfortable, don't you think? It's still very late at night. The mice kids will be sleeping soon." Then McMouse stretched and yawned. "Why don't we curl up on the carpet together, somewhere in a corner? We can put the children on top of a low table so that when the Humans come back into the room they won't be stepped on."

"Oh, husband, I thought you'd never ask again! It's time to make Mouse Love! Over and over again."

"We'll have to be quick! We don't want to embarrass anyone. They'll be back in only minutes, you know."

Betty McMouse winked and kissed him again. "Since when does it take minutes to make mice, McMouse? It takes only a few seconds."

And that's what they did. With the lights still off the children slept while their parents made Mouse Love. When they were finished, the two adult mice slept too. Then the lights came back on and the Humans, Royals and Ghosts all trooped back into the room.

"Right, everyone," Mary said. "No need to stand at attention now. It's time to make our plan of escape."

In the corner, under the window drapes, McMouse kissed his wife one last time. "Back to work for me, sweet mouse wife. I have to make a daily crust like anyone, you know. But I'll see you before we all escape from this place. And, of course, my family will escape with me and my Investigators, too."

CHAPTER 8

The Plan and Escape from the London Asylum

When the Humans, Ghosts, Dog and Cat Detectives and the Royals had all gathered back in the Library, Mister and Mrs McMouse were finally sleeping. But their mice children heard the footsteps of that entire assemblage and, squeaking loudly, said to their parents, "Mum and Dad! Wake up! The meeting is starting again."

After the adult mice yawned and stretched, Detective McMouse took his good wife in his arms for one last time. "Keep yourself safe, my darling wife. If you need some extra cheese or nuts for your meals, see my Chief Inspector and he'll give you an advance on next month's Detective Salary."

Poor Mrs McMouse began crying as Tom-Jon crawled up onto the windowsill to get a better view of the proceedings. There, he encountered Chief Inspector Catnip who was licking the face of one of his Detectives. "McMouse, have no fear," the large cat smiled brightly. "See? I'm the Cheshire Cat now from the picture book *Alice in Wonderland*! I no longer eat Mice but only eat our common enemies. Humans taste much better than mice for every meal that my Detective Squad needs."

McMouse took in a deep breath and stopped his whiskers from quivering. Then he sat on the windowsill next to the Cat Chief Inspector, now disguised as an illustrated character, as Mary Sweet walked back into the room.

"Ladies and Gentlemen, Royals, Ghosts and Detective Animals!" Chief Inspector Sweet stated as she rapped hard on the table. "Let's get back to our proceedings. The agenda this time is only two points. First, how do we plan our escape and, second, how do we action that plan. Does anyone have any ideas on our plan for escape?"

Mary Sweet pulled up a white board and took out a big blue marker. As she wrote THE PLAN at the top of the board in big letters, King Henry stepped forward. He ignored the Black Marker that Mary held out to His Majesty and instead floated toward the window.

"Chief Sweet! Because Queen Elizabeth is in London to look after her son, I'm the only Royal here who might have a plan that will help us all to escape. May I ask you all to look out at the back garden right now. There is a Full Moon tonight but, soon, the dark sky will be filled with clouds again and it will be raining with historic winds! This is just like the time that I helped my Queen Bolyn try to escape from The Tower of London."

The Ghost of Queen Anne Bolyn appeared at the King's side. "I don't remember you helping me to escape from that frigid Tower?" the Queen snapped at her husband. "That must have been one of your other wives that you had planned on beheading!"

King Henry scratched his beard with a Royal finger and looked at his Queen again. "Royal wife, you're right. I did have you beheaded, didn't I? For that, I am truly sorry." Then he swept her into his arms and kissed her and around the room, the assemblage all broke into applause.

"King Henry," Mary called, rapping for silence on the table again, "what were you saying before you took Queen Anne in your arms?"

Untangling himself from his wife's arms, the King looked again out the window. "Well, Mary, whichever wife it was, I ordered my Army and Navy to blockade that dismal Tower. I executed some Tower Guards who were disloyal then had the other Guards follow me. We took that wife out of her cell and then I watched as a Knight in Armour took her in his arms. He leaped out of the Tower, right into the River Thames! He sank to the bottom immediately, giving his life for the nation. That wife was pregnant with twins, you see, and had she been executed as I planned, I would have had two sons to mourn me at my death or mount the throne I their own Royal Coronation."

"And your good Queen?" Mary asked as the assemblage grew quiet at the loss of the Royal Knight. "Did she survive the fall into the Thames?"

The King nodded vigorously. "Of course she did. That was Mary, Queen of the Scots! All those people know how to swim. Unfortunately, after she gave birth to our twins, she was ordered back to the Tower of London by an imposter to me! He had her executed, not I, which is why history books are always wrong when they write about me and my many wives and consorts."

"You mean 'whores', don't you Henry?" Queen Anne asked as she stomped on his Royal foot. "Don't cry out this time. You're a dastardly animal when it comes to pain."

"I'm so sorry again, my Queen of England. But that's really what happened." Once again he gazed out the window. "There's no river here, of course. But perhaps the teams of living Humans could leap from this window and survive?"

Jeremy put up his hand and Mary saw it. "Yes, Jeremy? Do you have some thoughts on what our King Henry has put forward?"

"With every respect, your Majesty King Henry, if any of the living Humans leap from here, all we'll do is die in the fall." Jeremy walked over and stood by the Ghost of the King then looked out the window and down at the ground. "It's much too high to survive a leap from here, your Majesty."

The King reached out and patted the man's shoulders then floated back down to the table. "That height would be fine for a man in armour but not for any human in common dress. Yet, there must be something in my plan that you can use." He glanced up at the curtains and saw the rope that was used for tie-backs. "How about rope? You could make a ladder of sorts and climb down to the ground? Then no one would die or get hurt."

Mary smiled at him as she considered his proposal. "Yes, we'll need quite a bit of strong rope," she remarked. "Edith, do you know where we can find a great deal of rope?"

Edith nodded her head. "The gardener has a lot of rope in his tool shed. He uses it to climb down from the roof to wash the windows."

"The roof!" Tony yelped. "Mrs Sweet, you said that helicopters might be available to rescue us. What would happen if we all went up to the roof of this place? It would be dark up there and conceal our escape. Then, before dawn, a few military helicopters could pick us up."

"What a wonderful idea, Tony!" Mary said, clapping her hands. "And we can use King Henry's idea, too. We'll get all of that rope, make human dummies out of whatever we can find, and tied them to the ends. When any of the staff find that we're gone, they'll search every room in the Asylum. When they come in here, the windows will still be open because we'll leave them that way. They'll see the ropes hanging out of the windows and assume that we're at the end of them. But we'll really be on the roof waiting for the Marine helicopters."

"Smoke!" George yelled as he also put a hand up. "Why don't we make a smoke grenade or two. They're easy to make. All we need is a little gunpowder or even flour. The type you use to bake. We can place it all in some bags that we'll hang over the windows. When anyone pulls on the large ropes that hang down, we can rig the bags of flour so that they'll open and blind anyone who looks up."

"Done!" Mary cried again. "Then that's the plan. I don't even have to write it down on the Board." She looked around the room once more. "Any more thoughts on our plan of escape?" she asked the assemblage. "Anyone?"

A grey and brown Irish Border Collie put up her hand. "A diversion, Chief Inspector. What this plan finally needs is a great diversion to conceal our escape. And I have just the idea."

She looked across the room to Detective Bluebell who was feeding her pups. "What's your idea, Mrs Border Collie?" the white Mam Dog asked. "As you know, I have no intention of taking my puppies. I'm going to leave them in the care of some Humans I know not far from here. But I certainly plan to come in your helicopter, whatever that is."

"Talking dogs too, and talking cats as well, I bet!" Mary said as she started to laugh. "And you'll be very welcome to join us, Detective Bluebell. And your idea, Mrs Border Collie?"

"Puppies yelping," the black and white dog said. "Humans can't stand it if they think a puppy is in trouble. We'll contact that farmer friend that Mrs Bluebell speaks of then, when we're all ready, place those white pups in a place that only the farmer can find them.

Any staff from this place will forget about searching for humans and instead concentrate on finding those puppies."

"Done again!" Marry cried and stepped up onto the large Library table. "Then that's it! We have our plan to escape this place of imprisonment! Now all we have to do is implement it." One final time, she looked around the room. "Gather here right before dawn. Bring everything that we have on our lists. Communications and medical equipment, any firearms if you can find them, bags full of flour, ropes, food for the puppies, kittens and little mice children while we're gone, and clothing stuffed into pillow cases. Enough for a day or two. Also, make sure you eat something before we leave. We won't have time to eat or drink anything for hours, not until we're landed at Buckingham Palace. Does everyone understand?"

The entire assemblage nodded. "Good. Then get moving! I'll see you here in..." Mary looked hard at her watch, "one hour and twenty minutes and don't anyone be late or we'll be captured and placed into solitary confinement."

Then, as the assemblage was breaking up, another Ghost floated in through the window. "Why, it's my good Rector, Thomas Wolsey," King Henry cried as the great rector floated down to him dressed in his Royal Rector's gown. "Everyone here! I command you to bow your heads, even you animals. For this Royal Rector will now say a prayer to Christ for all of us."

The Rector Wolsey put up both hands and said in a mild voice, "Oh great Creator, our Lord on High, bless these humans, ghosts and pets. Let them live to see many a fine day and night and ensure that they have enough to eat. When they are rescued from this small dark palace, may they find safety in the English armies that will take them from here. And may they have the courage and wisdom to protect the Royal Family from destruction. In your name, I beg thee Oh Lord, let they good will be done. Amen."

When the Rector had disappeared in a flash of light, the assemblage clapped their hands. "Right!" Mary said, "Now we have to be back here in one hour even! Set your watches, and animals, mind the Humans. Take what time you need to eat but be back here in fifty-nine minutes, thirty-two seconds and counting!"

The Head Nurse of the London Asylum was helping other psychiatric nurses to make their rounds. Tulisha Gale used a bright white torch to check each bed in each Ward of the Sanitorium. Almost finished with the first floor, she opened the door of a Female Ward. As her torch swept the beds, a woman who had been sleeping suddenly woke up.

"Is that my John Roberts?" a sweet voice said into the bright light as she shielded her eyes with both hands. "Did you bring me the new puppy that you promised me?"

Nurse Gale walked up to the bed and, looking down at it, pointed the torch directly into the eyes of her patient. "Camille, go back to sleep!" she hissed. "It's not dawn yet and no, that creep you have for a husband is no longer allowed to see you much less bring you a puppy."

"But I want that new puppy, Nurse," Camille yelped in a loud voice. "He promised it over a year ago. Nurse, he's dead isn't he? My poor John is dead."

The Nurse smiled and nodded, then patted her patient on the arm. "That's right. But the only time I saw him I could tell that he was a horrible husband to you. So stop thinking about him, won't you Camille?"

The patient started to cry then to wail, and woke up the other Alzheimer's patients in the Ward. "Stop crying, for God's sake!" Nurse Gale said harshly. "Look what you've done? All the other patients have woken up!"

But as Camille kept crying, an old woman climbed out of bed and approached the Head Nurse. "Food!" she shouted. "We need food!"

"Food?" the Head Nurse said. "Why, it's not even breakfast time yet. You'll get your slice of toast and a mug of tea when it's time."

"That's what you said yesterday," the old woman replied. "We might be Alzheimer's patients but most of us still have our marbles. We didn't get any dinner yesterday nor tea, yet we saw all the staff Nurses eating at their stations earlier tonight. We know our rights!"

Turning toward the rest of the Ward, the old woman put up her arms and shouted, "Food! We want food!"

All of the women in the Ward began shouting as the old woman sat down next to Camille. "Camille, what that Head Bitch said isn't true. I saw your husband John only yesterday trying to sneak in past reception. But when the staff saw him, they threatened him with arrest! Now dry your eyes. Your husband isn't dead. He's very much alive."

The old woman watched as Camille dried her eyes with the back of her hand then looked up and glared at the Head Nurse. "Nurse Bitch, in that you have no intention of feeding us, turn out your torch and get out of our Ward and let us go back to sleep again."

The Head Nurse frowned down at that old woman and her other patient. She turned off her torch and stalked out of the Ward. Out in the hallway, she slammed the door then used all the many buttons to turn on all the lights in the Ward. "There! Let them try to sleep with all the lights on," she hissed as a male Psychiatric Nurse walked up to her. "Nurse Cleve, don't you dare turn out the lights in there. Those witches from hell are out of order and we may need to give them additional sedatives to make them sleep."

"But they've already had their sedatives for today," Nurse Cleve stated as he smiled in understanding. "But another one or two will ensure that they'll not only sleep but won't want anything to eat. And if a few of those old witches die, well, that's less work for all of us, isn't it?"

"I'm glad you understand, Cleve," the Head Nurse replied. "Now I need to go up to the next floor and check on that Mary Sweet and the rest of her insane friends." Sitting down on a cushioned chair, Tullisha looked up at her friend and winked. "Mary Sweet never even recognised me. Over ten years ago, she had me fired because someone said that I was bigoted against black and brown people. Yet that allegation was never proven. She's the one who's prejudiced against white women like me! You know because I've told you that I'll stop at nothing to see that woman ruined just as I was. When we both finish our rounds, meet me in my bedroom. We'll take a long nap together, how's that?"

"That would be wonderful!" Cleve replied as he sat down on the arm of the chair next to her. "I love it when we have sex."

"So do I, Cleve, so do I."

Upstairs, Mary Sweet and the rest of her Psychiatric Investigative Unit made up their beds with extra pillows and extra blankets. When they were all finished, Mary stood back and examined the many beds in their Ward. "That should fool that Bitch Tulisa Gale," she whispered to her Team. "The woman thinks that I don't recognise her but I do. She's the cruellest Psychiatric Nurse in all of the United Kingdom. She'll kill every patient in all the Wards of this Asylum but we'll stop her too, won't we?"

Nimmy Ursula, a black woman from Nigeria, looked up at Mary as she finished remaking her bed. "Chief, can I come with you, too? As you know, I was only admitted to this hospital full of crazy people late last night. But I heard you come into the Ward earlier and I'd love to help you and get even with that Head Nurse Bitch at the same time."

Mary stepped up to the black woman's bed and smiled. "Nimmy, isn't that your name? I heard George talking about you earlier. Head Nurse Gale had you involuntarily admitted for no reason, is that right?"

The Nigerian shook her head as her black hair fell across her eyes. "That's right, Chief Inspector Sweet. That Gale stated to the local police that I'd run a red light in a car that I'd stolen from a friend of hers. But that was impossible! I'm taking driving lessons right now and can't yet afford a car. But when I saw that Miss Scaly-eyed Gale speeding down the road toward a group of children, and stepped into the street to protect them, she swerved and hit a streetlight. She blamed me, of course, and the white Police Officer who took the report believed her. When I objected and told the truth, they said that I was resisting arrest for intoxication, even though I never take a drink of alcohol. Then, when I got angry, that Gale one said that she recognised me as an escapee from this nut house. That was it. The Police Officer brought me in here and I gather I'll be in here for a minimum of three months."

"Six months is the minimum sentence and I'm sorry about that," George stated as he stepped in through the door to the Ward. "Mary, the Head Nurse is walking up the stairs with that so-called loving friend of hers, Cleve. They'll be here in a few minutes after checking the male ward on this floor. I have my bed re-made just as you instructed, so let's get out of here now."

"Done!" Mary replied. "Nimmy, do please come with us. You're the final member of our team. Were you a nurse in Nigeria?"

"No, I was a Corporal with the Nigerian Army working as an explosives expert," Nimmy replied. "I served during many revolutions. I'm retired from the Army now and I'm studying to be an engineer at a London University."

"Explosives expert?" Mary said with wide eyes. "Done, done, done! We need a specialist just like you on our Team. Now come on, let's get out of here before Head Nurse Bitch finds us."

Stepping out into the hall, the three team members opened a small door and walked out onto a balcony. Using the ropes that George had left there, they slid down the wall of the Asylum and then, finding the Library window still open, climbed in.

The PIU had already gathered in the dim room. Someone started to turn on a light, but Mary motioned at her not to. "Staff might open the door!" she whispered. "Where's the Ghosts and the Animal Teams?"

Detective McMouse hopped up onto the Library table. "The Ghosts have already floated away toward London," he said in his squeaky English voice. "A legendary King named Arthur floated in very briefly. He had a meeting of the ancient Knights of the Roundtable and they agreed to help you, too. King Arthur has left Sir Lancelot and his white horse below in the garden. That great King told me that if anyone gets into trouble here, that fabled Knight will joust their enemies to death.

"As to the Animal Teams: the Cats and Dogs are now in the garden. The cats leapt down and, the dogs worried that the cats would think they were all afraid, leapt down, too."

"So that part of the plan is ready," Mary said softly to her entire Team. "George, do you have your smoke bombs prepared?"

"Flour bombs, isn't that what you mean?" Nimmy replied from the darkness. "No one can use real smoke bombs in here. They'd burn down the Sanitorium."

"Which is exactly why I made flour bombs," George said, turning to Edith. "That flour will make anyone who gets covered by it look like ghosts."

Edith laughed softly. "Where did you put them?"

George pointed above the table. "Hanging up there, just like we all agreed on."

"So that's done too!" Mary said, snapping her fingers twice. She looked at Nurse Jeremy, Tony and Maria. "And you're all ready too?"

"All set," Jeremy replied. "We've hung all the ropes from the Library windows. We've also placed two on the outside that look like strong ropes but that are actually made from cotton. If anyone tries to follow us, they're going to fall down to the ground and bust their stupid heads."

"The EMT Service in London is ready for us, too," Tony said. "As are all the helicopters. Edith, as communications officer, was already in touch with a Royal Marine Air Force General who said that he'd also send us a fighter escort."

Mary snapped her fingers again. "That's it. So why wait any longer? Let's get up to the roof and plan what we'll do when we get to London."

Just as they were preparing to step out of the Library, Edith saw the doorknob begin to turn. "Oh, God!" she whispered as softly as she could. "That's that Head Nurse finishing her rounds with that Cleve guy I can't stand. Now what do we do?"

"Everyone hide under the table!"

The entire team as well as McMouse crawled under the Library table just as the room lights were turned on. McMouse watched from his hiding place near the table leg as four shoes walked in on the soft carpet. Two were black shoes and two were white shoes, and he watched, holding his tiny breath, as the four feet made their way to the table. Turning to the Humans that were hiding with him, he held a tiny finger to his lips.

"Looks all right to me," a man's voice said. "Tullisha, there's no one here at all."

"I could swear I heard voices."

Next to Mary, George lay waiting holding four light chords of rope in his hands. Seeing him start to pull them, Mary put a finger on the back of his head. "Wait!" she said as silently as she could.

McMouse watched the pair of shoes head for the open window. "See? I told you someone was here, Cleve! And it looks like they've escaped!"

"It must have been that Nimmy woman you put in here yesterday. Or maybe that Mary bitch."

"But they were all asleep."

"You sure about that?"

"Cleve, I do those rounds every night. Of course, I'm sure. Let's close and lock all the windows in here then we'll call the police and they'll search the garden. I'm sure it was a pair of thieves who broke into the Library. I'll go call the local cops while you check to see if anything has been stolen in here."

As Mary watched the pair of white shoes walk toward the Library door, she rapped as loud as she could on the wood above her head. "What the hell was that?" Cleve said in a loud voice.

"What?" Nurse Gale answered. "I didn't hear anything."

Mary rapped on the wood, this time louder than she did before. "Get over here, Tullisha. It's above my head, whatever it is."

Tullisha's shoes walked across the carpet and stood next to Cleve's shoes. "Where, Cleve? I don't see anything. It's too dark up there."

"I think I see something hanging. Hold my hand and I'll take a look."

They all watched as Cleve's black shoes climbed up onto a chair, then heard him walking across the table. "Cleve, help me up too and we'll both look," Nurse Gale said, and they watched her white shoes climb up on the chair and heard her on the top of the table, too.

"I still can't see anything!" they all heard Clive say in frustration. "Where's your torch?"

"Upstairs in our bedroom. I didn't think to bring it with me."

Mary looked at George and smile. "On my count," she whispered. "Three. Two. One. Go!"

George pulled on the ropes. They could hear some fabric rip open. Then they heard Nurse Gale scream and Cleve begin to cough. "What the hell was that! Oh, my God! Tulli! Look, it's a ghost!"

"It's me, you big fool! It's your loving wife!"

"They're married now?" Edith whispered and started to laugh. "Good. They deserve one another."

"Okay, Team. When I count one, run for the door then the roof of this building as fast as you know how! One!"

The Team all crawled out from under the table and ran toward the door. Tony made it first and turned out the lights as he opened the Library door. He glanced toward the Library table as the four other members of his Team ran out. Then he stepped out and, as he was ready to close the door, turned off the lights again.

"Tulli! Where are you! I have something like baby powder in my eyes and can't see a thing."

"Me too! Don't fall off the table."

"Oh, shit! Oh, God, I can't see any… Tulli!"

"Cleve! Aaahhh!"

Tony smiled as, in the soft light coming in from the hall, he saw both Nurses fall off the table and onto the floor. "Get off me you fucking man!" the Head Nurse yelled as she kicked Cleve. "Get off or I'm going to bite your head off!"

"Don't talk to me like that. Edith told me you were a real bitch and finally, I believe her."

"I want a divorce, you scumbag."

"Divorce? We've only been married for two months."

"Yeah, and I'm pregnant again."

"Good Christ! Yes, I want a divorce right now!"

Closing the door and locking it, Tony ran past the empty reception desk and up the

stairway as fast as he could. On the roof, he saw Mary look out on the bright dawn that lit the eastern sky. He could see three small dark objects moving toward them at speed. "There!" he shouted, pointing to the eastern sky. "The Royal Marines!"

Below them, they heard a window slide open. Mary looked over the bricks of the roof and saw the top of two snow-white heads. "I'll go first," she heard Cleve say. "You watch up here. Did you phone the police?"

"Not yet. I'll phone them when I know you're safe on the ground."

Mary and the other Team members watched Cleve climb out onto the window ledge. One of the Cat Team members stood next to the Psychiatric Nurse's shoes. "Meow?" it said in Cat Team Language. "Meow, you stupid human being Nurse."

Cleve looked down at the cat who was rubbing against his ankles. "Puss, now's not the time to want a scratch. Get away from here until I descend to the ground on this rope." The cat jumped off the window ledge and Cleve, amazed, watched as it rolled itself up into a tight ball and bounce off the damp grass. Unrolling itself, the cat looked up at Cleve and said, this time in English, "Squire Nurse, I'd not trust that rope if I were you. Someone, maybe your wife, cut it so that, when you try to climb down here, it'll snap in two!"

Cleve rubbed his eyes at the Cat English and looked back into the room. "Tullisha, that fall did me more harm than I thought. Don't think I should climb down this rope. I'm dizzy."

"Dizzy! I'll give you dizzy. Now get down here and get out of my way."

The Team began to giggle as they saw Cleve climb back into the Library then the snow-white hair of a woman's head slid out onto the window ledge. Looking down, she saw a cat who looked back up at her. "I already told your husband, Nurse, not to trust that rope," the cat hissed in English. "Rope will break in two, ya' know?"

The Head Nurse only shook her fist at the cat. "Cats don't talk! Nor does my husband, not when I'm finished with him."

She picked up a pebble by her hand and threw it down at the furry animal. When it hit the grass inches from him, he stuck out his tongue at his assailant. "Cats don't throw stones, only Humans do. Besides, you missed because you're a very lousy shot." Cat bounded away and Nurse Gale picked up the rope with both hands. "Okay, lobster breath," she said to Cleve. "I'm going to drop to the ground on this. There's plenty of rope in the room at your feet. As I lean out, you let me down but slow, you hear me?"

"Sure I hear you, my pet," Cleve said and the Team could all hear the slyness in his voice. "By the way, lambchops, did you sign that insurance form that I left beside our bed?"

"I did Cleve. So send it in to the solicitor as soon as you can. What's yours is mine and mine is yours, that's what happens until death do us part, right?"

"Right. Now give us a little kissy-kiss."

Mary heard the two lips come together then part and then she saw that big white Nurse lean out from the ledge of the window. "Here we go Team. Four to one odds that the rope snaps in two when Cleve starts to lower her to the ground."

"Two to one," Edith replied. "She weighs a fucking tonne, that one does."

"One to one," George said, "or even lower. That bitch of a Nurse never gave me my breakfast three days ago when she was in charge of the Common Room. Which is why I made that cut a bit deeper with my trust Army knife."

He took the knife out of his pocket and Mary saw how sharp the blade was. Looking down from the roof again, she could see the Head Nurse begin to lean out. Mary could also hear the helicopters grow closer.

"Cleve, what the hell is that? Sounds to me like helicopters."

Mary and her Team saw Cleve look out the window. Looking to the east, they could see both eyes go wide. "That's the Royal Marines! Maybe the local Police have asked them to come to find the thieves!"

Just then, a Ghost sailed up in the air. General Patton stood on the window ledge, looking down at the living Humans. "Royal Marines, that's bullshit! That's the Army Air Corps!"

"Oh my God," they heard Cleve whisper. "Darling, that's an escaped patient of ours. He thinks he's General Patton."

"But did you see him fly up to this floor, Cleve? That's no patient. That's a..."

They heard both nurses scream and then, as the Head Nurse leaned out further, they all saw the rope snap in two.

"Down she goes," Patton stated as he stood at attention and saluted. "Such a brave soldier. She'll be buried with full military honours."

"But that's my wife!"

"Then if I were you, I'd fall with her, son. If you're lucky, you'll hit the ground first, get to your feet and catch that fallen one."

The Team watched as Cleve leaped off the window ledge. "Three! Two! One! Splat!" Mary heard Nimmy say and they all clapped. "They're both dead, don't you know it? A real pity because I was always quite fond of Cleve."

"Naw, see? They're both down there on the ground screaming in pain," George replied. "Tis a real pity. I can't stand either of them. That wet grass and all that manure the gardener put on last week? It made for a lake full of smelly muck."

"Least the flour is washed away," Mary said then, getting binoculars out of her bag, looked up at the choppers that were now headed straight for the roof. "Okay, Team. On your feet. They're inbound. Edith, see if you can raise the Captain on your satellite phone."

Edith took the phone out of her duffel bag and switched it on. Pointing it in the general direction of a satellite that was orbiting just above them, she keyed the Mic.

"Marine Rescue One, this is Team Delta PIU. Do you copy, over?"

"Copy you, Delta PIU. Get ready for evacuation."

"That's a roger, sir. I'll leave the line open." Looking up at Mary, she held her thumb in the air. "They're inbound all right. You and everyone else heard the Skipper."

"Okay, everyone. You know your duty now. Protect those inbound aircraft at all costs. Our enemies have heard that transmission. They'll track the Captain's signal and his transponder and will do everything they can to shoot those choppers down."

"Look!" Jeremy shouted. They all turned to the west. There, they could see a dozen streaks of white ascending toward the three Marine Helicopters. "They're going to get hit! There's too many missiles!"

"Tally-ho, my White Stallion Lucifer! To work we go by sailing forth, bound again for eternal glory!"

Looking down, Mary saw a knight in shining armour, riding on a white stallion, ascend from beneath the ground. Obviously a Ghost from time immemorial, she turned toward General Patton who still stood on the window ledge beneath them.

"General, who is that?"

"That's my ride, Madam," the general replied to Mary. "Sir Lancelot and his white horse Lucifer. Even better than my own Lipizzaner Stallions."

As the team watched, the Knight on horseback ascended toward the incoming missiles. Using the lance and sword that he carried, he slashed at the dangerous weapons. Instantly, three exploded. "That's four gone!" George shouted. "Only six more to go."

As Lancelot kept slashing with his sword and lance, a missile came in from the north. "Look at that one!" Tony roared. "Lancelot didn't see it. It's tracking one of the choppers."

Mary looked up to see one of the choppers begin to zig and zag. It fired some white-hot chaff from its fuselage then began to climb. "That's one hot pilot!" Mary said as they all looked up. "Let's hope that pilot is as good as we all hope he is."

The chopper turned on its tail as the missile passed it, now climbing for the sun. Then executed a one-hundred-and-eighty-degree turn, heading again for the Marine Helicopter.

They all heard Edith's satellite phone squawk. "Captain, I can't get rid of this one. It's right on my tail."

"Charlie Alpha, head right for the ground then turn around. I'll shoot it right up that burning stove pipe."

The Marine Chopper did as he was ordered. A few hundred feet above their heads, the Team watched as the helicopter came to a complete stop and turned around. From the Captain's helicopter, they saw all of its missiles and machine guns fire.

"That's a miss!" they heard the Captain shout. "Pilot, get your tail out of their or that missile will…"

Then they all saw an explosion as the missile hit the mid-section of the Helicopter. But Lancelot had seen that, too. Reaching out with his long lance, he placed it beneath the burning aircraft. Lowering it gently to the ground, he stood beside the burning hulk helping one Royal Marine after another get out before they were burned to death.

"Ah… Delta PIU, did you just see what I saw?"

Edith keyed her mic again. "That's a Roger, Sir."

"It looks like…no, he couldn't be."

"Sir Lancelot and his white horse? Yes Sir, that's what we're seeing now too."

"Good. Thought I'd have to commit myself in that asylum of yours." Then they all heard the Captain key his mic twice. "Alpha One to the rest of my command. Inbound right now while the skies are clear. Those other inbound weapons missed. Grab that Royal Team and evacuate them right now!"

The Team stood up and watched as the chopper began their final approach toward the rooftops of the Asylum. Mary watched as General Patton saluted Sir Lancelot. She looked down at the window ledge and saw Detective McMouse waving into the distance. Then, Lancelot, still on his white horse, picked up General Patton by the back of his coat and placed the Officer behind him. Finished with his rescue of the stricken Helicopter's crew, the General saluted the Marine Chopper Crew as Lancelot lifted his sword in goodbye. Floating toward the building that her Team still stood on, she watched as McMouse leaped onto the White Stallion's head. Nestling up in its white flowing mane, she could hear the little mouse cry, "Mary and the PIU Team! I'll see you in London! I'll meet you at Buckingham Palace when you all meet King Charles!"

"Okay, Team. You heard our McMouse friend. It's almost time to meet the King. We'll plan what happens in London when we get onboard the Choppers."

The Team huddled together in the downwash of the two Helicopters as they both landed on the roof. When the doors opened, the Team split into two small groups and ran inside the choppers. As the door of one Chopper started to close again, a woman ran toward it. She looked in through the door and saw Tony sitting next to Edith.

"Good thing I caught you, Tony," Maria sang in her strong voice. "I'll see you sometime soon in London Town. I have something wonderful to tell you!"

"Tony, is that really Maria, the wife who died in the fire?"

"One and the same, Edith," Tony replied as he took her hand in his. "Maria! I'll see you soon and can't wait for your wonderful news! I'll meet you at Buckingham Palace!"

Maria leaned in the door and kissed him on the cheek then gave Edith a quick kiss too. "Edith, take care of my Tony. He a good man but he so stressed out when he lose me and our children."

The door closed again and the two Choppers lifted into the air. Pivoting, they both headed to the west in close formation.

Standing on the grass of the Asylum's back garden, Cleve tried to stand up as did the Head Nurse. "Jesus Christ, that hurts. I think I've broken both of my legs."

"And I've broken my head! Oh, the pain!" the Nurse Gale said as she put her hands to her head. "Cleve, I think I'm going to check myself into our London Asylum for a month or more. I've seen and heard too many things that just aren't normal."

"So have I, my psychiatric Head Nurse. Maybe I'll check myself in, too."

"And we'll share the same bed," Tullisha said as she smiled. "I'm sorry for calling you names. I was upset again."

"And I'm sorry too," Cleve replied as he reached up to take her hand in his. "What a lovely bride you are. Don't try to help me to stand up, gorgeous. I'm too heavy and my legs really, really hurt."

"Oh, you sissy! Just stand up."

She pulled and the man started to scream again as the back doors opened and staff ran out onto the grass. When they saw the couple, they all stopped running. "Oh, it's just them," a nurse said as she turned to the rest of the staff. "Now, for you who don't know me. My name is Madam L'Pookey and I'm the new Psychiatric Head Nurse." The woman with the auburn hair and sunny smile placed both hands on her small hips. "Some of you think I'm a psychiatric patient on the first floor. But I was told by our management to find out who had been stealing from our various institutions." She pointed to the couple who were both lying flat on the ground. "Them, that's who, and you know exactly how." Then L'Pookey smiled again. "But I'm not going to report them to our management, not yet, anyway. First, let's treat them exactly like they've treated our patients and our staff members. How's that?"

"That's a deal!" a male nurse shouted. "Come on, everyone. Let's help our new guests to change their clothes and get something to eat."

The last that Ms L'Pookey saw that crazy, ignorant couple was the staff carrying Cleve and that Bitch of a Head Nurse into the Asylum. As the doors closed, she looked out of this page at you, the Reader of this novel, and smiled her charming L'Pookey smile. "To the author of this chapter and novel, here's a special wish for you," the wise woman said. "Believe me when I say I'm not dead. I'm right here in this novel waiting for you."

Then, like a Ghost or Spirit, L'Pookey became transparent and floated into the sky. She floated east, right past the helicopters and over The Tower of London. Looking down, she saw a white stallion carrying a knight and a General on its back. A tiny mouse looked up at her and waved. "Goodbye, Miss L'Pookey, and we'll all see you soon." Then, she was gone in a flash of light and the tiny rodent rubbed its small black eyes. "I'd say that was no ghost, was it Mister Stallion?" the mouse whispered into the horse's ear.

"No, it wasn't," the horse whinnied back. "That was a real true lover if I've ever seen one. Now let's get you down to the King because my stomach is empty. We've been fighting enemies for what seems like many, many seasons."

McMouse looked down and saw Buckingham Palace and a large crowd at the golden gates. He watched as the two helicopters landed in the nearby parade grounds. "Those Humans, what a great race!" Detective McMouse said to the horse. "Now, let's land too and we'll all have something to eat. Cheese for me and hay for you, and God knows what for the humans."

As they landed on four hooves right by the front door of the Palace, the mouse detective saw a man dressed in a bright yellow military uniform with a gold hat and red and black ruffles at his throat sitting on a horse at the front gate. He was talking to a Royal

Soldier who was climbing onto a black horse next to that British Army Officer.

"That's the Spy General, I'm sure of it!" the mouse said to the horse. "He's planning what to do next but so are we. Let me crawl down, Magical Stallion, and tell the rest of our many Teams that General Gusto Gatwick is already here and planning to execute again the King and Queen of Great Britain."

CHAPTER 9

Fighting Back the General's Attack

Inside Buckingham Palace, Mary Sweet and the members of her Team reviewed what they had planned in the helicopter.

"Now we must stick to the plan that we've drawn up," Mary stated as she placed a brand-new Chief Inspector's cap on her head. She looked across the large, elegant living room at her Inspector. "Inspector, did you have time to review the plan with the Ghosts who are now with us as well as the Animal Teams?"

"I did, Chief Inspector," Bernie said solemnly. "The Ghosts and all the Animal Teams know that the first thing they must do is find anyone dressed in Yellow and that includes so-called Officers in the Royal Military service who will be outside the Palace Gates to welcome the Royal Family to their London Home."

"Good, Inspector Bridgestone," she stated as she turned to the other Members of her Team. "Jennifer Markova, I'm glad you could join us, too. What news do you have to bring us?"

The woman, now dressed in a Captain's Interpol Uniform, stepped forward and saluted. "Chief Inspector Sweet, I bring you greetings from the Chief of Staff of Interpol as well as the French President. Both are fully aware of how the General tried to murder you and your Team members on the roof of the Asylum and how a number of Royal Marine soldiers and officers died when they tried to rescue you. They offer their assistance whenever you need it."

"That's good too," Mary stated as she shook the Captain's hand. "I'm so glad you received your promotion, Jennifer. You deserved it for always being there to help us."

"It's an honour to serve you, my friend," Jennifer replied. "We've been told of your plan by your Inspector. My Interpol officers and I will keep our eyelids open to find anyone dressed in Yellow."

Mary heard a tiny voice squeak in English, "But I've already seen that General Gatwick! He's on horseback and dressed in Yellow as an English Military Officer. He's right outside the gate and was talking to a man that was dressed as a common English Soldier wearing a Bright Yellow Sash."

Mary looked up to see the mouse standing on a golden table. "Detective McMouse, thank you for keeping your eyes open. Is Lancelot and his White Stallion here?"

"Just outside the Palace door," the mouse said. "I asked them both to use their eyes to track wherever that culprit goes on his dark horse."

The Chief Inspector looked at her Team. "Edith, keep monitoring all incoming transmissions. We need to know if the General is going to land more troops near the Palace. George, work with Edith but also talk to any Military officers and soldiers that you see. Tell them all we've spotted the General and tell them how he looks and that he's mounted on a dark horse. Tell them to look for anyone wearing anything Yellow." Mary looked next at Tony and

Nimmy. "Both of you be prepared to help any wounded that are hit by arms fire or explosives. Talk to the EMT's that you know in all the London hospitals. They must be prepared for hundreds of casualties in the event that the General orders his troops to fire before we catch him."

She spotted a number of Ghosts floating up through the Royal living room floor. "Ah, Mister Holmes and Doctor Watson. I'm so glad that you've joined us. Are the Royal Ghosts with you?"

"I'm sorry, Madam, but they're busy right now," Detective Sherlock Holmes replied as he brushed lint off his black jacket. "The last I saw of King Henry and his Queen Anne Bolyn, they were heading for the Tower of London. They told me that their, they'd keep a sharp lookout from the top of that Tower for anyone dressed in Yellow.

"Mister Holmes, my friend, don't forget to mention General Patton and that Hubert human. I saw them last floating down the Mall. They've spotted our major Quary dressed all in Yellow and riding on horseback, just as that little Mouse squeaked. If we're not quick enough, he'll escape our clutches before we can capture him."

"Then we must capture him now!" Mary said in a tough voice. "The King and Queen of England are scheduled to arrive in a small motorcade accompanied by the King's sons as well as Princes Diana who is arriving in an unseen special Rolls Royce with her present husband, Dodi Fayed who is, of course, also a Ghost. They have both told me in a Telegraph from Heaven that they will look for mines in all the London Parks as well as in any open spaces, gardens or buried in our London roads."

A Royal Secretary marched into the large room and bowed to Mary in greeting. He took a small white letter from a black box that he held and handed it to the Chief Inspector. Reading it, Mary held it up for all of her Team to see. "This is a message from King Charles and his good Queen. He will be here, in this Royal Room, to give each of you a CBE. We are ordered to wait here until the

Royal family arrives. That said, he also recognises the threat to his family as well as his subjects standing at the Palace gates. For that reason, he has ordered the Military and London Police to clear the streets of people as far away as Trafalgar Square. Following the presentations, he orders that we leave here at once to find that disloyal General and bring him to justice."

As her Team began to talk among themselves about the Royal orders, Detective McMouse jumped onto a Living Room window ledge. The window was cracked open, just enough for him to squeeze past the window frame and stand outside.

"Sir Lancelot, can you please trot over to me, Sir?" McMouse squeaked in Old English as loud as he could. When Lancelot, on horseback, stood next to him, the mouse jumped onto his open silver helmet visor. "Sir, I can go with you but the rest of the Team must wait for the current King and Queen. We're ordered to follow that fake Yellow Military Officer anywhere he might go and to also keep a close eye on anyone wearing Yellow. Do you understand, Knight Errant?"

"I am not a Knight Errant," Sir Lancelot replied. "You are confusing me with the Great Don Quixote who spent a lifetime chasing windmills with his trustworthy aid-de-camp Sancho."

"Forgive me, my Knight friend," the mouse said as it bowed. "I meant no offense to you. But do you understand our new orders?"

The knight closed his visor and kicked his steed gently in the sides with both heals of his silver boots. The horse began to trot toward the Golden Palace Gate. As they grew closer to that Gate of Gold, a soldier saw the Royal Knight. Saluting, he opened the gate and stood back as the horse trotted past him.

"That's one fine uniform," the uniformed soldier said to his mate who was standing next to him. "That Officer was dressed as the great Sir Lancelot, knight of King Arthur's Roundtable."

"What are you talking about," his friend replied. "I didn't understand why you were opening the Gate. It's too early for the Royal family to arrive." The man, a soldier in the Royal Navy, scratched his beard with a long finger. "Jack, my friend, you've been watching too much television."

"But I saw a knight in shining armour!" Jack replied to his best friend Mike. "He's right there! Can't you see him on his trusty white steed?"

Mike looked but all he saw was Royal Military soldiers and one officer dressed in Yellow with a circular ruffle around his throat. "Jack, what you need is a pint of Bitter and a meat pie," Mike said to his friend. "T'aint no knight in armour. Tis a man in yellow. See?"

Jack looked where the man pointed and saw the Military Officer dressed in a yellow uniform. Looking around the crowd, he couldn't find Sir Lancelot on his white stallion. "Ah, Mike, yer right. It's that rheumy eyed barkeep I visited last night. She gave me a pint of porter but it tasted like mud. Bet it was a shipment from Ireland that'd gone off that's making me see things."

Both men laughed and, walking past the crowds that were being told by the local Police Force to leave the area, Jack pointed to a pub across the street. "Not as good as The Shakespeare Pub, but that's miles from here. This one will have to do."

As they walked into the pub, arm in arm, a woman dressed in Yellow smiled at them. "My name is Josephin Svetlana. I am a military officer with the Ukrainian Army. Can I buy you both something to drink?"

Jack winked at Mike who winked back. "Lady, thank you but our wives would never understand it if she spotted us with a woman as beautiful as you," Mike said. "We'll buy you a glass of bitter but then we'll sit at the bar to eat."

The mysterious woman frowned at them. "It is your right to refuse a drink from such a simple officer as me," Ms Svetlana stated. "I will buy my own drink, you rude men!" Then she marched away from them and toward the Officer dressed in Yellow.

"Those foreign women are all a joke!" Jack howled to his friend. "Come on, Mike. Let's get in here before the crowd comes in."

CHAPTER 10

The Suspects in the King and Queens Murder Receive Royal Awards. Or Do They?

While Detective McMouse and Sir Lancelot kept their eyes on the Officer dressed in a Yellow Uniform, inside the Palace the Teams waited for the King and Queen to enter the Living Room. Captain Jennifer walked toward the window and looked out. On the other side of the room, Mary was talking to Bernie when she saw the Captain of Interpol take out her mobile phone. Jennifer started to talk on it and waved to someone outside.

"Bernie, who's Jennifer talking to? Her Interpol Officers are with the King and Queen right now."

"That woman isn't used to taking instructions anymore," Bernie grumbled as he munched on a cucumber sandwich. "I told everyone here to turn off any communications device they're carrying. That includes Edith and George. When the Royal couple arrive, we need to tighten all security."

Bernie looked at his watch as he kept grumbling. At the window, Jennifer still talked on her phone. "For all we know, that woman could still be working for the General. I know he was going to pay her handsomely for the murder of the King and Queen."

"But Jennifer said she'd always worked for Interpol," Mary reasoned. "She apologised for shooting Hubert, remember?"

"Apologies!" Bernie smirked. "Apologies are a very inexpensive way of covering a murderer's tracks. I think we should keep including her as a possible spy for that treacherous General." When he looked toward the window again, Jennifer had placed the phone back in her bag and started walking toward them.

"I am glad to see you are eating, Inspector," the Interpol Captain said as she picked up a sandwich from a plate on the table. "I was just talking to my commanding officer in charge of security for the King and Queen. They will be arriving in only three minutes."

"Three minutes?" Mary said as her face flushed red. "I'll actually get to meet them."

"And so you will," Bernie replied. "I'm sure the King will award you with a Knighthood, my great friend." Taking her hand in his, she squeezed it and, leaning over, kissed her on each cheek. "You will be the first woman in all of British history to receive a Knighthood from our King. Females are always awarded the title of Damehood but from the moment the King taps you on your shoulder, you will be the only woman to ever be given the title 'Sir'. Mary, you deserve such an honour. You've been our leader since the day your husband was murdered." He glared at Jennifer who simply smiled at him. Bernie took out his wallet and opened it. When he looked into it, his eyes went as wide as two saucers. "Somone's stolen the cash I had in here! I had over two-hundred pounds! I was going to buy us dinner tonight but, well, it looks like I'm broke." His eyes moved up to Mary's as he smiled at her. "Chief, is there any way I could receive an advance on next month's salary? It's almost the beginning of the new month and I only need a few hundred to see me through."

Mary looked at his smiling lips and couldn't help but wonder why he didn't seem more upset. Then she glanced at Jennifer who frowned back at her. "Bernie, are you really that skint? If you want, I can have an officer drive you to an ATM right after the Royal visit."

Bernie shook his head and sighed. "No, that won't work, I'm afraid. I've had all sorts of bills to pay over the past few years. When my wife was dying of heart failure, I took out a few loans to pay the doctors' and surgeons' bills, as well as all the hospital bills. I mortgaged my home to the banks for some of those bills but I had even more bills to pay so I took out those loans, too."

Mary blinked twice. "But Bernie, we have the NHS here. Most of those costs are covered by the government. Why did you need to take out any loans?"

Bernie began to cry. "Esmerelda was living in the United States when I met her. We were married there then moved back here. Over two years ago, before I met you, we agreed to move back there for a year. Then, my fiancé became very ill and we rushed her to a local hospital in Texas. That's when I learned she was dying of heart failure and die she did."

"I didn't know you were married," Mary replied as Bernie kept on crying. "You told me you were never married or engaged."

"I've been so upset I forgot to mention it," she said, drying his eyes with a clean white handkerchief. "I ended up staying in Texas until Esmerelda passed on, then moved back here. Those moves interrupted my time in service which is why I'll need to work for at least another ten years."

Jennifer took another sandwich from the table. "Inspector, may I ask you something? If Esmerelda was your fiancé and your both English, why didn't you bring her back here to have her operations? As the Chief Inspector said, all the bills would have been covered by the government."

Bernie blinked not once but five time. "I never even thought of that. She was in so much pain and the Texas doctors said she needed surgery immediately. So that's what I did."

Jennifer smiled and patted him on the arm. "You're a good man, Inspector Bridgestone. I'm sure you still miss your fiancé so very much." Finished with her sandwich, she moved away from the table and walked to the window again. There, she once more took out her phone. Bernie frowned and started to walk toward her but Mary took his hand and pulled him back to the table.

"Let her talk, Inspector Bridgestone. She's responsible for the safety of the King and Queen, is she not?" When he nodded, Mary pecked him on the cheek. "I'll ask the man responsible for our salaries to give you an advance, just like you asked for. Don't worry, we'll figure out your debts. That's what friends are for, isn't it?" She looked around the room and arched her eyebrows. "If there's a thief in here, we'll soon catch him and get your money back."

"I hope you do," Bernie said through clenched teeth. "We have enough to worry about without having to concern ourselves with that lot."

He smiled at Mary then walked toward the front door. When he was out of earshot, Jennifer walked back to the table. "The Royal couple are now one minute away," Jennifer said. "When I got off the phone with my commander, I put a phone call into Belgium about Bernie Bridgestone. We have detailed records on all police officers working on all the forces across Europe. Our records say that Bernie Bridgestone was never in the United States, nor was he in Texas. He's been in the UK for over thirty years and has never travelled outside its borders."

Mary's face went white as she looked across the room at her friend. When he turned toward her she waved at him then looked back at Jennifer. "Maybe there are more than one Bernie Bridgestone. Bridgestone is a common surname and Bernie is a common first name.

"I am sorry, my Chief Inspector. Perhaps this Bernie man has a good explanation but our records state categorically that there is only one Bernie Bridgestone in all of Europe. They also state that he lost all of his family fortunes when he became addicted to gambling and alcohol many years ago. As for his wallet, look what I found on the carpet under the table?"

The Captain held up some English notes. Mary took it and counted it. "Two hundred pounds. Exactly what he said was stolen from him." She looked across the room and smiled, waving the notes at Bernie. When he rushed back over, she gave them to him. "See what Jennifer found under the table? Your cash!"

Bernie smiled broadly as he put the money back into his wallet. "What a relief!" he stated as he wiped his brow with the handkerchief. "I honestly thought someone had stolen it!"

Mary's eyes wandered all over his face and body. "Bernie, can I ask you something? For some reason, did you ever change your name?"

Looking embarrassed, he nodded. "Thirty years ago, I got into some trouble. I was accused of gambling my family's fortune and alcoholism but that couldn't be proven by the courts. As it turned out, someone had stolen my identification. I changed my name to join the police force. Why do you ask?"

"I was just curious, Bernie," Mary replied as she looked at Jennifer. "That's a very simple answer to a very simple question."

A trumpet began to blare as the front door opened. The Royal secretary came into the Living Room and bowed before the many guests in the room. "Announcing the arrival of the Royal couple!" the man shouted above the trumpet's wonderful Royal song. "Bow, when the King and Queen enter!"

They could all hear the clatter of hooves just beyond the door. Mary saw Detective McMouse hop up through the door just as a group of Royal Guards marched into the room. When the mouse crawled up onto Mary's shoulder, he had a good view of the entire room. Then the Royal couple walked in and everyone in the room curtsied or bowed.

"My friends, I am so very fortunate to be here today," the King said to his audience. "Let us begin this ceremony and we'll take our time for each person as I call their name." The secretary gave King Charles a short list and the King started to read out the names of the honoured men and women.

"May I call the entire Team led by Chief Inspector Mary Sweet forward!"

In the room, Mary's PIU Team walked in a loose formation toward the King and Queen. Since disembarking from the helicopters, they had all changed into new official PIU uniforms. With their official caps under their arms, they bowed or curtsied when they faced the Royal couple.

"George Smith, Nurse Edith, Nurse Jeremy," the King continued as he smiled at them, "Toy Enwenopa and Nimmy Ursula, may I present each of you with a medal to honour each of you as new members of the Order of the British Empire!" As the trumpeter was joined by two other trumpets, they began to play a Royal march. Then the Queen gave each of the Team a certificate and a bronze plaque. "Be it known to all the people in the United Kingdom and the Commonwealth that these people have been chosen by me due to their outstanding service, their bravery, fortitude and discretion in protecting me, Charles the Second, and my Queen!"

The trumpets stopped blaring and the other people in the room broke into loud applause. Mary watched as Ghosts drifted in from the open door. Most bowed toward the King and Queen then Queen Elizabeth the Second followed by Henry the Eighth and Anne Bolyn. Queen Elizebeth floated over to her son and gave him a kiss on the cheek. Taking his hand in hers, she whispered to him, "What an intelligent and brave son I have, Charles." Charles looked to his Queen Camilla and smiled.

"Why, thank you Camilla. That was more than nice of you to whisper those words to me."

"What words, Charles?" she said as she leaned toward him. "I never whispered one word to you."

"What a fine new wife you have here, and a wonderful Queen, too," Queen Elizabeth said to her son in a loud voice. "Charles, open your eyes. By my command, you will see me again."

King Charles blinked and did as he was bid. He closed his eyes, counted to three, and opened them. Queen Camilla watched as her husband's mouth opened wide then shut again. His face wore an odd expression then he smiled. "By command, is that what you said my Queen?"

"By whose command, Charles?" the living Queen replied. "Yes, I make commands sometimes. But only to those who serve us."

Stepping away from the crowd, Charles turned back to see his mother float toward him. Turning away from the other people in the room, Charles poured himself a cup of tea from a silver teapot that sat on the table. "Mother, is that really you?" he asked as he added some milk to his tea. "Or am I seeing things?"

Queen Elizabeth laughed. "Charlie, you're not seeing things. It really is me. Now, a Royal Command this time. Someday soon, our Mary Sweet will confide in you and you'll pay close attention to her. She'll tell you that she sometimes sees and hears things that most people can't. When she tells you exactly who and what she sees, you'll now believe her because you can both see me as can a few more in this room."

The King smiled as he looked sideways at his Royal mother. "Mumsy, I'm a very lucky man, aren't I?"

"We both are," his mother said. "And don't forget about honouring Mary Sweet. She's the sweetest Chief Inspector this jolly old England and Great Britain has ever had in employment."

The King felt his mother put her hand on his shoulder. Kissing him on the cheek again, he watched as she took her place behind Queen Camilla. Taking a final sip of tea, he walked back to stand beside his wife.

"Forgive me but I needed some tea to clear my throat," the King said to the audience. "Now, and before today's events become history, will Chief Inspector Sweet step forward."

Mary looked to Bernie who stood beside her again. Her hands started to sweat and he gave her a handkerchief. "Me, Bernie? But what have I done to deserve an OBE?"

"You?" he smiled. "Why nothing, Mary, nothing at all."

The audience was silent as Mary marched up to the King. She curtsied and he took her hand. "Mary Sweet, are you ready to be conferred as Knight of the Realm?"

Mary wanted to die. Shaking his hand as firmly as she could, he looked up at his tall figure and could swear that she saw Hubert floating over his shoulder. The King's secretary brought the Royal Sword to the King, resting on a purple pillow. Taking the sword, the King smiled again down at Mary as a cushion was placed before him by one of his grand-daughters. "Mary Sweet, God has commanded that you kneel before me." When Mary kneeled before him, he placed the sword on her left shoulder. "By my command I make thee, Mary Sweet, a Royal Knight of Britain." Then he placed the sword on the other shoulder. "Should anyone try to harm you, your good Team or any member of the Royal Family, or any officer I appoint to serve me or you, then from this day forward you shall use this sword to kill or main any of our common enemies."

The secretary leaned forward and whispered, "Mary, kiss the sword then the King's ring," which Mary did.

"Rise, Sir Mary Sweet," the King commanded.

As Mary rose from the cushion, the King held out his hand and helped her to stand up. Applause broke out from the entire audience as well as all the Humans who stood at the door to watch the ceremony. Animal Teams clapped with their paws and the Ghosts clapped with their hands. Even Queen Camilla and King Charles began to clap. Sir Lancelot floated in through the door mounted on his White Stallion as McMouse hopped from Mary's shoulder down to the table then back up onto Lancelot's open helmet visor.

"Sir Lancelot, what an honour for Mary Sweet to receive!" the mouse whispered as the audience still clapped.

"'Tis truly," replied the Knight. "When King Arthur bid me such an honour, t'was the greatest day in my life!"

McMouse turns toward you, the reader of this Royal part of the novel. "And so it 'tis for Mary Sweet. As long as she is alive, and through all of Eternity, she will remember this as the greatest memory of her long life." The mouse smiles at you as he clears his throat and starts to laugh. "And wait until King Charles hears me squeak in an English accent and words that he can also understand! And wait until the rest of the Team and even that horrible traitor the General also hear me squeak with words they can understand! But that's for the next chapter in this tale of Knighthood, honour, bravery, murder, death and war."

Detective McMouse looked down on Mary Sweet from his high place on the Silver Knight. Both watched as Mary burst into tears. King Charles and Bernie, as well as ghostly Hubert all offered her handkerchiefs. Mary took all of them as the King took her arm on one side and the living Queen took her other arm. Leading her toward the door, Mary looked up at McMouse. "My little friend, what an honour God and this King have bestowed on a poor woman like me."

"Yes, you've been Honoured, Mary Sweet," Sir Lancelot said as he floated a silver handkerchief toward her. When she caught it in one hand, she looked back up as he said, "Tell the present King that he can also hear me. Soon, the Knights of the Roundtable will be here to defend not only him and the Royal family, but also all of England and what he calls Great Britain. See, Sir Mary Sweet? The King has heard me."

King Charles looked up at the Silver clad Knight and smiled. Squeezing Mary's arm, he bent over and whispered to her, "I can hear and see that Royal fellow. Is that really Sir Lancelot made famous by the stories from T.H. White?"

"No, I am not the same Knight," Sir Lancelot continued. "That was only a fairytale. King, I am yours to command but I am the ghost of the real Lancelot who was the son of the Noblest King in all the land, King Arthur."

"You're the son of Arthur?" the living King gasped. "But that means that Guenevere was…"

"And is," the Knight again continued. "She is my mother and no, I never wanted to marry her. That is rubbish and all made up by that writer you speak of."

Mary glanced up at Lancelot and winked then smiled at King Charles. "Tis a mighty Knight you see and hear now, is it not Your Majesty?"

"I'm a lucky man again," King Charles whispered to her. "Not only did I see my mother again and talk to her, but now a

Royal Knight will help to defend me, as well as many of his Royal soldiers."

As Mary and the Royal couple went out the front door, she saw a man dressed in Yellow sitting on a horse quite near to her. When she studied his face, he placed his hands over it and pretended to cough. 'Tis the General,' she thought to herself and began to laugh. 'What unnoble things is he thinking in that horrid little mind of his.'

She smiled again up at the King and Queen as they escorted her to their Royal coach, then the Royal couple climbed in beside her. As the coach was pulled away by its pair of white horses and toward the Mall, the crowds began to roar as marching bands started to play Royal music. "What a life I've led," Mary said to the King of Great Britain. "I'll never forget today. Thank you, Your Royal Majesty.

She blew her nose on the Silver Handkerchief and when she was folding it back up, noticed that it was embroidered in gold thread with her new Royal title as well as her initials.

"SIR-MS," she whispered. "Sir Mary Sweet." Then she placed it in her lap as through the open window she could hear the crowds still cheering and above her, jet aircraft whistled through the sky overhead trailing thin clouds of blue, white and red.

CHAPTER II

The Capture of the General and the Apparent Death of Jennifer Markova

Once again clinging to the mane of Sir Lancelot's White Stallion, Detective McMouse reached into his vest pocket and took out the pocket watch his wife had given him last Christmas. Opening it, he saw that it was almost 6PM. When he heard the bells of Saint Peter's clang as well as all of the other church bells in London, he grimaced and looked up at the silver helmet of the Knight.

"Sir, we've lost that Yellow Uniformed Officer in the crowd. Could you kindly float us up above London so we can find him again?" When Lancelot nodded, the steel of his helmet creaking, he shut his visor then gently kicked the Stallion and up into the sky they flew again. Looking down on London, the mouse spotted a number of people in the crowd dressed all in Yellow. "Look down there, my Knight in Shining Armour. See how those people in Yellow are all gathering in front of The Tower of London? Doesn't that mean something to you?"

The Knight looked down and saw what his tiny friend had observed. Kicking the white charger into a gallop, Sir Lancelot whispered into the horse's ear, "Duke Goldenrod, you are the fastest, most powerful stallion in all of the known world. You can fly and gallop almost anywhere I ask you to. Now listen to what I order. Place me and this mouse man down on Earth again, in a way that those Humans in Yellow below us will never see us. When we dismount, fly like the wind to find King Arthur and his Knights of the Roundtable. Tell him that I sent thee and that soon, there will be War here. We need the King as well as his Knights to fight these desperate people and protect the living King and Queen from all of their evil!"

When the horse nodded its head three times to tell his Master that he had understood, Goldenrod circled above the Humans in Yellow then descended as fast as he could. McMouse clung to the horse's mane, thinking he would be airsick, as the flying Stallion approached The Tower of London. Landing on its roof, its silver hooves clattering on the tiles, the Knight and mouse jumped to the ground and watched as the White Stallion took to the air again.

"Thank-you Duke Goldenrod!" Detective McMouse yelled as he waved goodbye. "We'll see you as soon as you bring back the Once and Future King and his mystical Knights!" Reaching this time into his coat pocket, the Mouse Detective withdrew a tiny mobile phone and dialled. When Mary Sweet answered, he spoke carefully and distinctly in English so that she would understand.

"Chief Inspector, this is Detective McMouse. Together with Sir Lancelot, I am on the roof of The Tower of London. Do you read me, over?"

"Detective, this is your Chief. Have you successfully tracked the Officer wearing Yellow?"

The mouse looked up at the Knight who picked the poor animal up by the tail. Lifting him as high as he could, McMouse took out a pair of Mouse Army regulation binoculars from his coat pocket. Focusing on the crowd below, he spotted his target. "Yes, Chief. I have him in sight! He's with a number of other uniformed English troops all wearing Yellow colours including badges, scarves and military uniforms. Hold on a second. Who's that I see?" The mouse saw a tall woman dressed all in Yellow. Focusing his binoculars again, he thought he saw Captain Jennifer but realised that he was wrong.

"Chief, this is McMouse again. I thought I saw our Captain Jennifer of Interpol near the primary target. But it is not, and I repeat, not Jennifer. It's someone who looks very much like her and I think I know who it is." Placing the binoculars back in his pocket, he took a small notebook from his vest jacket. Quickly paging through it, he found a picture of a woman who looked almost exactly like Jennifer but was actually a man. "Sir, this is McMouse again," he said into his phone. "Our next important quarry is a man, and I repeat, a man not a woman. His name is," and he squinted at the tiny lettering on the page he held in his paw, "Colonel Francis McOuvre aka the Yellow Egg. He's a spy from Russia but we'd been told he had defected many years ago to spy for England."

At the London Police Station Mary Sweet, now back in her standard Uniform, looked down at the phone that she held tight in one hand. Lifting it to her ear again, she walked away from her Team as she said, "McMouse, that man was a Spy for the old Soviet Union. When the wall fell in Berlin, we brought him in. He was actually a double-agent. His real name is Francis Assisi, an Italian by descent but Irish by birth. He's agreed to help us find and capture that General Blister. Do not, and I repeat, do not approach him at all or you'll blow his cover."

"Roger that," she heard McMouse answer. "We'll continue to track all of the Humans below us. We should have reinforcements up here within an hour. McMouse out."

Slipping her phone back into her bag, Mary considered the new situation. If Assisi was on the General's tail then where was Captain Jennifer and the rest of her officers? And where was her Inspector Bernie Bridgestone? For that matter, where was Edith and George? Looking around the Interrogation Room which she was using now as a Meeting Room for her various Teams, she saw Tony Enwenopa coming in the door with his wife, Maria.

"Tony, can you come here for a moment with Maria?" When they walked up, she motioned them to a chair in the corner of the room. "I want you to talk quietly with Sherlock Holmes and Doctor Watson. As you know as well as I do, there's a traitor in our midst. It could be anyone of a half-dozen people, animals or ghosts who are members of our Teams. Ask those fine English Human Detectives if they've been able to discover who is working with the General and who is that traitor or traitors who are lying to us."

"We'll do just that, Chief," Tony replied as he buttoned up his EMT coat. "Maria and I will talk to the Detectives. But we have our own suspicions."

"Do you really?" Mary stated as she crossed her arms across her chest. "And who do you think would be so ruthless that they'd turn on their own friends and family?"

"Mary Sweet, I know who it is not," Maria said with ice in her eyes. "It is not Captain Jennifer. I'm sure of that because, years ago, she and I had the chance to work together in London when she was training to be a nurse just as I was. Nor is it George or Edith. The two of them are out near The Tower of London, tracking that madman General. Nor is it Nimmy Ursula. Have you noticed? She's not here, either."

"No I didn't," the Chief replied. "I hadn't noticed that she's also missing. Where is she, do you know?"

Tony nodded his head. "Nimmy is now standing with that Mister Assisi, you're old friend and counter-revolutionary. They are both single, as you know, and the last time I saw them together, Nimmy was holding that man's hand."

"Really? Honestly?" Mary smiled. "I love both of them and hope that a relationship blossoms between them. I wonder if Francis knows that Nimmy has five children?"

They all laughed then Maria and Tony got up and walked over to see the two English Ghost Detectives. When Mary saw Doctor Watson frown, she walked over, too. "Doctor Watson, is there a problem, Sir?"

"Why Mary Sweet, of course there is a problem," the great Doctor stated primly. "These two Human people are also suspected of being the traitors that we're looking for."

Sherlock Holmes tapped out his pipe on his pale palm. "Miss Sweet, if I were you I'd lock these two characters up in jail pending a trial for conspiracy and attempted murder. I am certain that they're on the run, the two of them." Holmes rose from his leather chair and stepped toward the window. "Many years ago, I caught Professor Moriarity attempting to kill the King of England. When I tried to stop him, he shot me in the leg and dived into the River Thames. He escaped and has been on the run ever since." Facing Tony and Maria, the best Detective and Forensic Scientist in all of history held up a tiny tube filled with blood. "This morning, when this man who I will still call Tony, was seeing the present King of England, I took this blood sample from the back of his hand when he wasn't looking."

Tony immediately looked at the back of his hand. He rubbed it once then a second time and stood, looking down on his Chief. "Chief Inspector, look at my hand. There's no sign of a needle puncture. That Ghost of a man has mistaken me for someone else."

Mary looked from Sherlock Holmes to her trusted Team Member. "Mister Holmes, perhaps this man is correct. Are you sure you took the blood sample from him?"

Holmes looked to Watson who looked back at him. "Perhaps she's right, Holmes," the Doctor said. "Did you accidentally take it from someone else?"

The great Detective rubbed his long jaw in thought. "Perhaps I did, Watson. If you'll remember, the Palace Living Room was crowded. A Captain of Interpol stepped in between me and my target as well as a number of other Humans including the King and Queen of England. I could have taken the sample from any of them."

"Sir, why is the sample important?" Mary asked. "Does it have a bearing on this present mission?"

"It does, Madam," Holmes replied, his thin lips compressing. "When I talked to your husband, he said that his murderer, a woman, was bleeding. But he also said that a man that looked very much like this Tony was there dressed as an EMT. Now, we both believe that either this man Tony, who is actually my enemy Professor Moriarity, or the woman in Yellow is intent on executing the present King and Queen of England."

Mary walked up to the great Detective Holmes and shook his hand. "Thank you for your quick analysis of this situation. But may I point out that if your arch-enemy, the Professor, is still alive he would be well over one hundred years old? He was older than you or Doctor Watson in your crime stories. Can you explain that?"

Doctor Watson frowned at Holmes who also frowned. "What you say is true, Miss Chief Inspector. Moriarity would be much older than this Tony if he was still alive. I and Watson have been dead for many years, so we look the same as we did the day we were both murdered by our common enemy."

"Which is a woman, might I remind you Holmes?" the Doctor interjected and turned to Mary. "The woman was wearing Yellow when she shot us, Miss Sweet. Mind you, many women today wear yellow. It's a common colour. Whereas, in the England of our day, yellow…"

"Wasn't so common," Mary replied and began pacing the room. "Which leaves us exactly where we started. Someone is working with the General to kill the King and Queen. If we don't stop them…"

"Then God help us," Hubert said as he floated into the room and joined them. "It certainly isn't me, is it, sweet?"

"No, it's not Hubert," Mary said, smiling. "I'd better start a list of those I think could truly be traitors. I'll cross the names off that list as I decide who is innocent and who isn't."

"Maybe it's that McMouse character," Watson stated sternly. "I never liked mice too much. Filthy beasts. They were responsible for the plague, you know."

"It was rats, not mice, Watson," Holmes stated. "Though they are both rodents. Filthy beasts, the lot of them."

Mary smiled at the two of them. "I'll have to think about all that you've said. But I can cross Tony off the list, as well as his wife. Don't you agree?"

"Done," Holmes muttered. "I'll continue with my forensic analysis. Perhaps the traitor is someone we've not yet even met."

"Which is a decided possibility, don't you concur, Mister Watson?" Mary asked the Doctor. When he nodded, she walked to the middle of the room and climbed up on the table. "Attention everyone! All humans, Ghosts and animals. I'll have a major briefing here in exactly thirty-seven minutes. Get yourselves a cup of tea and something to eat because it's going to be a long night. And," she said to everyone who was looking up at her, "for all real men, women and animals in this room, the Great Sherlock Holmes might ask you for a blood sample, fingerprint, or paw print. I hope you'll comply with his request."

When she climbed off the table, Mary turned to her husband. "Sweet, have you seen Mum and that Simpla one recently?"

"They're at The Tower of London," the Ghost husband said with a smirk. "They think they can help catch the Spy and murderous General."

"Do they now? Again?" Mary replied. "You're not joking are you. You never joke about my mother or that simple one."

Sighing, she put a hand to her head and felt the room spinning again. "I need to eat something and have a lie-down. Hubert, is it in your power to bring me a bit of dinner and cuppa to my office?"

"It certainly is, dear," he replied and kissed her on the cheek. "I'll be with you in only moments."

When he disappeared in a flash of light, Mary walked out of the Meeting Room then to her office. Lying down on a couch that was there, she fell asleep in seconds. When Huburt drifted in with her meal and found her sleeping, he couldn't help but smile. "My little hen is all tuckered out," he whispered. "I'll place the tray full of her dinner on the desk and let her sleep for a few minutes. Then, I'll wake her up so she can eat something before she captures the General. And of that, I'm certain she will."

In the apartment in 221B Baker Street, Sherlock Holmes stood by the open fire as Doctor Watson sat in a comfortable armchair. Watson had a glass of whiskey in one hand as Holmes walked over and added some water from a crystal cannister. Walking back to the fire, the great Detective stared up at the ceiling.

"Holmes, my friend, do you have any idea who is trying to murder the King and Queen?" Watson asked as he took a sip of his drink. "Or do you believe that your reasoning has been again reduced to rubble because of the Cocaine that you've started to take again?"

"Cocaine has nothing to do with my reasoning, Watson. If nothing else, that white powder makes the cases clearer." Holmes looked down at Watson and noticed his muddy boots. "I see you've been back home, again, my dear friend."

"Why do you say that? I could have been anywhere. London streets are always muddy when it rains."

"Yes, they used to be in times gone by. But now they're not muddy, they are bone dry." Holmes smiled at his friend. "Did you see your wife again? And if so, did you get rid of that revolting maid you had? In my estimation, the answer to both questions is a decided 'No'."

Watson chuckled as he smoothed his jacket. "You're right, of course. Yes, I saw my wife. And no, I didn't fire the maid. She's been working for us for many years. I have no reason to fire her."

"But you do, Watson! What's that on your coat?" The great Sherlock Holmes walked back over to his friend and picked a piece of yellow thread from the man's lapel. "Yellow thread and mud on your boots? Were you down by the Thames by chance? There are places near the water where a person, even a maid, can step into mud."

Watson took the piece of thread in two fingers and studied it. "The maid took my boots to dry before the fire two days ago or so," the man replied. "When I told her I needed them for my visit to you tonight, she said she had moved them outside and they were soaked. Yet, when I looked beneath one of those modern radiators, I found that she had tucked them beneath them so I couldn't see either of my boots."

"Take off your boots, Watson."

The doctor untied the laces and Holmes stooped over and picked them up. Taking them to an oil lamp he had lit which stood on his desk, he closely examined each of them. "See here, my friend?" Holmes stated as he pointed to some deep scratches in the leather right near the soles of each boot. "These are the slashes made by dog teeth. I deduce that a large black dog, a Labrador, made them when he was attempting to eat the shoe leather."

"But Holmes, why do you think that?" Watson asked as he walked to the desk and leaned over his friend's shoulder. "Those could be the mark of a knife or anything sharp."

Holmes held one of the boots closer to the lamp. "See those two deep slashes there, Watson? Those were made by a surgical knife." The Detective looked into that boot and with a long pair of silver tweezers, drew out two long strands, one dull yellow and the other white. "The yellow is a piece of blonde hair from a female. The white is a thread from a nurse's uniform."

"Truly, you can't deduce that simply by holding those strands to the lamp, can you?"

Holmes waved the strand of white thread over the lamp then held it to his nose. "Perfume! Men don't wear perfume, Watson. Some wear aftershave but never perfume, not ever! This strand of white is definitely part of the woven cotton fabric from a nurse's uniform. The other? A strand of female blonde hair. We must get ourselves back to the London Police Station to meet with the Chief Inspector. My deductions will tell her exactly who to look for. This is the woman in Yellow! This right here!" He again picked up the short strand of Yellow thread. "We're looking for a woman dressed in Yellow with blonde hair and somehow wearing a nursing uniform. She'll have a black dog, probably a Labrador, with her. She'll have muddy boots because after your maid had given her to this suspect, we'll call the Woman in White and Yellow, she gave them back to the maid who hid them in an attempt to make certain you couldn't find them. Which means, of course, that the maid is in on the series of crimes, too!"

Watson stepped back to his chair to retrieve his glass of whiskey. Downing it in a single long drink, he patted his wet lips and moustache then looked back at his dear friend. "Holmes, it's been much too long since we worked on a crime together. Get your coat on and we'll float back to the Police Station again."

When Holmes and Watson were both ready, they heard a noise in the adjacent room. The door to Sherlock Holmes' Chamber opened and a man carrying a torch walked in. Flashing the lamp around the room, he walked to the open fire, his mouth dropping open.

"Why, this fire hasn't been lit in years, not since the great Sir Arthur Conan Doyle lived here."

A woman wearing a nightdress stepped into the room and stood next to her husband. "Lawrence, there be ghosts in this room. I've told you that for years and years."

"Many years, and you're right, Petya. People say that Holmes and Watson are fiction but we've never believed that, have we?"

The wife took her husband's hand and squeezed it as her eyes glittered in the firelight. "No, we never did. And a good thing too. That great Detective is probably working on a new case to save the lives of the King and Queen."

Holmes looked to Watson and smiled. "Shall we let them see us?"

"No, my friend. If they did, they'd both scream and then where would we be? No, let's get back to the Station."

As the couple turned to go back out of the small room, a great flash of Light and thunder ripped through the old Chamber.

The wife looked to her husband and smiled. "That's them, Lawrence. Them, for sure!"

"Yer right, Petya. That was them in that flash of light! I swear by my dead mother and father that I caught a glimpse of them as those great Detectives went up the chimbley." Lawrence looked around the room again and in the dying fire, caught sight of an empty whiskey glass sitting on the dusty surface of the ancient desk. Picking it up, he put his nose into it then using his finger, he tasted the remaining liquid. "That be whiskey for sure! Irish whiskey. Legends say that Watson was oh so fond of a drop of Irish Whiskey."

He took his wife's hand and led her from the Chamber as the fire finally died. He closed the door and as he did there was another flash of bright white Light. A hand reached out from the fireplace flu and grabbed an umbrella from the top of the desk. Opening, the black umbrella sailed up the chimley as a voice said, "Watson, you almost forgot your umbrella again!"

Then, the house shook with a final clap of thunder as, over it, two Ghostly figures sailed through the night sky, one clutching tight to the end of a black, opened umbrella.

As the sun climbed higher overhead, Chief Inspector Mary Sweet climbed up the steep ladder that led from the River Thames. Looking down, she saw a handful of local Police and Detectives walking through the Tidal Mud. Climbing onto the cement path that lay next to the street along the river, Mary stamped her Official Boots free of the mud and black muck and walked across the street to the French Restaurant which had been completely refurbished since the time that her husband was murdered. Looking inside, she could see her mother and that Simpleton Simpsa sitting together at the bar. Glancing up at the large clock on the wall, she saw that it was just after Noon.

"Mother's half-drunk already," she whispered to Holmes and Watson who floated beside her. "I'll have someone keep them both amused while we try to find the General and his gang of Spies."

Watson looked at Mary's mother and smiled. "A drop of alcohol for a woman as apparently old as she is can never be a bad thing, Ms Sweet."

"A drop? That's the problem. She'll drink the entire bar dry!" Mary countered as she looked over to Holmes. "Detective, thank you for your deductions. They're all we need to catch this gang of Perpetrators."

Holmes doffed his Deerstalker hat and bowed his head slightly. "It's always a pleasure to help rid London of any criminals whatsoever," he said and smiled. "Now, dear lady, if it's all right with you, Watson and I will observe the proceedings from The Tower of London. If you need me, just clap and I'll be right beside you."

Mary closed her eyes but this time there was no flash of light. Opening them, she saw the two Detectives floating high over London as they made their way for the nearby Tower. Pulling out her radio, she keyed the mic. "Detective McMouse. Come in, please. Over."

On the roof of the Tower, the short mouse yawned and stretched from the nest it had built in the White Stallions long mane. Putting the radio to his fluffy ear, he keyed his mic. "McMouse here, Chief. I read you. Over."

"McMouse, we know who the real perpetrator is now. We're looking for a woman wearing White and Yellow. From now on, we'll call this simple woman, Tully Gale White Yellow. Do you read me? We need all eyes on the River Thames. Look over the brick parapet of the Tower and I'll send up a red flare."

The mouse looked over the Tower bricks from its high position on the white horse. He saw a streak of white then a 'Bang' and a red flare blossomed. He took out his Mouse Army binoculars and focused them on the River right below the flare. "Chief, McMouse here! I see her! A woman dressed in Yellow and White and…Oh, gracious me! It's that Tullisha Gale from the Asylum! She's walking along the cement path with a black dog. Beside her is a man holding her hand. Good gracious me, again! It's that jerk, Nurse Cleve!"

Outside the French Restaurant, Mary smiled. She turned to Hubert and Inspector Bernie. "Inspector, where are the King and Queen right now?"

"Ma'am, they're both still in Buckingham Palace. The King has decided to transport his family and his staff to Windsor Castle for the duration and until we can catch the General and his spies."

"Very good, Bernie. Now here's what I want you to do. There are many men and women who enjoy imitating the King and Queen. We have many theatres right near us. Order a London Police Officer to go to a few theatres and find two volunteers."

"Will do, Chief," Berne replied as he saluted her. "I'll do that job myself, if you don't mind. In fact, I've played the King many times in the past at Pantomime Performances each and every Christmas for years!"

"Really Inspector? Then you're the King. Now all you have to do is find your Queen."

"But I already have a Queen, remember? And you're it!" He laughed and clapped his hands twice. Holmes appeared at his shoulder immediately.

"Can I be of service?" the Detective asked as he floated near them. "I'm now a simple apparition. The real Sherlock Holmes is still with Watson on the roof of The Tower of London. We saw your red explosive float through the air above our Perpetrators. Now all you have to do is flush them out and arrest them before anyone is injured or killed."

"Which is absolutely correct," Mary said. "Inspector, can you please get us both costumes. I'm sure you know where to find them. Tell the King and Queen what we're doing which is to lure our prey to us before we grab them all. I'll meet you back here in a few minutes."

When the apparition of Holmes had disappeared, and Bernie had left to find costumes, Mary Sweet decided to get a better look at her quarry. "Hubert, can you take me up there?" she asked her husband as she pointed to the London Eye. "That would be a great place to keep a look out for the General and to keep an eye on Tully and Cleve."

"Certainly, darling," he replied as he took her hand. Floating over the River Thames, he landed her gently in one of the egg-shaped plastic enclosures housing the long customer seats. When the giant wheel began to turn, Mary picked up her radio again. "Mary Sweet calling! Tell the operator of the London Eye to stop all equipment until I tell them to. I need to keep watch on the River Thames for our Perpetrators."

A London Police officer came back to her immediately stating he would carry out the order. Sitting down on a seat with Hubert next to her, Mary took out her binoculars again and focused on the foot traffic that passed back and forth on the cement path just across the River.

"Hubert, look! It's the General. And with him are two, not one, but two women in Yellow!"

As she watched, the General climbed off his horse and approached both women. She also saw a man costumed as a White Egg walk toward them. When he lifted both hands, she knew immediately that it was Colonel Francis Assisi. "Hubert, that's Francis down there! He promise that he would help us protect the King and Queen, and he is. And one of the Women in Yellow has to be Captain Jennifer! She's talking to the General. See? What the hell is she up to?"

Hubert floated out of the plastic egg-shaped car and toward the people in Yellow. As he did, Mary watched through her binoculars as Jennifer drew a small hand-gun and aimed it at the head of the General. Putting up his hands, Mary saw many people dressed in Interpol Uniforms rush toward him. "She's caught him just like she swore she would!" Mary yelled. "Now all I have to do is get down from here to help her and her soldiers."

Just as she was getting out her radio again, she heard shots being fired. Looking toward the Restaurant, she watched as Jennifer slumped to the ground. Looking through her binoculars again, she saw the General and the other woman in Yellow look toward the River Thames. Tully Gale and Cleve jogged into view and the Chief Inspector saw that both carried handguns. "That bitch! She killed my friend and she'll never get away with it! It'll be me who kills you or arrests you before the day is done."

Mary keyed her radio mic and ordered the operators of the Eye to restart the machinery. As she approached the ground, Mary heard a number of explosions. Looking across the River, she could see that the road itself was the source of those loud bangs. As people screamed and started to run in panic, the Chief Inspector watched as more explosions blew out portions of the main street, killing and injuring many civilians.

"Mines! Just as Princess Diana warned me about in my dreams! This means that all of the public places of London as well as its roads and streets could also be filled with mines!" Now near the ground, Mary jumped from the car to the cement path and ran toward London Bridge. As she neared it, she saw Sir Lancelot and his White Steed Goldenrod float toward the ground. McMouse clung to the main of the horse.

"Detective McMouse! Call all the animal Teams! Have them sniff for explosive devices in the roads, streets, parks and public place across our City. Do it now, sir, before more people are killed!"

Lancelot took his sword from its scabbard. "Tally-ho we go again! And into battle!" As Mary watched, he began to float away across the Thames high on the back of his trusty stallion. Then, hearing a noise like the rushing of a hurricane, she looked up and saw what appeared to be a hundred knights on horseback. In the lead was the glint of a large sword and a King that she also knew held it high into the air.

"Knights! Protect Sir Lancelot! Gawaine, take the lead now. Lead our knights and the Knights of the Roundtable into bloody battle against the enemies of the living King and Queen!"

The Knights left King Arthur as they swept to both sides of Sir Lancelot and the mighty White Stallion Goldenrod. Then, she heard small arms fire from a road behind her. Turning around, Mary saw herself face to face with a dozen people holding handguns and automatic weapons in their hands. "McMouse! Get down!" she cried as bullets rained down on them. They pinged against the cement path and, one of them ricocheting off of it, McMouse doubled over in agony.

"Chief, I've been hit in my tiny tummy!" he squeaked.

The Chief Inspector got on her radio again. "This is the Chief!" she yelled over the rat-tat-tat of gunfire. "Get an ambulance over here, quick! McMouse has been hit and could be dying. I repeat, make that quick!" When she looked up, she could see more automatic firing. Getting out her handgun, she picked up McMouse in the other hand and, seeing the blood all over his uniform coat, started running toward the Thames. Arms fire and small explosives followed her as she leaped over a concrete barrier and lay, sprawled, on a walking pathway planted with grass.

"McMouse! Are you alive?" she said into his ears. The wounded mouse opened his small eyes.

"Chief, I'm alive but barely. I have a letter to my wife and small family in my vest pocket. If I die and go to Mouse Heaven, give it to her."

The he closed his eyes again. Mary could tell he was still breathing because his small chest still went up and down. Then she heard the wail of an ambulance, and looking toward London Bridge, saw it and its blinking blue lights with Police Armour Plated Vehicles on both sides. "McMouse, they're coming here right now! Hold on. It'll only be a few seconds."

The Armoured Escort returned fire with its Fifty Calibre Machine Guns as Mary checked the chamber of her automatic Glock Handgun. Pointing it at London Bridge and the Spies who were trying to kill her, she returned fire. A figure dressed with a Yellow Sash screamed and fell from the bridge into the River below. The mouse opened its eyes and tried to smile. "They're coming? Is that what you said?" he whispered. When Mary nodded, he closed his eyes again and his arms flopped to his side.

"McMouse! Stay with me, do you hear? The Ambulance is here!"

The white ambulance with its Red Cross pulled up beside her as did one of the Armoured Cars. Two EMT specialists climbed out under a hail of gunfire. One of them picked up McMouse in her hand and placed him on a tiny roller bed. Escorted back to the Ambulance, Mary followed protected by the Defensive Machine Guns that the Police fired from the giant Car. Climbing inside with McMouse and the Specialists, she watched as one of them inserted a small needle into the mouse's arm while another placed a Human oxygen mask over the mice's entire body and turned on the flow of gas.

"Breathe, McMouse. Just breathe!" Mary begged as she fired back at the enemy on the bridge. Then she heard a roar of pain and looked into the sky. She could see Sir Lancelot on his White Stallion being hit in his armoured chest. Blood spilled from his body as, bent over on his flying horse, the Stallion Goldenrod was hit by a number of bullets in the head. Down toward the ground they both plummeted as King Arthur grabbed the Stallion's white halter.

"Stallion, thou shalt wake from your midnight sleep now!" the King shouted as he placed his sword Excaliber on the wounds. Mary watched in wonder as all the wounds sealed shut and the blood stopped flying from Goldenrod's head. Opening its eyes, it began galloping through the sky again and up into the Heavens. Mary could see the Once and Future King lift off his gallant Knight's helmet. Sir Lancelot's head slumped over and she could hear a mighty cry from the King as other Knights joined in the chorus of grief and anger.

"Sir Lancelot be dead! The Gallant Knight is Dead! Onward to Avalon we shall fly with our Knight where, before he goeth, he shall meet the great real love of his life and his Queen in Heaven."

The Might King Arthur descended to the ground. Climbing off his great Horse Hengeron, the King walked through a panicking crowd of his subjects before finding the woman in Yellow lying on the ground. He watched as a number of men and women used some sort of strange objects as one of them said, "She's dead. Mark the time of death as…"

The King placed his sword Excaliber upon her many wounds. When her eyes opened, she gazed up at a stately figure dressed as a King. "Are you… are you the Egg man?"

"No, I'm here." A short man in a blue coat with his hood up walked forward. Looking up at the man Captain Jennifer had called King, he immediately recognised him from the books that he had read. "You're King Arthur, are you not my King and Liege?" When the King nodded, Francis sank to his knees. "Sir, I am your new small knight. I am Francis but you can call me by whatever name you desire."

King Arthur smiled down at the small figure. "You are called Francis? Then I shall also call you by that name." He placed the Sword Excaliber on the man's shoulder. "I dub thee Sir Francis of London and Dublin. Is that not correct? My Squire tells me that you live both here and in that great city to the West, just before the island of Avalon where my Knights now take Sir Lancelot."

"That I true, my King. I live in both great cities."

"Then I entrust them to your care for you have shown great bravery, my new Knight. I saw you from my flying Horse Hengeron as you defended these subjects of ours. And I saw you tried to use that strange weapon you have hidden beneath that horrible coat of armour to kill the men and women who killed this Queen I have made alive again. Rise, Sir Francis."

Francis did as he was told as the King looked down on Jennifer. "Woman, I bid you rise with me. You are now Queen of Avalon and Sir Lancelot's true loving bride. With him, you shall rule not only Avalon but all the islands and great continents to the West as far as it is until the great Ocean be filled with dragons. Now rise with me, Queen Jennifer, and take my hand and I shall ride thee to your welcome wedding."

Captain Jennifer, now Queen Jennifer, rose with the help of the EMT specialists and Police that had surrounded her. First taking Francis's hand, then the King's, her body suddenly shuddered as her clothes were stripped off by unseen hands who also hid her body from view. Then, behind the many white and dark hands, Francis watched as they sewed a Queen's white and gold wedding gown right onto her body. When they were finished, the hands disappeared as if they'd never been there.

"What am I wearing?" the new Queen said. "Where am I? Who am I?"

"This King says that you're now a Queen!" Francis stated as he pointed to the sky above them. "You will soon meet Sir Lancelot on his special Island. There, it neither rains, hails or snows until the two of you command it. Some call Avalon 'Camelot' and, well, I think it's true! Find out what it's like and let us know, Jennifer."

Nodding her head in confusion, the EMTs and Police watch, astounded, as Queen Jennifer floated into the arms of a King flying on a white and gold Stallion. "We shall fly now to Avalon where the sun never sets until I order it to!" the King roared. "Onward, my gold and white stallion. Queen Jennifer, take the two reins. You must learn to ride and jump as well as your faithful, loving husband!"

Then, joined by other Knights that flew in formation around them, and heading toward a flying boat that had Lancelot's body on it, they heard King Arthur order, "Lancelot, thou shalt open your eyes and see your bride, a Queen beyond compare!" Then, there was a flash of white and gold Light and the King, his Knights, Jennifer, all the flying Stallions and Flying Boat disappeared.

Near the River Thames, Mary watched through the back of the ambulance door as all of these many miracles transpired. She looked back at the EMT specialists who were taking care of McMouse. When the vehicle door closed, the door was peppered by enemy fire. But through the back and front windows, Mary could see an assortment of jet aircraft fly toward London Bridge accompanied by Knights flying on horseback, who all flew in close formation with the aircraft. The jets strafed the bridge a number of times as the Knights slew people with their swords and lances. When the smoke had cleared, the Ambulance driver stared the engine and she could feel it bounce along the grass toward the street.

"McMouse, we're getting you to a nearby hospital. We'll be there in only minutes. Can you hear me, Tom-Jon? Are you there?"

The mouse opened his eyes and really smiled. "Yes, I feel that we're moving and I feel much, much better. See?"

The tiny rodent lifted up his soaked vest. Underneath, the bullet-proof vest that he always wore to work was shot through with one single large hole. "It missed my heart," the mouse said to Mary. "You can't keep a mouse Detective down forever, can you?"

Mary smiled. "No, mouse, you can't. But it's time for a good rest, and I think I'll join you for a day or two just as I promised my doctor and Surgeon many months ago. But first, I have to make certain that the Police have apprehended the true suspects in our case."

When the ambulance turned onto London Bridge, Mary climbed out and jogged back down the stairs and the hill that led to the River Thames and the French Restaurant. Hurrying up to a large crowd, she saw that the Police had, indeed, captured General Gusto Gatwick, Tully Gale and Cleve. A large black Labrador, tied to a rope that a Police Officer held, barked at Mary as she stepped through the thick crowd toward the apprehended criminals.

"You have them at last, Detective," she stated to a Detective Officer standing next to the three criminals.

"Indeed, we do, Chief Inspector," he replied with a twinkle in his brown eyes. "We've also captured and killed a number of this disloyal General's spies and troops."

General Gusto glared at Mary and tore the ruffles from his throat with both of his handcuffed hands. "You've caught me but I'll be free soon! You watch, you murderous bitch!"

Mary just stood there smiling as the sun came out from behind the clouds again. Turning around, she saw the other pair of criminals. Stepping up to face Tully Gale, Mary smiled and then, without a thought, spit into the woman's face.

"There, bitch. Take that back! You thought you had us fooled, didn't you? But you never fooled some of us. Same thing for you, Cleve! You two were never nurses at all. I've had time to do some research on both of you. Cleve, you were once a loyal member of Britain's armed forces but you were first demoted from Captain to Private for insubordination. Then you were tried for murdering a woman who you said made you do it, and found guilty. With nothing else to do, you learned to be a psychiatric nurse while serving time in a military prison in Wales. Then, having met this Tully woman there who had also been sentenced for murder, the two of you escaped."

Turning to Tully, Mary Sweet smiled as brightly as she could. "And as for you: once upon a time, you were a Russian agent. You always worked for the Russians until you met the General who was at the prison trying to help out an old friend of his. When the two of you met, it was love at first sight because human lives mean nothing to either of you."

Turning back to the Detective, Mary said, "Take them away, Detective, and make sure that they're always guarded by the best that you have. They're both very slippery customers."

As the Detective started to lead them away, Tully Gale who had also been handcuffed, reached for Cleve and, lifting his coat, grabbed a small handgun that he had concealed there. When he looked up, smiling at her, Gale shot him once in the face. Turning around, she opened fire on the Detective who fell with a wound in his throat and chest. Mary reacted as quickly as she could. Reaching for her own weapon, she discovered that it was empty. Rolling to the ground, she reloaded as she watched Tully Gale run for the River Thames. Finally reloaded, Mary got up and followed her. She fired a number of times as Gale climbed up on the steel fence that overlooked the River and, avoiding the bullets, made a leap for freedom.

Hours later, Mary Sweet lay in a bed beside the smaller bed of McMouse. When the door opened, a male nurse came in carrying a tray of tea and scones. Seeing that her Detective mouse had fallen asleep, Mary told the nurse to place the large tray down on the table beside her. Buttering her scone and adding some jam, she poured herself some tea from a small silver teapot and added a bit of milk to it. She sipped the hot tea and nibbled at a scone. "I'll save some of this scone for McMouse. When he wakes up I'm sure that he'll be hungry. I know I am."

When she finished, she also fell asleep. In her sleep, Mary dreamed that she was being followed by Tully Gale. She tried to shoot Mary with a large handgun but Mary returned fire and the woman fell down. This time, that crazy woman was wearing red, not white or yellow or even gold clothing. Smiling in her sleep, Mary realized she'd seen the next disguise of the criminal who was now on the run from justice.

'Red,' Mary thought to herself as she continued to dream. 'Red. The colour of Russia. If I see red again, I'll know what it means.'

Finally sleeping without dreaming, she didn't notice as the door opened and her entire Human Team walked in. One of them carried a small vase filled with white and orange flowers. Another one held a small flower with a note pinned to it which had been written that day by Mrs McMouse. Because both patients were asleep, the Team left the flowers and note on the table beside the scones and, walking as quietly as they could from the room, closed the door behind them.

McMouse was dreaming too, as he slept beside Mary. But he dreamed a much different dream. 'I see a beast that's as beautiful as anyone or anything I've ever seen before,' he said to himself in his dream. 'I wonder if it's a dragon or perhaps another dragon spy I'll get to know soon? Whatever it is, I hope it leaves us all alone.'

Then the mouse rolled over on his side and, as both of the patients snored softly, slept the sleep of a thousand small lives.

CHAPTER 12

The Maskarova that Fools London and Paris

Back in her home in London, Mary Sweet tried to sleep in the large double bed that Hubert used to sleep in, too. Her hand slid under his pillow and all she could do was imagine that he was alive again. She looked at the new travel alarm clock that Bernie had bought her after she and Detective McMouse had left hospital and saw that it was only 6AM in the morning. Having had a poor night's sleep, Mary rolled over and closed her eyes again but all she could image was her husband making love to her again.

"Fuck this stuff!" Mary yelled to the darkness. "I'm getting up."

She'd already kicked off the bedclothes in her sleep and, her face covered with sweat, jumped out of bed then pulled the curtains back. Now almost Christmas again, she looked across the street and saw that a neighbour had already put up their Christmas tree. "Look at the tree lights, Detective! They're beautiful again this year."

McMouse, who had been asleep in a drawer filled with Hubert's socks, stretched and sat up. "Yes, I can see them from here too, Chief Inspector. Look! Some of them are blinking!" He looked at Mary's new alarm clock and saw the time as well. "Time for me to get up. My wife told me to buy her the smallest Christmas tree I could find around here. She and the children are moving to this street. She'll live with her mother and all of her London relatives."

"McMouse, why have them all live on the street in a tiny nest that will be so cold this time of year? Have them all live here! This is a big house and we've lots of space for mice in many of our rooms. They also have drawers and we can stuff them with old clothes that I'll find in the attic. And as for a tiny Christmas tree? Why not share our large one! All of your mouse children can hang their stockings on the mantle above our fireplace."

McMouse started to giggle then he laughed, clapping his two small paws together. "Mary Sweet, that would be wonderful! It will be so warm in this home, much warmer than living in a tiny nest I was going to build beneath the eve of that house across the street. Does Saint Nicholas still visit you here?"

Mary walked to the bureau and pulled open the bottom drawer. Pulling out a red Saint Nicholas jacket, she put it on and turned to her mouse friend. "See what I found in the attic? Hubert used to wear this on Christmas Eve. He'd creep into this room with one Christmas present for me and, though I pretended to be asleep, I'd watch as he hid it beneath the bed. Then, I'd pull the sheet over my head and jump up. Hubert would be so frightened that he'd faint and hit his head on the wooden floor. I could pretend to be Saint Nicholas for your children this Christmas Eve, if you wanted me to."

McMouse shook his head. "But I thought Saint Nicholas was alive. Is the Saint of Christmas truly dead?"

"Not at all, Detective. It's just that we get so little snow and ice on the roof that his reindeer have trouble landing here."

The mouse laughed again. "That's easy to solve! I'll make snow and ice with a big machine that I found not far from here. Someone abandoned it and the Council is going to pick it up soon and destroy it. I'll use that and have one of the stronger Ghosts help me to fly it up to the roof a few days before Christmas."

`"That's perfect, mouse. Saint Nicholas can fly right to our home on Christmas Eve! We can use strings of coloured lights to provide him with directions to our small landing strip on our roof."

Just then she heard a roar from downstairs. "Child, where is my breakfast! I want a complete fry up including tea and toast!"

"Here we go again, mouse," Mary sighed. "Hubert could deal with that cold-hearted woman. Now, with him gone on to Paris for a Ghostly conference, I guess I'll have to deal with her."

"Not at all, Chief. Let me talk to that dear woman you call your mother but, as it turns out, isn't your mother at all!"

"She's not my mother?" Mary whispered in disbelief. "But she has my birth certificate. It was signed by the doctor attending my birth as well as her and my father. But Dad, of course, died many years ago."

"Not true!" McMouse roared. "That Gertrude Johnson is a fake name. She tried to kill your father the day that he brought you home to this house. She pushed him out of the only window in this bedroom. But, as he fell, his long coat caught on a loose gutter right below the window. Hanging there and looking down, and seeing only the streets and a line of metal fencing, the poor man started to scream! Neighbours stepped out and saw your Dad in grave danger so someone ran to get the fire brigade. They rescued him but only after he fell to the ground, hitting his head on the stones of the front garden. When he woke up in a London Hospital, his doctor quickly discovered that your father was suffering from amnesia."

"My father's still alive?" Mary said with a loud voice that filled the room. "Where is he now, Detective McMouse."

"I'm having the Mouse Team trying to track him down right now. We should have him home for Christmas."

"And what about my real mother? Who is she?"

"Her name is Abigail Johnson. Gertrude's real surname is Jansen. That's why it was so easy to forge your mother's signature. She simply used an old eraser that she had in her pocket to erase a few letters of your mother's last name and change it with her own surname. And as to where she is now? Well, Mary, that's easy. She's living down the block, only a few doors down. We were able to track her down as soon as we learned about Gertrude."

Mary's face broke into a large smile just as Gertrude again roared, "Where is my breakfast! I want it now, do you hear me! Right now!"

"Detective, can you please call our London Police Station? Have them send one uniformed officer here as soon as possible. As for that Simpsa character, is she a maid or what is she, mouse?"

The Detective's face also broke into a large smile. "No maid was she ever, Chief Inspector. She's Gertrude's younger sister. That Simpsa's name is really Susan Deegna, who's been on the run for many years because of the theft of a great deal of cash from Barkley's Bank, your local branch. Shall I ask the Officer to arrest her, too?"

"By all means, mouse. If there's a reward for either of them, you keep it then split it up and give it to your Mouse Team as a Christmas Bonus. Now I'm going to get dressed. I'll have a shower later." Mary rubbed her hands together. "It's time to confront those Bitches who think they can live here for free! Haha! We both know, mouse, that nothing in live is ever free."

Mary walked to her closet and quickly dressed in her new Chief Inspector's Uniform. It now had a Saint George medal hanging from her coat pocket and embroidered on the left sleeve of her jacket uniform. "That was so kind of the King to give me this,

McMouse. Yes, I was brave but so were all the other members of our Teams."

"The King sent one to every member of all of your Teams," the mouse explained as he held up his Detective uniform coat. "See? I received one too by special delivery only last night."

Mary put on her uniform coat and, touching the medal with her finger, reached up into the closet and took down a white box that she'd filled with important papers. Opening it, she quickly found what she was looking for. "There it is. My birth certificate! This is a copy, Detective. The real one is in a safe down in the basement where Hubert has his office."

Taking out the copy of the birth certificate, she studied Gertrude's signature. "Here, Detective McMouse. Look at this signature! You can see where some of the letters have been rubbed out by that false mother and replaced with a few other letters."

McMouse studied the official document and smiled again. "Yes, Mary. That's definitely been erased then forged by this so-called mother of yours."

"I'll be back in a few minutes. When I leave, please call the Police."

Mary walked out the door and down the stairs. She found Gertrude in the kitchen waiting at the table, with a fork and knife in each hand. "So, daughter, you finally decided to come make my breakfast."

"Where's Simpsa, mother? Is she late again."

"Oh, forget Simpsa! I'm going to fire her today. Now get me my breakfast, daughter, before I scream again!"

All that Mary did was smile. Taking her birth certificate from her pocket, she unfolded it then thrust it in front of Gertrude's long snivelling nose. "Read it, you Bitch! You're not my mother. Your real name is Gertrude Jansen. That signature right there? That's a forgery you made a few days after I was born. Moreover, I've also learned that you pushed my father, Daniel Johnson, out my bedroom window many years ago! We're tracking down his whereabouts right now. And as for my real mother? Her name is Abigail Johnson. She lives just down the street from here."

Gertrude rose, her face red with anger and shock. "Mary Sweet! I am your real mother. Ask anyone we both know. Even that dead bastard husband Hubert knows that I'm your mother."

The back door opened and the kitchen filled with a cold, icy wind as Simpsa walked in. She looked first at Gertrude and then at Mary and realized that something was terribly wrong.

"Let me get you both some breakfast," she tried to say in a very flat voice. "All I need is a pan and a few eggs. But I'll make tea first."

As Gertrude's sister stepped to the kitchen sink, the door opened again. A uniformed Police Officer walked in holding up his official ID. "Gertrude Jansen and Susan Deegna? I'm placing you both under arrest." Walking up to Gertrude, he handcuffed her. "Gertrude Jansen I'm arresting you for attempted murder, child theft, money laundering, fraud, theft of cash that you stole from Mr and Mrs Hubert Sweet, unpaid rent and any number of misdemeanours." Pushing the old woman to Mary, the officer walked up to Simpsa.

"Simpsa. Ah. Well, that's not your real name is it, Ms Deegna?" the officer asked coldly. "Your real name is Susan Deegna and you've been wanted for many years. You stole a few million pounds from Barclay's Bank but now I have you in custody. Turn around, please." As the so-called Simpsa turned around, her wig fell off.

"My God, the woman is a man!" Mary shouted as she reached for a pair of handcuffs she had in her uniform jacket. "Officer, do you know her real name? She had all of us fooled!"

"You mean 'he' don't you my dear?" the man said and, when Mary handcuffed him and turned the man toward her, she gasped. "Why, if it isn't General Gusto Gatwick! You thought you'd escaped from us, didn't you? But now I have you in custody."

"So you do, Mary Sweet, so you do," the General replied. "My woman's disguise fooled you and your husband for years, didn't it! It was the perfect ruse that I used so I could spy on you at any time of day, and wherever Gertrude showed up when I instructed her to."

He winked at Gertrude and, as the Police Officer led him out the door, the General turned back to Mary and tried to salute her but found that he couldn't. "I salute you, Chief Inspector, for being smarter than I am at least this one time. But have no fear! I'll be back soon."

"Not if I have anything to do for it," Mary replied. "You can rot in jail for all I care. Take him away, officer. Ask our Inspector Bridgestone to order a judge to try this man as soon as possible. Do I make myself clear, Officer?"

The Officer nodded and smiled. "That's an order, Chief, and I'll carry it out as soon as I book these spies in at the station." Looking from one to the other, the Police Officer frowned. "I'm going to add espionage to your list of crimes," the officer stated. "That should keep you in prison for at least the rest of your natural lives."

When the Officer walked out, McMouse scampered down the stairs. "Chief, did the Officer take them away? That's really amazing! I phoned the station only a few minutes ago."

"That's right, McMouse. Case closed, as far as I'm concerned. That General and his Spy will never get out of jail. Now, let's get to work, shall we my mouse friend?"

Just as Mary was sitting down at the table, she heard gunfire coming from the street. Reaching under the kitchen sink, she held up Hubert's police revolver. Checking the chambers, she knew that the gun was full of ammunition."

"Do you have any weapons on you, Detective?" Mary asked as she ran toward the door. Seeing the mouse nod its tiny head, Mary climbed the few steps then ran through the garden and out onto the street. The Police Officer lay dead in a pool of blood coming from his head. In the near distance, she could see the two criminals running down the street.

"General, Gertrude, stop right where you are or I'll blow your heads off!" Mary yelled as she ran after them. Quickly catching up to Gertrude, she aimed the gun at the woman's stomach. "Get on your knees or I'll fire this at you. You'll die an agonising death, not that I will ever give a good damn."

As Gertrude fell to her knees, Detective McMouse ran up carrying a small looking side arm. "Gertrude, that weapon is small but it holds standard Mouse Army ammunition. Detective, if that woman moves blow her head off!"

"It would be a pleasure, Chief," the mouse squeaked as it cocked the pistol and held it at Gertrude's head.

"Now, all I have left to do is catch the General." Mary ran as fast as she could up the street and found the General lying on the ground. He looked up at her and smiled. "Wrong again, Mary Sweet. I'm not the General after all. My name is really Susan Deegna and I'm a spy for the General and on his payroll."

"Then you're going down for murder, Deegna," Mary stated as she cocked her weapon. "Get up or I'll shoot you right here and now."

Susan Deegna rose to her feet. As she did, the mask that she wore to impersonate General Gatwick slid off. It exposed a beautiful woman's face and her cold black hair and black eyes. "You don't have to shoot me, Chief Inspector," the woman said in her English accent. "I will do it myself. See?"

As Mary watched, the woman turned away from her. She had already taken off the handcuffs using the key that the Police Officer had in his jacket. She pulled the Officer's pistol from her pocket. Pointing the gun first at Mary Sweet, Susan Deegna smiled. "I have spent many years in jail for various offences including the so-called Valentine's Day Massacre. I don't like prison. Would you?"

The woman named Susan Deegna then pointed the gun at her head and fired one time. The air filled with pieces of brain, bone and a mist of blood as the criminal fell to the ground on her back. When Mary made sure that she was dead by taking the pulse in her neck, she looked back at Detective McMouse who waved at her. Jogging back the mouse and Gertrude, Mary smiled down at them.

"That's one criminal gone, Gertrude Jansen," Mary said as she pointed the Police Officer's weapon at the old woman's head. "Now, are you disguised as anyone or are you really Gertrude Jansen?"

The woman smiled up at her. "Jansen, that's who I am, Chief," the woman said. "And no, I'm not your mother. Your mother is standing on the steps of her front door, right over there."

Mary looked to her right. Standing on the steps of a familiar looking home, the woman waved then ran over. "Chief Inspector Sweet, can I be of help?" the woman asked and then she smiled when seeing Gertrude in handcuffs. "You finally caught up to her, didn't you?" she asked in her sweet voice. "And if that's so, then you know who she is and who I really am. Mary, I'm sorry I couldn't tell you many years ago, but that Bitch of an old woman would have killed you just as she tried to kill your father."

Mary found herself crying as Police cars and Ambulances roared by all of them. She watched as they lifted Gertrude to her feet and threw her into the Police car. The ambulance stopped by the body of her Police Officer. An EMT Specialist ran out and Mary saw the man raise his right hand. "Chief! This officer is still alive! I'm taking him to hospital as fast as I can."

Mary kept crying, even louder then, as her Mother Abigail took her in a big hug. Pushing back from her, Mary dried her eyes with the back of a hand then turned to McMouse. "Detective, what an early Christmas present I've received," she said to the tiny Detective. "Tell the Teams that I'm taking one more day off. It's time that I got to know my mother, don't you think so Mum?"

The older woman, an image of Mary, smiled back and wiped the tears from her eyes. Taking her daughter's hand, the mouse watched as they walked into the small front garden, through the back door, and into what he knew had to be the kitchen.

"That Mary Sweet, what an Early Christmas present, indeed!" the mouse whispered then, when he heard some tiny squeaks, he turned around as quick as he could. An entire family of mice children tried to leap into his arms as his wife, Betty McMouse, gazed up at him. "The children want to know when you're coming home, husband," his wife said and all he did was smile.

"We need to talk, good wife," McMouse replied as he took her tiny paw in his. "Mary Sweet says that our entire family including your mother and all of our relatives, can live in her house starting right now!"

His wife looked ready to faint as, leading the tiny line of mice up the street, McMouse pointed to the house. "See, wife? Now you're the mouse woman of that new home of ours. You'll love it, don't you think so?"

She stepped up on her toes to kiss his furry cheek and smiled. "And so I will, darling mouse man and husband. Now, let's get the children inside. They're all hungry and so am I. You are too, aren't you?"

"Famished," McMouse replied and, as he led his family down the steps toward the kitchen, he heard a ghostly voice yell, "Ho-ho-ho! And a Happy Early Christmas to the McMouse family!"

"Christmas," the two mouse adults said at the same time. "I can't believe it's so close." McMouse picked his wife up in both small arms and carried her through the open door. "And a happy early Christmas to all of us," the McMouse's say to all of you reading these few words. "We all love Christmas! And even if you don't celebrate that occasion where you leave, then from all of us to you, may there be peace on our good Earth wherever you may live, work or roam."

CHAPTER 13

The Paris Peace Conference: A Prelude to Global War

When Chief Inspector Mary Sweet and her Teams of Humans, Ghosts and Animals stepped down the ramp from the C-5 Globemaster Aircraft operated by the Royal Airforce, the first thing she did was order the Ramp Personnel to start looking for anyone wearing Red.

"You're the ramp manager, aren't you?" Mary asked a French woman at a secret Parisian Airforce base. "Start looking for anyone wearing Red. That will be a sign that General Gusto Gatwick is here in your capital to assassinate your President Macron."

"Oui, Madam, I am ze ramp agent," the young French woman yelled over the turbine engines that howled from jets and helicopters that could be heard across the airfield. "But remember, most of us wear red, blue and white. It is the colours of the French flag, non?"

Mary turned away from the woman as a large Military Cargo aircraft taxied near them. The jet engine blast was warm despite the fact that it was below zero outside. When the airplane had passed, the Chief Inspector faced the ramp agent again.

"Merci, mademoiselle, Je parle francaise un peu," Mary said in stuttering French. "I know a little French and I want to apologise for my silly statement. Of course, those are the colours of the French, British and American flags. But if you or your fellow ramp agents see an aircraft taxiing in painted all in red, or with any red paint on it whatsoever, please contact me. I'll be at the local Gendarme for the duration."

A French military General walked out. Saluting the Chief Inspector, he walked her toward the military terminal. Behind them marched her various teams.

"Madame Chief Inspector, I am General Pierre Bonaparte, an ancestor of the Great Napolean Bonaparte. I have come here to meet you and say Salut and Bonjour from President Macron. He will meet you soon at the Elise Palace accompanied by his wife and family."

"*Bon*, and please tell your President *Merci Beaucoup*. I and my Teams look forward to meeting them."

The General looked over his shoulder at all the animals that marched behind them. Turning to his uninvited Guest, he said, "Madam Sweet, some of the President's relative are allergic to cats and dogs. For that reason, when you visit them, you may *not* bring them into the Palace."

Mary considered the order as they marched up to the Terminal door. As she entered, a military marching band began to play the French National Anthem, *La Marseillaise*. When they were finished, a British Colonel walked up to the Band Conductor.

"Monsieur, I am a member of the British Consulate. Why do you not play the British National Anthem to welcome our guest, the great Chief Inspector Sweet? She has been knighted by King Charles. Are you such a fool as to not know international protocol?"

"Mon dieu!" the French officer said as his eyes rolled. "Sir, you do not understand. This Mary Sweet one, she was not invited by our government to visit the President. Your King announced to us that she was flying her only this morning. And yes, I know global protocol. If you want us to play your national anthem, then you will have to direct my band yourself because if I do, I will show disrespect to my President and my flag, as well."

The British officer held out his hand. As Mary and the French General watched, he took hold of the baton and turned to the Military Band. "Ladies and gentlemen. If you please, play the British National Anthem." He swung the baton but not a single musician played. "Don't you know God Save the King? For God's sake! It's known the world over!"

A British Sargent marched up and saluted the Colonel. "Sir, I have our marching band behind us. By order of the King, we have been asked to play both national anthems to welcome Sir Mary Sweet to France."

The British Band marched out into the large area of the terminal. As the Sargent swung his white baton, they began playing the French National Anthem. A French Sargent marched up carrying the Tri-colour of Francoise as a British Soldier stepped up carrying the English Flag and the Royal Army colours. When they were finished playing both anthems, Mary Sweet was asked by the General to step up to the podium and say a few words to the few officers and journalists that were in the room.

"Ladies and gentlemen, I don't have much French so I will stick to English and I hope you'll forgive me. I come here due to the direct orders of King Charles. He bids you peace, prosperity and solidarity. I have been told by the King to hunt down the Russian spy General Gusto Gatwick."

"Madam Chief Inspector, is not Gatwick the name of an airport near London?" a French journalist asked.

"It is, Miss, but that fake General decided to name himself after that airport to confuse both the English military and anyone looking for him." Looking back over the crowd, she saw Hubert floating in and landing near the podium. As she watched, he turned away from the small crowd and, coughing three times into his hand, he turned back and to her shock, was alive again.

"Ladies and gentlemen of the press," he said into the microphone. "My name is Hubert Sweet. I'm the retired Chief Inspector of England but now work for Scotland Yard. I also bid my wife welcome to France. I was instructed to come here earlier with a number of well-known people I'm sure you know. Don't be shocked. They are not fake or in costume. They have been away in Lagos, Nigeria getting their health back. Some you think are long dead but I swear to you that they are as alive as I am. Please welcome them as they arrive off their special flight from Africa and the United Kingdom!"

As Mary and her Teams watched, the door to the Terminal opened. Through it a number of Ghosts she now knew well but who were as alive as Hubert, walked in. "That's Napolean Boneparte, my ancestor!" the French General said as he marched up to the long-dead General and saluted. "Mon grand-pere! Tu ca va?"

"Oui!" Napolean Boneparte said as he saluted back. When the small crowd began to applaud and scream at the appearance of such a famous General, a photographer started to take pictures but the famous Napolean wouldn't hear of it. "Non, si'vou plais! Non!"

Later, when the photographer looked into his digital camera, he discovered that the pictures were all dark. All that he could see was a French Tri-colour and a hazy distortion of what appeared to be a Ghost.

The Generals turned as more living people walked up to the podium. "There's Sherlock Holmes and Doctor Watson! There's Princess Diana with Queen Elizabeth! But they're all dead!" journalists shouted as Mary started talking again.

"No, they've not departed. They're as alive as I and my husband," Mary said smiling as Hubert gave her a kiss on the cheek. "Now that everyone is here, I must bid you adieu. General?" she asked as she looked for Pierre Bonaparte. "With your permission I must now go to the Palace. I will leave the Animal Teams in the care of our staff at the British Embassy. Merci, my Generals. And to both bands, I thank you too and all of you for welcoming us here."

When the Chief Inspector walked out the front door of the Terminal holding Hubert's hand, she found Inspector Bernie Bridgestone waiting for her. "Hubert Sweet! Look at you. You look wonderful, Chief!"

Hubert smiled and shook the Inspector's hand. "Don't you worry, my good friend. I've retired from the force when that traitor General murdered me. I'm now with a division of Scotland Yard that has offices in three locations: in Paris, in London and in Heaven. I'll not stay too long and certainly won't get in the way of your loving relationship with our Mary Sweet."

"But Hubert, you've just come back to me!" Mary said as she was escorted to a waiting limousine by a French Aid-de-camp. "You aren't saying that you're going away again."

"As soon as we catch the spies and executioners who want to kill the French President and the King of Britain," Hubert answered. "I won't be coming to the Palace. The Inspector and I have other more important tasks to complete while you talk to the French President on behalf of our King."

When Mary climbed into the black limo, two British Army Officers, one a Major and the other a Colonel, sat on both sides of her. Looking down at the large black bag she had brought with her from London, she saw Detective McMouse look out with a smile on his furry face. "Mary Sweet," he whispered so that only the Chief Inspector could hear him, "I'll stay in your bag. I have a listening device with me, the very latest Mouse technology. We'll record what President Macron has to say to you and play that to King Charles so he'll be kept up to date on what will soon become Peace Negotiations. We'll talk more of this when we reach the Palace."

As the long black car drove away from the Terminal, Mary turned around to see both Hubert and Bernie waving at her. "Good luck, sweetheart!" she heard them call through the open window. "You'll be wonderful again!"

The Army Major closed the window and Mary found that it was growing hot even though the air conditioning was on. "Sir, would you mind opening the window a little? I'm getting very warm."

The Officer looked down at Mary and smiled. "Madam Chief Inspector, I apologise. But there are people who want to assassinate you, too. This is an armoured car, the best that the King could buy. The windows are made of toughened glass so that in the event of an attack, anyone in the car will survive."

It was then that Mary truly began to think. 'I'm in danger, too? But of course I'm in danger. That General Bull-Gusto knows that if I find him, I'll kill him. Just like I killed that traitorous woman in front of my real mother's house."

Leaving the airport, the limousine sped onto a motorway accompanied by rows of French gendarmes all on motorcycles and wearing white and black helmets. As they began to drive into the French countryside, a motorcycle Policeman drew close to Mary's window. Looking out at him, she could see that his helmet was painted with three long Red stripes over the black and white. "That's one of the General's spies!" she stated firmly to the Army Officer. "Sir, call our Military Police. Have them arrest that so-called French motorcycle cop."

The Colonel looked out the window and, seeing the man in the red-stripped helmet, waved at him. "Madam, that's actually one of our Military Police. He's a Sargent in our Army. He wears three stripes on his helmet so we can recognise him."

"Oh, he's in the British Army, too," Mary replied and, as the limo sped on down the motorway, she leaned back and was soon fast asleep.

The Meeting with President Macron and

the Declaration of War on Great Britian The banquet room of the Elysee Palace was already crowded with dignitaries when the French Police motorcycle escort came into the courtyard and stopped at the long red carpet President Macron had ordered for his uninvited guest. The Police escort was immediately followed by Mary Sweet's British Army Motorcyclist and limousine which, when it abruptly halted tossing Mary forward in the rear passenger seat, the Sargent pulled out his sidearm and aimed it at his feet.

"That motorcycle Sargent is wearing red gloves!" Mary whispered to McMouse who was looking up at her again. "In fact, the Army Officers beside me are also wearing red leather gloves."

"I'm sorry, did you say something to me?" the Colonel asked her. "I'm sorry but I never heard you."

"Colonel, I was just looking for a lipstick in my bag," she replied. "Let's see. Where is it?"

As Mary dug into the bag with both hands, McMouse handed her the lipstick tube with both paws. "There, I found it at!" she said to the Colonel. "I'll need to use the lady's room when we get into the Palace."

"Sir, the Sargent is signalling that you should all get out of the car," the driver said primly. "He along with the French Police will now escort Mary Sweet as well as you both into the Palace."

The passenger doors on both sides of the limo opened. Mary saw that the Sargent was going to take her hand but she waved him away. "Sargent, I'm perfectly capable of climbing out of a limousine." When he reached for her large black bag, Mary frowned up at him. "Leave that to me. There are letters from the Prime Minister and the King in there. I'm to deliver them directly to President Macron and have been ordered that the bag should never leave my side."

When the Sargent stood back, Mary grabbed her bag by both handles. Stepping across the legs of the Colonel, Mary climbed out where she was greeted by a number of reporters. When they started to ask her question, she held up a hand.

"Members of the press, I'm sorry but I'm not in a position to comment at this time. When I've finished talking to the French President, I hope that we can issue a joint statement." As the crowd of reporters tried to follow her up the red carpet, the French Police stood in a line, refusing them admittance to the Palace door. They were replaced as escorts by a line of French Military Officers who all held up their swords in honour of her rank. Followed by the Colonel, Major and the Sargent, she walked as quickly as she could to the door where she was met by a man in a black suit with a white, blue and red tie.

"Chief Inspector Mary Sweet, President Macron apologises deeply. My name is George Charles de Gaul and I am the newly appointed Minister for Defence. The President is feeling very unwell. He promises that he will meet with you before you depart back to Great Britain."

Mary shook the man's hand and as they entered the Palace through the golden doors held open by Palace staff wearing formal attire, the Minister of Defence looked up as a woman wearing a dark blue formal dress walked toward him. "Chief Inspector, may I introduce you to my wife, Clarissa. She and I have only recently been married."

"Mrs de Gaul, I am so happy for you," Mary said to the woman as they both shook hands. "I'm certain the wedding was a wonderful celebration."

Clarissa smiled and leaned forward. "Yes, it was wonderful, Mrs Sweet. I hear that your husband is coming, too, to meet you here?"

"Unfortunately, Hubert has been delayed at the instructions of our Prime Minister and King Charles. He is currently traveling to the Ukraine where he will give reassurances to President Volodymyr Zelenskyi that Great Britain will support them in their long war effort by sending them fighter jets, more tanks and officers who will provide training."

The Secretary of Defence furrowed his brow as his wife looked at him, confused by what Mary had stated.

"Mary Sweet, your government can be impossible!" the Minister stated. "You know that we were planning on a joint statement with all members nations of the European Union. What your government is doing is an insult to our President, the French government and the governments of all of Europe."

Mary smiled sweetly as she studied his face. "Sir, I am definitely not a diplomat I'm only a Chief Inspector in Great Britain. Might I suggest that you contact our embassy which, as you know, is located in Paris? Or perhaps she's been invited here, too."

"*Non*, the British Ambassador is not invited to this occasion. As you know, you were not invited her either. What your government is doing by sending you here without an invitation is both perplexing and also an insult."

A man wearing a long black tuxedo walked toward them. He bowed and, taking Mary Sweet by the elbow, led her away from the Minister for Defence and his wife and toward the formal dining room.

"Mrs Sweet, I am Douglas Martin. I work directly for our Ambassador and am her Chief Advisor. The Ambassador sends greetings to you and hopes to see you before you go back to London. Don't be offended by the Minister for Defence. He's helping his President run for re-election again so must defend the record of Mister Macron."

Mary looked up at the Chief Advisor and, as she did, she heard Detective McMouse squeak, "Do exactly what that man next to you tells you to do, Chief. He is also a spy working for our government and is helping us track down the General."

Nodding down at her bag, Mary let herself be led toward a pair of tall mahogany doors. As they opened, she stared into the luxurious dining room noting that only a few people were seating at a few tables. "This room could hold a thousand guests!" Mary exclaimed to Douglas Martin. "How many guests have been invited for my meeting with the President which, of course, is now with his Minister?"

"Not including your teams, only eleven others from Britain," the man stated. "And if I sound angry, I am, Mrs Sweet. This meeting is very, very important as you know. President Macron already suspects that General Gusto Gatwick is working for your King and the British Navy as a spy for them. Macron firmly believes that we are positioning troops in Germany and Italy and will soon invade France. He is also convinced that soon we will declare war on this country."

"But that's impossible, Douglas. The British have always supported France. We have been at peace with them for, what, three hundred years or more?"

"Yes but Macron fears for his life. The story never made the press, not even the French press because that story was quashed by Macron's many supporters and friends. Chief Inspector, you must believe there was an attempt on his life recently, as well as his wife."

"It was Gusto or one of his Spies, wasn't it?"

He stopped walking and, reaching to his throat, adjusted his bowtie. "Yes, we believe it was the General or someone dressed exactly like him. All we know is what we've been told by Interpol. A woman phoned me using my private phone number. The only person who has that is our Ambassador to France, the Prime Minister and a few members of Interpol. She identified herself as Major Jennifer Lance. She told me that she'd found a red leather scarf and a red leather glove outside of the Maron's apartment."

"Jennifer Lance?" Mary said in a hushed voice then smiled. "She must be back on duty! That's wonderful news that she's also been promoted. Douglas, she's the best officer in Interpol. With her on duty, we'll finally solve this case and will also prevent war between France, Great Britain, members of the EU and the Americans."

"Don't forget the Russians," Douglas replied as trumpets began to blare from inside the dining room. "They're calling us all inside. When we sit down at our table, let me introduce you in French. Then you can talk to the other guests in English."

"Sounds perfectly sensible, Chief Advisor."

Douglas took Mary's arm again and led her into the dining room. When they were seated alone at a table, a waiter wearing a red sash began to pour them red wine but Mary waved him off. "None for me, thank you," she said firmly. "I'll have wine later when I'm finished with this meeting."

When the Chief Advisor to the Ambassador of France stood up, all eyes were on him. Turning to the Minister for Defence, he took out a prepared speech. Mary pretended to listen to his French words as she placed her black bag on the empty chair next to her. Detective McMouse scurried out and, sitting on Mary's lap, turned on his recording device.

"I don't know any French either, Chief," the mouse squeaked in a whisper as he held up the small device with a fury paw. "My mouse Team has a translator standing by. Put this tiny earpiece in your ear and you can understand what they will say."

When the mouse handed her a little acorn nut, Mary put it into her right ear. She could hear the voice of a mouse translating in a small voice. "McMouse, how do I turn up the volume? I can barely hear her."

"Push that tiny button on the end of the nut."

When Mary did, she could hear the voice clearly. "And now may I introduce you to Chief Inspector Mary Sweet," the mouse voice said as the Chief Advisor turned to her. When she rose to her feet, she saw the other Members of her Human and Ghost Teams sit down at a number of tables. Winking at them, she saw the tiny paws of a number of mice and the larger paws of cats and dogs sitting beneath the tables. One large black cat sat at her feet looking up at her. Mary turned to the Minister of Defence and his wife and smiled, then bowed her head.

"Minister and Mrs de Gaul, the members of the Press who have been allowed to attend this meeting, and other guests and friends. Thank you for your kind invitation to meet with President Macron. I understand that he cannot attend because he and his wife are quite ill. Too, I also understand that he believes that I have not been invited but that's a simple misunderstanding. An invitation from the President of France was delivered to me by special courier only two days ago. Anyway, now that this misunderstanding is cleared up, may I send greetings from my country's Prime Minister as well as King Charles."

As Mary continued to talk, McMouse scampered down the table and sat on the Black Cat's head. "Detective McMouse get off my head, I'm trying to listen, too."

"But I can't see if I'm sitting on the floor," the mouse said in Cat language. "Besides, it's warm and cosy sitting on your fur."

The big cat sighed and began to lick its paws as McMouse continued to listen to Mary. When she was finished with her brief speech, he saw her pick up the black bag from where she had placed it on the chair. "Minister, I bear two letters for the personal attention of your President," Mary stated as McMouse watched her feet walk toward another table. "One is from the Prime Minister and the other is from King Charles. In that your President can't attend this meeting, may I ask you to open them and read them?"

McMouse listened to two envelopes being torn open. He heard the ruffle of paper and the Minister clearing his throat. "Mrs Sweet, I cannot read English very well. But my wife can. May I have her read these to me?"

McMouse heard someone push back their chair. "Dear President Macron. As the Prime Minister of Great Britain I ask you to understand that we have no intention of ever declaring War on your country or any other country except Russia but only as a last resort. Chief Inspector Sweet is visiting you to deliver my short message to you. With your permission, I will soon visit your country with members of my staff and together, we can find the source of this misunderstanding. Mrs Sweet, by my instructions, is also hunting down the man who tried to assassinate our King and Queen but who is also responsible for any number of deaths and injuries in London. As you know, he caused that mayhem twice in recent months. It is also my understanding that this man and a friend of his that he now calls his wife, could be responsible for your attempted assassination. I wish you peace and continuing prosperity."

McMouse heard some papers being shuffled around. A woman cleared her throat again and started to read the letter from King Charles. When she started that long letter, McMouse scampered back up the leg of the table and sat again on Mary's black bag.

"Is she almost finished?" the mouse whispered to Mary? "I hope so because I'm getting hungry."

"Me too, McMouse," Mary replied. "I wonder what's for dinner?"

When Mrs de Gaul had finished reading the letter from the King, she walked up to Mary and gave her a kiss on both cheeks. "You're Prime Minister and King must be wonderful men," she said. "Please tell them we wish them well. We will give the letters to the President as soon as we can. We will have them scanned and sent over a secure channel to the President's office and apartment in just a few minutes."

When the two women had shaken hands again, Mary watched as Mrs de Gaul walked back to her table and sat down next to her husband. Then two back doors opened and a group of waiters walked out. Some carried plates of wonderful looking food and others carried two bottles, one of red wine and the other of white wine.

"Look, mouse. There's food coming right now! They might not have cheese yet but they'll have something you can eat. I'm sure of the. French food is divine!"

Serving the Minister of Defence and his wife wine first, Mary watched as they both chose red wine. When the waiter looked at their glasses, he shook his head and picked up both of them. Polishing each glass inside and out with a snow-white linen napkin, he placed both glasses back on the table and filled each with wine.

"Mary, you'd better take a glass of wine and toast the Minister of Defence," Douglas said to her. "Otherwise…"

"It will be construed as an insult," Mary replied. "I know, Douglas. I know."

When another waiter came up to the table, Mary and Douglas both chose white wine, not red. When the waiter had finished filling their glasses, Mary stood up and raised her glass toward the Minister for Defence. "Minister, may I offer this toast of greeting to you, your wife and the President. I hope he gets well soon as does his wife. And please accept our apologies for the unfortunate misunderstanding regarding my visit to see you all."

The Minister for Defence and his wife raised their glasses of red wine. As Mary sipped her glass of white wine, the couple drank a half a glass of red wine each in one long swallow. Still sitting in their chairs Mary, who was still wearing her acorn device, could hear the mouse translator say, "My husband, I do not feel very well." Right after that, Mary heard the translator state, "Nor do I, my wife. In fact, I feel…"

As she watched, Mary watched as both heads slumped down to the table, right into a bowl of soup that had just been placed there. Running to them, Mary looked up in alarm as the few guests began to shout. "What's happened to the Minister and his wife?" she heard an American reporter ask. "Someone, call a medic!"

As more people began to shout, Mary took the pulse of the Minister. Looking to McMouse who had scampered up her arm so he could be with her, she shook her head. "He's dead, Detective, as I'm sure is his wife." Putting on latex gloves she had in her uniform pocket, Mary picked up the Ministers glass of wine. "He only drank a half of the glass and he died. I'll have the Team analyse both the glass as well as the contents."

Sherlock Holmes and Doctor Watson ran up to her. "We're so very sorry we're late, Chief Inspector," Watson said as he took a stethoscope out of his black bag. "We were in the Ukraine with your Inspector. As you can see, Holmes and I are now human again and I've received additional training in modern medicines."

Sherlock Holmes took a pair of gloves from the Doctor's medical bag and carefully picked up the glass that had been used by the Minister's wife. Sniffing the contents, he looked toward Watson and then turned to Mary. "Chief Inspector, I don't smell anything at all. Yet as I understand it, both this man and woman died within seconds of taking a drink."

As Mary nodded, a team of medical personnel ran into the room. Running to the table, two of them tried to revive the Minister by placing him on the floor and pumping his chest with two hands as one held a mask to his face. "Careful, my friends," Holmes said to the two medics. "Do you speak English because my French can be faulty at times." When one of them nodded, the great detective stepped up to her then carefully took the oxygen mask away from the Minister's face. "From a simple deduction, I will now tell you that your Minister of Defence and his wife have died of arsenic poisoning."

"Mon dieu!" she replied as she stripped off both of her medical gloves. Standing up again, they all watched as she ran out of the room.

"Toilette," the male nurse replied. Running to the door as did the other medic, Holmes turned to Watson.

"A simple deduction, wasn't it, Doctor?" Holmes asked as his friend nodded. "Most other poisons have some sort of strong odour. Arsenic has none. And yet, it can kill a human being in only seconds."

Doctor Watson picked up both glasses which were filled with poisoned wine and placed both of them in a plastic container that he took from his medical bag. Closing it, Mary heard it sigh. "Automatic sealing, what will medical science dream up next!" the Doctor said as he placed the container back in his bag. "Chief Inspector, please tell anyone approaching the bodies that they should not touch their faces or their hands. Ideally, they will place both bodies in plastic bags and take them away where they, too, can be analysed for arsenic poisoning with a simple blood test."

As Mary nodded, she saw Douglas Martin on his private mobile telephone. When he hung up, he walked over to her. She saw from his face that he was not only angry but frightened. "That was President Macron. He just learned of the death of the Minister and his wife. He believes that it was caused by the same murdering General that not only tried to murder him but also his wife and children. He told me that the General has left some sort of red leather clothe either on the table or near it."

Mary's eyes looked across the table then fell to the chair next to the one used by the Minister. As he eyes grew wide, the great Sherlock Holmes picked up a red leather glove. He also picked up a red scarf. On each piece of clothing, an emblem had been stitched in by hand. "Very interesting, don't you think so, Doctor Watson?"

"Very interesting, indeed!" the Doctor answered as he took the glove in his hand. "That emblem is one I know well. It is a diamond, is it not my friend?"

"A ruby red diamond. As far as I know, there's only one in all the world like that."

"Which diamond?" Mary asked as he took the glove from the Doctor. "I don't know any red diamonds."

"I had the pleasure of catching the great Professor Moriarity attempting to steal that from the Parisian branch of the Bank of France," Holmes said in a dry voice. "I caught him red-handed. The gemstone is at least eighty carrots. The red is caused by light refraction due to a small fracture in the gem. I gave it to the then French President who, in turn, gave it to a Paris museum. I gather that this General must have stolen it?"

"He did," a reporter said as she walked up to the table. "Madam and Monsieur, I am with a French newspaper. We reported on that theft about six months ago. La Figaro also ran that report."

Mary looked from the reporter to Holmes, Watson and the Chief Advisor. "But the General was in London six months ago. Maybe one of his Spies stole it."

"Perhaps," Holmes said as she stroked his narrow chin. "Or perhaps it was him. We shall see. I must now examine the museum from which the gem was taken."

More medics came into the room carrying two stretchers. As a group of them placed Mr and Mrs de Gaul into body bags and zipped them tight, then placed the bags onto the stretchers, Mary noticed a small flash of light as a man in an historic French General's Uniform, wearing a hat she immediately recognised, appeared and floated high above the body bags.

"My great-great grandson, the honourable George Charles de Gaul is morte?" the General asked Mary. When she nodded, she could see the anger in the Great General de Gaul's glowing red eyes. "Morte! My relative is dead. Then I will declare war on the man or men who have killed not only him but his wife!"

When he disappeared in a flash of light, Mary looked down at Detective McMouse. "Tom-Jon, my friend, it looks like we'll have more help than we asked for."

"You know it, Chief," the mouse said as he climbed up Mary's arm to sit on her shoulder. "But Mary, what about some dinner? I'm really, really hungry now."

Smiling at him, she carried him back to her table and placed him on the white linen tablecloth. "Here, McMouse. Have some of my dinner. See? That's roasted salmon but that on the side? That's famous French cheese sauce. Melted cheese mixed with a little white wine. You'll love it."

As the mouse begin to lick at the plate, Mary sat down and began to sip at her soup. "It's gone cold but I don't care. I'm starved!" Looking at the other tables, she saw that her Team member were also eating. "I'll have to give them a brand-new brief,

McMouse," she said as she finished her soup. "Then we can find that cowardly man who calls himself a General and whoever else is with him."

A waiter came over to her table carrying another plate of dinner. Sitting it beside the one the mouse was using, the waiter looked at the tiny mouse and smiled. "Misteer McMouse like French Cuisine?" When Mary nodded, he patted the mouse on his head and, picking up the empty soup bowl, bowed to her and walked toward Holmes and Watson.

"They get to eat now too, don't they McMouse?" Mary said to her tiny friend as she watched the Great Detectives begin to sup at their bowls of soup. "And they'll need to sleep, too. Speaking of which, when we finish our dinners, I'll ask the Palace staff if I can curl up for a nap on a couch somewhere. It's too far a drive to go back to Paris right now."

Mary heard some shouting and the roar of a machine gun. Looking out the window, she watched as the Army Colonel that had escorted her to the Palace raised a machine gun and pointed it at her. When he opened fire, the glass shattered and everyone dived under the table. Mary watched as a French Police Sargent pointed his gun at the Colonel and pulled the trigger. The Colonel fell to the ground as French Police came running up. The British Army Major was running across the red carpet toward a waiting red car. As Mary crawled toward the shattered window, she watched as the British Sargent also gunned him down. Dropping his sidearm and holding up his hands, he was immediately surrounded by the French Police.

"Mary Sweet! Mary Sweet! It's Sargent Benjamin Adams! Remember, you trained me years ago in London as a Police Officer."

Mary waved out the window and standing up again, called through the window. "Sargent, they'll have to arrest you but you know that. I'll see you tonight at the Police station where they'll be holding you. Do you hear me?"

As the French Police handcuffed the Sargent, Mary waved again to him and then walked back to her table.

"Just another day at the office, isn't it, McMouse," she said as she yawned. "Time for this Mary to go to sleep for an hour. I'll see you soon."

The tiny mouse watched his Chief walk out the door as he finished his first real meal of the day. Seeing the acorn device on the table where Mary had left it, he placed it in his coat pocket then climbed into her black bag. "A day like any other," the mouse said as he stretched out on a lace handkerchief that Mary kept in her bag. "I'll be glad to get into a bed. That would be the end of a great day." And in seconds, he was asleep.

CHAPTER 14

France Declares War on Britain

Two days later, Mary Sweet's entire PIU Team as well as all of her Animal and Ghost teams were aboard a Royal Marine C-130 enroute to Saint Petersburg, Russia. As the four-engine aircraft, flying low over the eastern Baltic Sea between Estonia and Finland, the Sargent in charge of parachuting the Teams on their secret mission to Moskva came out of the cockpit and ran down the entire length of the hold to where the teams were strapped into their seats.

"When you see this light turn orange, stand up!" the Sargent yelled over the roar of the engines. "When this light turns red, hook your parachute's ripcord line onto this wire! When that light turns green, that large ramp will open and I'll order you to jump!"

When a light turned to yellow, George Smith stood up. "Alright you blighters! Get to your feet like the Sargent ordered!"

"That means us!" Nurse Edith said to her new husband, Nurse Jeremy. "Stand up, husband, and I'll show you how to hook up your ripcord to that long wire." When they booth stood up, some turbulence hit the aircraft. When both of them stumbled, Jeremy grabbed the wire and placed his hands on his wife's shoulder.

"My God it's choppy," he said as she placed the hook of his ripcord on the silver wire. "Hope it gets calmer soon."

George, standing just in front of them, laughed. "When you start to freefall through the air, you won't care if it's choppy or not. Just enjoy the ride because it's going to be a short one."

Helping his wife Maud to her feet, he attached her ripcord to the wire then checked her main chute and her reserve chute. "Looks good, wife!" he yelled, giving her a thumbs up. Then, Tony Enwenopa and his wife Maria stood up. Both hooking up their ripcords to the wire, they checked each other's parachutes then gave each other a warm hug. Nimmy Ursula and Francis Assisi also stood up and as Nimmy hooked their ripcords to the wire, she looked at the man she'd become very close to over the past few weeks and, before he pulled on his black helmet, kissed him gently on top of his bald head.

"Are you nervous, my darling?" she asked him seeing the sweat course down his cheeks. "I've never jumped from an airplane but I hear that many Nurses and Doctors from Nigeria have to do that when they're visiting their patients located in Africa's dense tropical rain forests."

Francis looked up at her and tried to smile. "Me? Nervous? Of course I'm nervous! I told Mary Sweet I was not going to jump out of any airplane whatsoever but she replied that I had to jump or we wouldn't get the danger pay she promised all of us!"

As Nimmy helped her new boyfriend put on his helmet and pulled on her own, Detective McMouse crawled into Francis's jumpsuit pocket and looked up at him. "Colonel McOuvre, remember me? My name is Tom-Jon McMouse! We have a number of mutual friends back in Ireland."

"My surname is Assisi, mouse," Francis said as he looked down at the tiny rodent looking back at him from the deep pocket. "McOuvre is my aka name. But yes, I am a Colonel in the Irish military. I order you, McMouse, to get out of my pocket. I hate rodents, snakes and most human beings except Nimmy."

McMouse simply smiled up at him. "Mary Sweet told me to ride to the ground with you. She ordered me to protect you because you're nothing but a big chicken! Just zip up the pocket and I won't bother you until we're all safe on the ground."

As Francis zipped his pocket, the Animal Teams got ready to make the big jump. Chief Inspector Claws and Mama Bluebell crawled into separate black bags as the rest of the dogs and cats followed. Bluebell saw one of her puppies trying to crawl into the Cat Unit bag but, picking him up by the fur of his neck, she placed him in the bag next to her. "Hold on to my fur with your teeth," she growled to her son as he shivered next to her. "It won't be long until we're in a warm home, okay my boy?" When the puppy nodded, Bluebell saw a human hand close the zipper on the large black bag.

"Right," the British Sargent said as he zippered shut the black bag of the Cat Unit. "I'm going to hook the Animal Team's bags to the wire. George Smith? You're retired from the British Military and Police Force, aren't you? Look after these two squads of animals. That's your job."

When George nodded, the Sargent spread his legs wide and faced the George and the rest of the Human Team. "PIU Team! Animal Teams! Are you ready to jump?"

The humans nodded and the Sargent heard some dogs and cats bark and meow. "Right. Take your stations now!" he yelled as the Green Light came on. The ramp at the back of the C-130 opened and George looked into the twilight. "See that white snow over there, Edith? That's Finland!"

Edith smiled back at George as wind tore through the entire storage compartment of the large aircraft. The British Sargent stood back from the ramp. Placing his hand on the first parachute jumper, he screamed into George's face, "Jump feet first! You hear me?" Taking a breath, George jumped. As he fell from the ramp, he felt his ripcord snap and, as he turned around in the air, the parachutist looked to see Edith jumping. As she fell toward him, he saw his parachute open up in a black rectangular silhouette. Then he was looking down at the sea and saw a number of rubber boats floating on the ocean below him.

"RIBs!" he shouted into his helmet radio mic. "Edith, do you see those RIBs below us? That's the British Navy that's come to pick us up."

As he touched the water feet first, George hit the round silver buckle on his chest. Swimming in the cold waters of the Black Sea, he unbuckled his reserve parachute, swam away from his main parachute, and pulled the rope on his life vest. As air hissed into it, George found himself floating on his back. "Edith, I see you! Pull the handle on the left side so you'll land close to me."

In the twilight, George watched as Edith pulled on the handle. Her entire main chute tilted toward him and, when her feet touched the water, he rolled over on his belly and began to swim toward her.

"That's my great woman!" he shouted as he punched her buckle and helped her untangle herself from the web of ropes that covered her. "I'll take off the reserve chute. Pull that rope to activate your life vest."

As Edith and George struggled in the water, other Team Members touched down. Looking up again, he saw the two black bags attached to a single large parachute hitting the water near him. Leaving Edith when he was sure she was safe, he swam to the bags and activated the large flotation device that kept them from sinking into the sea. When he was sure they were also safe, he looked toward the two RIBs that were speeding toward him and, reaching into his pocket, pulled out a flare and, taking off its top, lit it by pulling a small cord. Holding the flare high over his head, he began to wave it and shouted, "Here! We're here!"

Both RIBs turned toward him and he could hear the roar of their outboard engines. Swimming back to Edith, he pulled off his helmet and helped her off with her helmet. "George, I did it!" she cried as she came into his arms. "That was so much fun! Let's do it again sometime."

George grinned back and, as he looked at her and saw the excitement in her eyes, he whispered in her ear, "Edith, you know that Maud, my good wife, has landed with the Team, too. She and I had a long talk and when we're done with this Mission, she wants to go back to Heaven. She met a good man there and he asked her to marry him. She said yes, thinking she wouldn't see me for many, many years. But then? Well, you know what happened."

"Yes, George, I know what happened. Jeremy and I also had a good talk. You know, he asked me to marry him but, having had months to think about it, we both decided we're much too similar. Kack White, Jeremy's wife, has been looking after him from Heaven for years. He had a word with her in his prayers, and she's agreed to come down to Earth if God approves of the idea."

"Which He will," George said as the RIBs approached. "We won't have time along for God knows how many days. And I just wanted to tell you this. Edith, I more than like and respect you. I...well, you of all people know how I feel."

"I feel the same way, George Smith." Kissing him quickly on the lips, she watched a RIB drive toward them. "We'll have so much time together when we're finished with this Putin and Macron job."

George nodded then, as the RIB pulled up to him and stopped, he helped Edith over the wide rubber gunwale then climbed in himself. Sitting down next to a British sailor dressed in a black camouflage uniform, he watched as another British sailor pulled both of the Team's black bags into the boat. The other RIB had already picked up the other Team members except for Frank Assisi who was screaming in the twilight about some damned thing or other.

"Francis, where are you?" George yelled. "We can't see you at all. Light your flare!"

When he saw the sudden appearance of a red flare in the darkness, all he could hear from Frank screaming again. "Get this damned mouse out of my pocket! He's been peeing all the way down from that feckin' airplane!"

George began to laugh and turned toward Edith. "Looks like we're getting back to something approaching normal, my girl. That Francis one, he was in an Asylum like ours years ago. Met him when I was a London Police Officer on an exchange programme in Dublin, Ireland."

"Francis was in an Asylum?" Edith replied. "He sounds like he's rather in need of help."

"In constant need, Edith. I'll tell you more about him later."

In the east, the thin sliver of dawn appeared in the open sky as both RIBs restarted their engines. Turning toward the coastline of Estonia, they drove at high speed toward the waiting group of British Marine Commandoes that waited for them.

In a hardened bunker buried deep beneath Moscow's Red Square, the man who had disguised himself for years as a British General stood before a bathroom mirror as he shaved his large white beard and moustache off with a sharp barber's razor. As the door opened, he turned around and saw the woman who had become his next wife only three days before.

"Gusto, are you ready to see our President?" the blonde woman asked. "Don't forget to wash the white lather off your face."

"Come here, my one true love," Gusto Gatwick replied as he opened his arms. Tully Gale flew to him and kissed him, first on the cheek and then on his thin lips. Pushing her away from him, he started laughing. "Now we both have lather on our face. Perhaps on our next mission, we'll both pretend to be barbers to Spy on the Americans. They're always getting their hair done."

Smiling, she took his hand in her strong fingers. "We can't keep President Putin waiting. The appointment is only fifteen minutes from now. In that I know some Russian, let me translate for all of us. Now come into the living room and see the next plan that I set up while you were taking your shower."

Pulling him into the bedroom and through a steel nuclear blast door, she led him to a console of computers that were all aglow with green lights. "See those red blips just off Estonia? That's our fake Russian submarine fleet. And those blue triangles over there, moving quickly toward our Russian ghost ships? Those are American and British aircraft carriers who have been ordered to track them. This means that those nations have very little in reserve to defend the United Kingdom from a pre-emptive nuclear strike which I've already set on stand-bye." Pointing to a red button behind a small glass window, she opened it and turned a single silver key. Immediately, an automated woman's voice began to say: "Внимание! Внимание! Обратный отсчет до запуска начался!"

"Which means, my love?" the Russian four-star General asked his wife. "The first two words both mean 'Attention!'. But as to the rest?"

"Countdown to launch has begun."

Rubbing his hands together, General Gatwick clapped three times. "I take it that means that, when you or I push that red button, the missiles will launch in thirty seconds?"

"That's right, my sweet Russian General."

"And the targets?"

Moving to another monitor, Tully pointed again at the glowing monitor. "Do you see that large map of the entire world? Watch it when I activate the paths of our Multiple Re-entry Vehicle Rockets." Pushing a black button, a group of five white lines moved quickly from a location in Siberia. Two lines tracked quickly west. Then from one of the two lines, a series of small red blips moved toward the United Kingdom. Blossoming into large white circles of bright light, the automated female voice stated: "Уничтожено. Лондон, Белфаст, Бирмингем, Портсмут, Эдинборо, Базы атомных подводных лодок в Шотландии."

"And that means exactly what?" Gusto asked.

"Obliterated, darling. You heard the names of all the targets that have been destroyed. London, Belfast, Birmingham, Portsmouth, Edinburgh and all the submarine bases in Scotland. Now watch the tracks of the other MIRV missiles."

As Gusto and his wife watched, brilliant white circles lit up all over the world.

"That's Washington D.C., New York City, Chicago, Lost Angeles, Seattle and San Francisco gone!" Gusto said as he clapped with glee. "And there's Beijing, Seoul, Pyongyang, Kyiv, Paris, Berlin and last but not least?" he yelled as the last brilliant circle lit up over Moscow, "the Capital of our country, itself! What a wonderful woman you are, my Tully."

Looking at him, she smiled and clapped her hands five times. "Yes. And that's your ultimate plan, isn't it? With all the western capitals gone except those in Australia and in all of Africa, you'll go live on television from this bunker and tell what remains of the world that it was all Putin's doing. They'll make you King, my darling! You'll be the King of the World!"

"That's a certainty," the Russian General said as his wife helped him on with his Uniform jacket. "Now, let's get to this idiot President's apartment now and tell him that he has no alternative but to make peace with Kyiv and the rest of the world before the Americans, English, France and Israel attack him with nuclear bombs."

"Oh, my darling? We forgot one large country that also has nuclear capabilities."

"Do you mean Israel? Don't worry about them. They are too concerned about the Palestinian question. They won't be interested in what happens to the western world except for America. But by then, I'll be in control and will help them."

"And India? Are you forgetting them?"

Gusto waved a dismissive hand in the air. "The Indians? They have too much trouble running their own country and are so concerned about Pakistan that, like Israel, they won't care what happens over here."

Brushing a piece of lint from his jacket lapel, Tully Gale put on her own Russian Uniform coat. "Don't I cut a lovely figure in my new Captain's uniform?"

"Soon, my wife, I'll give you a big promotion! Then we'll both be Generals. And when this short war is over, you'll be my Queen forever."

As they left the room, another glowing monitor began to flash. The automated voice stated, "Внимание! Самолет противника приближается к границе России. Автоматизированное слежение за ракетами теперь на вооружении!Attention! Enemy aircraft approaching the Russian boarder. Automated missile tracking now armed!"

Mary a Royal Navy Sweet was flying in Gulfstream VI

when the cockpit door opened. A pilot walked down the aisle to her and handed her a white envelope. "This is urgent, Chief Inspector. We just received this over our encrypted radio. It's from the Prime Minister. Ma'am, I'm sorry. We all know you're exhausted by your trip to Paris but we've been ordered to fly immediately to the capital of Estonia, Tallin. There, you will be met by the President of France."

When the Royal Navy Captain had walked back into the cockpit, Mary tore the letter open and saw a written note from the Prime Minister.

"Dear Chief Constable. I have just received a telephone call from President Macron. He is incensed at what happened in the Palace and for that reason, he has recommended to his cabinet that his country declare war on the United Kingdom and any allies that attempt to defend us. He offers no promises of a swift resolution to this crisis but would like to meet you at your earliest convenience to help all of us negotiate a truce and lasting peace. For that reason, I as well as Our King and my cabinet order you to meet with him. Your pilot will tell you the final destination."

When she was finished reading the note, Mary smiled and looked out the window as the aircraft continued to the east. "I'll be meeting my McMouse and the rest of my Teams soon," she said to her reflection in the window then looked at her watch. "If our plan is working out, they should be heading to Moscow just about now."

The PA crackled as the Captain came on. "Chief Inspector, we have a fighter escort launched from the aircraft carriers. They are only a few miles out. If you see them make a pass by your window, it's the Americans and British. We're increasing our throttle settings and expect to be in Tallin, or any other destination we're ordered to fly to, in only a few hours."

Settling back in her seat, Mary couldn't help but giggle. "Another destination? That has to be dear Inspector Bernie Bridgestone. He knows I hate being cooped up. I bet we land on one of those big aircraft carriers and I'm taken to my final destination by a jet fighter! Oh, how I'd love that."

Fifteen minutes later, Mary's Gulfstream made a quick turn and began descending as the PA came alive again. "Mrs Sweet please buckle your seatbelt. We'll be making a short approach and will be landing on the USS Dwight D Eisenhower. It was redeployed and is now steaming just beneath us. This aircraft has been fitted with an arrestor hook so landing on that flat top is standard procedure for us."

Mary buckled her seatbelt as through the window she could see the flaps start to roll out and heard the engines roar. Biting her lip, she felt the entire plane tilt up and rock back and forth. Then she felt the violent jolt as the wheels of the Gulfstream touched the surface of a steel deck and an even louder jolt and noise as the engines were put into full reverse and the arrester hook pulled the airplane to a sudden stop.

Ten minutes later, having changed her official Chief Constables' Uniform for a Military Uniform with the rank of Major on the arms of her camouflage jacket, Mary climbed into an F-18 United States Navy fighter. Helped into the back seat by a Chief Petty Officer, he pulled all of her seatbelts tight and showed her around the cramped backseat cockpit.

"Sir, this hear's the instrument set up used by the backseat armament specialist. So, because you're flying in the rear seat, if an alarm goes off and the Pilot-in-Command orders you too, push this button here and all four Sparrow missiles will be fired."

"That button?" Mary replied as she pointed to a red button with her finger.

"Yes, Ma'am. But never push it unless you're ordered to."

"That's just fine. I won't, not ever, until I hear the order."

Then he helped her on with the Navy helmet and showed her how to put on her oxygen mask. "Sir, you'll be flying at twenty-thousand feet at least until you get over your final destination. When the Pilot says for you to don it, do it right now."

"Yes, Sir, Chief!" Mary said as she saluted him and he saluted back. Then she watched the Pilot-in-Command climb aboard. Putting on his helmet, he keyed his mic.

"Welcome aboard, Major Sweet. Name's Lieutenant Brian Jones. I'll be your Pilot today."

"Thank you, Sir. The Chief showed me all around the cockpit. So I know exactly what to do if you order it."

"That's a Wilco, Sir. Stand-by while we start up her engines."

Mary heard the loud roar as the twin turbines wound up. Then she saw the Chief wave them into position on the aircraft carrier's deck. "Bravo-two-seven, this is the Control Tower. You're cleared for take-off," she heard through her helmet's speakers.

"Major, brace yourself for take-off," her pilot said. Mary held onto two large handles as she felt the jolt of the Eisenhower's catapult system throw the aircraft forward. As Mary looked out the window, she suddenly saw that she was already hundreds of feet in the air. When she keyed her mic, she simply said, "This is the Major testing my mic. Do you read me Brian, over?"

"Yes Ma'am. That's an affirmative."

"And please call me Mary. Brian, no loop-the-loops, okay? I've had enough excitement for the rest of my life."

Hearing him laugh in both of her ears, she heard some high-pitched chatter and a voice came onto the radio. "Detective McMouse here. Chief Inspector, do you read me, over?"

"Who's that?" Brian asked. "What's a McMouse."

"Just a member of my special Teams, and a real leader."

"McMouse. An odd name for a Team leader."

"Oh, he's a mouse all right until he's in a combat situation. Then he's a lion. Brian, can you tell me our final destination?"

"Sure I can, Mary. I make it about an hour from here at Mach Two. We're flying you to a secret airport just north of Moscow. Got us special equipment on-board so we shouldn't be detected by even the best radar systems the Russians can buy from China or the Iranian sons-of-bitches."

"Got that, Brian. Moscow it is."

She felt the sudden acceleration of the aircraft and it began to climb almost vertically. Hearing Brian order her to don her oxygen mask, she did that as she looked up into the deep blue of the sky. "How high are we going to fly, Brian."

"Oh, I'd make it about Angels Eight Zero or so. That's eighty-thousand feet."

"Good, Lord! I'll be almost in Heaven."

"Let's hope not, Ma'am. I got my orders to get you there I one piece and back again when this mission is all over. Me too, as well as the aircraft, for that matter."

Within only minutes, Mary could see bright lights below her. Then she saw a pair of yellow and white trails streaking toward her. The radar scope in front of her flashed with bright letters. WARNING. INCOMING.

"Major Sweet, them's Russians just let go two missiles at us. Release our defensive counter measures now by pushing the green button and then the red button to launch all missiles. This pilot's gonna fly a bit higher then turn around. But those incomers are gonna get destroyed or my name ain't Lieutenant Brian Jones."

Mary pushed both buttons as ordered then sat back as Brian pulled the aircraft into another vertical climb. The sky became full of dim stars then the aircraft flipped over and all that Mary could see was two bright lights as the fighter's missiles destroyed the Russian missiles.

"Scratch two bogeys," Brian said. "Now, let's get you out of here and to that airfield as soon as we can."

Detective McMouse, dressed in a Mouse Army camouflage uniform, looked through his new sniper rifle's telescope at the ornate door Sherlock Holmes and Doctor Watson had discovered which led to Putin's apartment complex. Adjusting the site, the little mouse smiled as the door opened and General Gusto and Nurse Tully Gale walked out.

"This is McMouse," the mouse said into his tiny radio fitted to his wrist. "I have our customers in sight. Repeat. I have both customers in my site."

The radio crackled then a familiar English voice replied, "McMouse, this is Chief Alpha. Take the customers out. Did you hear me? Do it now!"

Behind the mouse, Sherlock Holmes and Doctor Watson floated just above him. "It's so good to be ghosts again," Watson said to his good friend. "Mouse, there's the ticket. Shoot the bastard in the throat as well as that goat of a woman Spy."

McMouse let out his breath. He estimated the distance between him and his targets at just over one statute mile. Adjusting the site again, he slipped two explosive rounds into two chambers at the top of the Mouse Special Forces Weapon. Steadying himself again, he slowly squeezed the trigger. The small rifle fired.

"Wait, now, Sherlock Holmes," the mouse said. "It will take about a minute for the rounds to reach the target."

In front of Putin's apartment door, Tully Gale squeezed her husband's arm. "That Putin! What a screaming idiot! He swallowed all the lies we both told him."

"In spades, my darling. In spades."

Kissing his wife on the lips, General Gusto turned away when he heard a sudden whoosh coming toward him. "That sounds so familiar," he whispered.

Suddenly, he was covered by blood and bone fragments. Ducking, the wall behind him exploded in the dust of rock and cement. He turned back to Tully just as she fell toward him. Catching her in his arms, he stared at the bloody neck and uniform jacket.

"Her head's been blown completely off!" he yelled into the bright streets of Red Square. "My wife is dead! Someone has killed her. Sound the alarm. The enemy is coming. Tell Putin to hide in his personal bunker."

Russian troops stormed toward him. Some opened the President's apartment door and Gusto could hear a woman scream. "Putin is gone! Someone has taken him!"

"That's English!" Gusto stated. "But his entire family knows English. I have to get out of here before I'm killed, too."

McMouse looked through his site at the growing chaos in the streets. He fired two more rounds at the fleeing Russian General. Then he keyed his tiny radio again. "This is McMouse. Scratch one, I repeat, one customer. Bag-a-Bones Gusto is fleeing the area, over?"

"McMouse, you killed Tully Gale?" Mary said from the cockpit of her fighter jet that was on final approach to their secret airfield. "Congratulations. Have no fear, my mouse friend. We'll kill or capture the General tonight."

"What about the Russian President?"

"Our Teams have just captured him and are now interrogating him. We'll have him transported back to Paris where he will be tried by the International Court of Justice for his many war crimes it the Ukraine."

Just then, the mouse heard a siren begin to wail. "Mister Holmes, that sounds like the alarms we both heard when we were Ghost Detectives during World War Two. Does that signify incoming German bombers?"

"No, Watson, that it doesn't," Holmes replied. "That would be incoming rockets, I deduce, based on what I've already read about global historic affairs."

"Gentlemen, let's hope you're both wrong," McMouse squeaked as he packed up his weapon. "Let's get out of here right now and go to see Mary Sweet. She will explain it all to us."

"Mister McMouse, please take my hand again," Watson said as he held out a transparent hand. "Scamper up my arm and sit in my jacket pocket. It won't be long until we find our sweet Mary Sweet."

The mouse did as he was instructed. Closing his eyes as he climbed into the Detective's pocket, he felt a flash of heat on his furry skin. Opening them, he looked down to see a short runway hidden in a dense forest. A single jet aircraft was sitting on the concrete.

"There she is," McMouse yelled in his high-pitched voice. "Chief, up here!

Standing next to the jet fighter, Mary looked up and waved. As she watched Doctor Watson touch the ground and saw her mouse friend scamper off his arm and run toward her, she heard a siren begin to wail.

"Major, that's the siren for incoming missiles," Brian Jones said as he climbed out of the fighter. "I have to skedaddle and get airborne again. Got me to load some rockets before I fly out of here. You gotta bet your pretty ass into a nuclear shelter. It's right under the control tower."

As Brian ran to a hanger to find some Sparrow and Sidewinder missiles, Mary picked up McMouse in one hand and ran toward the control tower.

"It's the General again," she gasped as she ran through a door. An on-duty US Marine soldier waved at her from his position next to the open steel blast door. "We have to stop him or the world will be destroyed by that insane beast."

"Mary, let us float you back to Moscow with that wee McMouse creature," Watson said. He and Holmes had followed her in through the door and they floated, invisible, right next to her.

"If you don't, and based on more extensive research, the next flash you see may be that of a single megaton nuclear warhead exploding right above you," Sherlock Holmes stated as he read a US Military manual. "We must depart within twenty seconds at most! Otherwise, that General will launch his missiles. What you hear is a warning that his missiles are ready to launch."

"But we don't know where that General bastard Gusto is hiding!" Mary gasped as she walked quickly toward the Marine Corps soldier. "He could be anywhere in Moscow."

"Ah, but Holmes knows where he is," Doctor Watson said. "Don't you, my superlative Detective."

`"Simple deduction, Watson," Holmes replied. "He is in an old fall-out shelter used during what modern people called the Cold War. That shelter has been dug right below the Kremlin. I found that using another manual printed by the old Soviet Union during the Cold War."

"But wasn't that printed in Russian?" Mary asked. "You know Russian, too, my dear Mister Holmes?"

The Ghost of Sherlock shrugged both shoulders. "Yes, Chief Inspector Sweet. I know enough Russian and most modern languages to research my many suspects."

"Then let's get out of here!" Mary stopped walking toward the Marine Corps soldier. "Soldier, get your ass into that shelter and close the door now! And that's an order."

"Yes, Major," he replied and, returning the salute, marched through the door and shut it with a solid clang.

"Mary, take my hand. Mouse, climb into her Uniform pocket and we'll leave right now and at the speed of light before time runs out!"

Mary and the mouse did again what they were instructed. Taking the hands of Holmes and Watson, Mary saw the flash of light. Blinking rapidly, she found herself standing in Red Square just outside the Kremlin Gates. When Sherlock Holmes pointed toward a door cut into the stone wall that surrounded the Kremlin, Mary Sweet walked up to it. She tried to find a keypad but nothing like that could be seen. "That steel door is an old fashioned one, my friends," Mary pondered as she looked toward the two Ghosts floating next to her. "See? All it has is a keyhole but I don't have the key."

"Elementary, my old girl!" Holmes said and reached into his vest pocket. Drawing out a long black key, he handed it to her. "When I found the door, I used some plasticine to make a mould of the lock. Then Watson changed back into a living person and took that to the local locksmith. I whispered the Russian translation into Watson's ear and the key was made in only minutes! So Voila again, we both say! Find that bugger of a General and arrest him now!"

"Gentlemen, I'll do exactly as you say but first I'll order in some reinforcements from my Teams. That General invariably has a number of soldiers with him, all armed with automatic weapons."

They all heard the wail of Kremlin sirens and, in the twilight, Mary watched as the roads were cleared by Russian soldiers and Police Officers.

"McMouse, call all the Teams. Get them in here except for those who are holding Putin." Looking up at the mighty Detectives, Mary smiled. "Gentlemen, you should know that the entire escapade of France declaring war on the UK was nothing but a Maskarova launched by Captain Jennifer Markova, the Interpol Officer and our current Spy in the Kremlin. That mask included President Macron. While he was truly annoyed at the murder of his Minister of Defence, we soon proved that it was Putin who ordered that assassination, and not anyone in the United Kingdom."

"We salute you, Mrs Sweet!" Holmes and Watson said together as they began floating up over Red Square. "You call it a Maskarova, Russian for *a mask*? We call it a pre-ordained stroke of genius! No wonder soon you will be made the Queen of a new country that King Charles himself shall name for you. We bid you farewell for now and good luck for your quest of capturing that murderous General before he kills anyone else!"

CHAPTER 15

Capture or Suicide: The Final Question

The Chief Inspector and Detective McMouse crouched behind a wall near the steel door. As the mouse detective took out his radio, they both heard heavy boots hit the ground near them.

"McMouse, that has to be the Russian Army," Mary whispered to her tiny friend. "There's no place to hide and Doctor Watson and Sherlock Holmes have disappeared into the twilight skies."

"I will not surrender!" McMouse said to his good friend. "See? I have a tiny tablet of cyanide. Rather than be captured, I will bite it with my teeth to prevent those Russian soldiers from interrogating me and capturing my friends, family and our Teams!"

"Mouse, I agree," Mary replied as she peered around the corner. "There's a whole platoon coming and they're all carrying automatic weapons. Give a tablet to me otherwise they'll find out the location where we're holding Putin!"

As the mouse dug into his tiny black bag looking for his spare tablet of cyanide, a woman's voice yelled from the twilight near them, "Shoot to kill! Don't take any of those Russian bastards alive!" They heard the pop-pop-pop of automatic fire and when there was silence again, Captain Jennifer Markova stepped around the corner and saluted. "My Chief Inspector and Detective Mouse. I have carried out my orders from Interpol and our Prime Minister to the best of my ability. I have left that son-of-a-bitch Putin as well as the General in the care of our Soldiers who will kill them should they try to escape."

Then there was a wail of the Moscow Nuclear Defence Sirens. "Captain, we are in desperate need of your help. Our intelligence states that the control systems to fire the nuclear missiles that the General has stolen are located just beyond that door. I have a key to it but we need some protection and backup in case the General has left a small platoon from the Wagner Army down there."

"We shall follow you, Mary Sweet and mouse. We also have studied the architectural plans of this bomb shelter. We must descend down many flights of steps as taking the elevator would put us all at significant risk if the Wagner Army has planted explosive devices on or in it."

As Mary was unlocking the door with the key that Doctor Watson had given to her, all of Red Square lit up. As she, McMouse and the Captain looked up, they could see the bright yellow tail of a missile streaking up over the Kremlin. "That bastard has done it!" Mary seethed as she unlocked the door. "He's fired a nuclear missile from its position beneath the Kremlin. God knows where it will eventually strike and how many innocent people will die!"

As she entered a dark hallway, McMouse climbed up onto her shoulder. Lighting a small flare he took out of his black bag, the damp area lit in bright yellow and red. "There's the door to the stairwell," Mary whispered to McMouse and the Captain. "Jennifer, place a guard at that elevator door over there to the right. If that door opens, shoot anyone who comes out. The rest of you, follow us."

The Captain waved back toward the entry door and her platoon of Interpol soldiers crept in. When the elevator door suddenly opened and a man dressed in black and red came running out, an Interpol soldier opened fire. Falling to the ground, another soldier kicked him once in the side to make certain he was dead.

"Now let's get down to the control room before we run out of time," Mary breathed to McMouse. Opening a steel door, they found the stairwell which was lit by a number of overhead lamps. "Follow us, everyone. Be quiet and don't make a sound as we make our way down."

In Putin's apartment next to the Kremlin, the General looked at his watch and smiled again. "My dear President, we saw the first missile leave its secret launching silo only moments ago. That missile is headed to London where it will let many MIRV warheads loose from an altitude of approximately two-hundred thousand feet. Then, you will be in a position to demand the surrender of the many countries that you want to preside over."

"My friend, don't take me for a fool," Putin shot back. "The only way to make certain that I win is to get to that control room of yours. Then we can track that missile and make sure that the other missiles are let loose on time, as we both planned."

Looking around the ornate apartment living room, Putin walked up to his desk and sat down in the armchair that had been made for Czar Nicholas the Second. His face set, he turned his head toward one an Interpol Officer who was guarding him and the General with an automatic weapon. "You, you betraying officer.

Are you the only one who is guarding us? Don't you know that this General and I are both trained in hand-to-hand combat?"

"I am not authorised to talk to you," she said with a stone-cold face. "Sit quietly or I will be forced to shoot you."

"Shoot us? Then you might as well do it now before your soldiers come back," the General said with a laugh. "Where are they anyway? Getting sick in the toilet? Or are they as frightened as that Czar Nicholas was the day the Russian Revolutionaries shot him and his family."

"I am an ancestor of the Czar, the rightful ruler of Mother Russia," the officer stated as she pointed her weapon at the General's head. "You will be so frightened when I begin to fire that you'll pee all over yourself and so will that Dictator Putin."

Aiming her weapon at the General's legs, President Putin realized that her anger had distracted her from her duty. Reaching under his desk with both hands, he quickly detached the two Glock handguns from the latches that had been holding them there. Pulling them out at the same time, he fired at the Interpol Officer. Hitting her in the head, she died immediately.

"Grab her weapon," Putin roared as he headed to the apartment's front door. "We'll be out of her soon. We'll head for the basement where I have built a secret tunnel between here and that bomb shelter of yours."

Within two minutes, the General with Putin were in the basement. "Thank you, General, for saving my life," Putin said as he wiped his brow. "I never saw those other Interpol troops coming up the steps toward us."

"No problem my great good friend," the General said as he changed the clip in his weapon. Then he looked at his watch. "We must be at the control desk in exactly three minutes or we will not be able to control the Nuclear Missiles or their warheads."

"Then go!" Putin shouted. "Through that door then turn left! Follow the small red lights on the ceiling. They will lead us to the shelter."

Hiding on a river bank near Red Square, Master Sargent George Smith looked down at a map he held in his hand. As Edith used a small torch, lighting the map, the other Human Team members crouched around them to look.

"That Holmes and Watson said that Mary Sweet, McMouse and an Interpol Squad are in here," George whispered. "I've already contacted our Animal Teams and the other members of our Human Team that were relieved from guarding Putin and the General. We need to get in through that door before something fires another bloody missile."

"Do you think Russian soldiers will be guarding the entrance to the tunnel?" Francis Assisi asked as he held tight to Nimmy Ursula's hand.

"Unlikely," George replied. "If Interpol is there, so is their Captain as well as Mary Sweet. Anyone on Putin's side is already flattened dead."

Picking up his automatic weapon and the bag of hand grenades that lay by his side, Geore stood up and looked at the wall near the Kremlin. "Looks clear of anyone," George said. "Let's go! We're due to meet the Animal Teams in exactly two minutes."

As they ran, crouching, over the river bank, Edith saw the teams of animals running and scampering across Red Square to meet them. "That Bluebell is far too white to attack in darkness," she whispered to George. "Why not station her just inside the door and she and her puppies can bark to warn us if anyone tries to get in to attack us."

"Great idea, Edith," he replied as he took her hand. "We're almost there."

Having made it to the open steel door, the Teams of Animals and Humans made their way into the hallway. George saw the body of a Wagner Army soldier lying on the cold stone floor then he turned to Bluebell and her puppies. "Blue! You and your pups guard the front door. Bark if anyone tries to enter."

"Yes, Master Sargent," the small white dog growled. "We will bark should any human person or animal try to get in. Oh, and congratulations for your field promotion."

"Save the congrats for later," George replied and looked at his map again. "Okay, people and animals. It's through that steel door then down seven flights of stairs. Guard our backs. I'll take the lead. Francis, you and Nimmy lead up the rear. Maud, Tony and Maria, you're in the middle. Check your weapons now to make sure they're all loaded."

When the humans and animals were finished checking their weapons, a tiny mouse crawled across the floor and stood up on its two hind legs. "See, Master Sargent?" the mouse squeaked. "We have lots and lots of Acorn grenades made by our Teams of Mouse Explosives Experts!" The little man held up a large burlap bag and taking one out, held it up. "Miss Edith, please shine that torch here. See? All you have to do is bite the end of the Acorn and the fuse will start. You have ten human seconds to through it before it explodes."

George took the nut in his hand and examined it. "Clever geniuses, those Mouse Engineers." He looked down at the mouse and gave the nut back to him. "Sir, I have my own grenades in this black bag. Please distribute your explosives to anyone who wants them."

As the mouse finished handing out the Acorns, George opened the steel door. "Ready troops! Let's get to Mary and her soldiers right now!"

Now down in the control room, the Chief Inspector and Captain Jennifer walked up to the line of control monitors. "Look at that!" Mary hissed as she saw a streak of white light make its way toward England. "In a few minutes they'll all be dead! Jennifer, did you bring a satellite telephone?"

"I did, Chief. Here, take it."

Mary took the phone in a shaking hand. She quickly unfolded it and attached the small satellite dish. Hearing the strong signal on the speaker, she dialled the number.

"Major Mary Sweet calling Lieutenant Brian Jones. Do you read! Brian, I need you! Come in!"

In his cockpit of the F-18, Brian heard the distorted hiss of a signal coming in through his helmet earphones. Reaching out to adjust the gain on the aircraft's satellite radio, he keyed his mic.

"This is Brian. Do you read, Major? Come in, over?"

"Brian, you are authorised to shoot down a nuclear missile that's headed toward England. We can only suspect that it's one of the MIRVs that the General has fired. Do you have a weapon that can reach such a high altitude?"

Looking at his radar, the Lieutenant grinned. "Yes, Ma'am, 'course I got one of them brand new satellite missiles on board. Only got me one such missile. It's sorta like a hypersonic Tomahawk and can fly all the way into outer space, if required."

Mary looked over to Jennifer, relief on her face. "Brian, when you're within range, shoot the damned thing down! Got that?"

"Sure do, Ma'am." Looking again at the radar, he keyed the mic. "Major, that missile will be right overhead in four minutes. Gonna have to climb as high as this big beautiful bird will fly and then I'll fire the tiny chick this here mother hen is carrying."

"Got that, Brian. Good luck and let us know if you're successful. London and NATO will be tracking that, too. This is Mary Sweet. I'll leave the phone on Standby."

"That is so very good," Jennifer said as she moved to the consoles. "Mary Sweet! We are in more trouble. Look at that clock count down!"

Mary Sweet looked at the clock on a glowing blue console. "That reads 75:00 and I don't think that means minutes. That's seconds! Jennifer, have you and your troops help me find some sort of deactivation button. I'm sure one's here. Something that will blow up any missile that's fired."

As they began their frantic search, the door opened and Mary looked up as George and his Teams marched in. "Mary Sweet we're all here safe and sound and just as ordered."

"George, look for any kind of button around here. Red, green or white! The missiles are going to fire in only a few seconds."

An alarm went off as the female automated voice said in English but with a distinctly Russian accent, "Good day, Mary Sweet and we are so glad you found us. I should warn you that the clock has been set incorrectly. The rest of the missiles will fire right now! I am your terrible friend. General Gusto, the Russian Agent."

The Alarm went off again. As Mary and Jennifer watched, more streaks of light left from a dark place which they both knew must be somewhere in Siberia.

"We're fucked!" Mary screamed. "That ass the General has fucked the world. Teams, find those buttons now!"

As the Teams of humans and animals kept looking for the secreted button that would disarm the missiles, a back door to the bunker opened. Vladimir Putin and the General stepped out and pointed their weapons at Mary Sweet and Captain Jennifer. "Stop whatever it is you are doing!" Putin roared as he ran over to stand by Mary. Pointing one of his Glock handguns at the Chief Inspector's head, he cocked the trigger. "If you do not obey me and this Russian General, I will kill her then this Interpol Captain. Now, place your weapons on the ground and hold up your hands."

"If I were you, Mary Sweet, I'd do just as the President has ordered," the General said as he pointed his Kalashnikov at her Human Team. "You! On the floor and put your hands behind your back!" he yelled at the Master Sargent. "Do it, or I will kill this woman who is standing next to you."

George looked first at Edith then at Mary. "Chief, better do what he says or we're all dead," George sighed as he fell to his knees. "This would-be English General is such a traitor he'll never know what hits him when we take him to England." As he lay down on his belly he turned his head and winked up to Edith. "Hon, lay that rifle of yours on the ground as well as your sidearm."

"My sidearm, George?" Edith replied with a wry smile on her face. "Why, I forgot to bring my sidearm. I left it back in England."

"You two. Shut up!" Putin roared again as he cocked his other Glock and pointed it at Captain Jennifer's heart. "If you do not be quiet, I kill these two bitches!"

Edith threw her weapon on the ground and fell to her knees next to George. Seeing the Police revolver that he always concealed by sliding it into the back of his Army trousers, she put her hands on his lower back and, feeling the weapon there, slowly slid it from his Army fatigues.

"Now we begin the real countdown!" the General stated as he punched the surface of one of the consoles. "See that big clock there, the glowing Orange one? That is all the time your Royal family, the Prime Minister, Parliament and all of your citizens and friends have to live. Very soon, our other Russian missiles will strike all the big cities in the United Kingdom, most European capitals,

North Korea, China and America. Millions will die due to the stupidity of Mary Sweet and her Team of crazy peoples!"

As the alarm went off again, Edith pulled out the handgun and aimed it at the General. Squeezing the trigger, she fired, hitting her target in the arm. "You silly, silly girl!" the General screamed as he dropped the Kalashnikov. "You have merely wounded me! Now we will kill all of your Teams."

Chief Inspector Claws Catnip, who had been watching all of this unfold from his position at the front door, hissed and stood up on his hind legs. "Acorn throwers! Throw your explosives at those two enemies. Mice and other cats and dogs, take aim with any weapon you have and fire!"

At once, the Animal Teams began firing. The Acorn grenades exploded on a number of the consoles. As they caught fire and filled the room with smoke, Animal handguns and automatic weapons also opened fire. "You bitches! I will now kill you all!" Mary heard Putin roar through the dense smoke. Picking up the General's automatic weapon from where she'd dropped it, she pointed it at Vladimir Putin.

"Mister Russian President, if I were you I'd throw your weapon to the ground," Mary Sweet yelled over the small arms fire. "We have you surrounded on three sides. See? Even Captain Jennifer now has a weapon she has taken from the General."

Looking over at the Captain, Putin could see that she held a handgun at the General's head. "You can have him but you will never take me alive!" Putin cried as he opened fire. The room filled with automatic fire as the Animal Teams moved closer to Mary through the dense smoke. Another alarm filled the room as the automated voice said, "Time to targets in the European nations, ten minutes and counting."

"Get on the floor, Putin!" Mary screamed as she ran toward him. "You're now surrounded. You have nowhere to run anymore."

The President of Russia considered his situation and began to laugh. Pointing the nozzle of a Glock at his head, he squinted through the smoke to find Mary looking back at him. "Miss Chief Inspector I must say that I wish you and your teams were Russian. You would have made a good General to replace the one that I am now losing." He pointed the other Glock at the General and fired twice. Mary turned to see the General falling to the ground in a pool of blood. "Putin, you're under arrest. Drop that weapon and lie flat on the ground. Or don't. Shoot yourself for all I care. It will save all of us the expense of a very short and certain trial and execution for the murders you have committed."

Putin stared at her and his mouth opened wide. Putting the barrel of the Glock into his mouth, Mary watched as he started to squeeze the trigger. Then she saw how the colour drained from his face. Coughing loudly, he fell to his knees in a pool of his own vomit and the stench of the urine that streamed out of his trousers.

"You are a chicken too, aren't you?" George said as he stood up again. Picking up his automatic weapon from the ground, he stormed toward the captive President. "You could have killed all of my friends right here. Why should I let you live?"

"Because you must," the General whispered from his prone position on the floor. "If you kill the Russian President, there will be destruction among all nations. Rather than do that, you must tend to my wounds and I will destroy the many warheads that fly back down to Earth."

In his F-18 jet fighter, Brian Jones once again looked at his radar. Outside the glass windshield that protected him, he could see the glow of stars as well as planets. Keying his mic, he smiled one more time. "Major Sweet, this is Jones again. I'm now at an acceptable altitude and am about to fire my hen's chick." Depressing a single white button next to his right leg, Brian Jones felt his fighter's fuselage tremble as the rocket engine started up. "Firing now!"

The jet leaped as the rocket left the wing of his aircraft. Satisfied that the rocket was on target, Jones pulled back the throttles and began a slow descent. "So pretty up here," he said to himself. "Always wanted to be one of them NASA astronauts but I'm too old now, I guess. Maybe that wonderful Major can help me out someday."

As he watched his radar, his Satellite Killer locked on to the Nuclear Missile that was streaking west right above him. Looking over his shoulder, Jones saw a sudden white explosion as if a nearby small sun had gone into a bright nova. "Well, look at that!" Brian said as he continued his descent back toward the Dwight D. Eisenhower. "Looks like the Russians have brought a little more light to this side of the world."

Throttling up, Brian pulled up when his altimeter read fifty-thousand feet. Looking out over the bright waters of the Black Sea, he keyed his aircrafts mic. "Dwight control, this is special flight Alpha one-one-zero. I'm now a hundred miles from the carrier. Fuel onboard is near zero. If I end up in the drink, please send out a couple of your choppers."

"Roger Alpha One, his is the carrier. We're all prepared to receive you. The Prime Minister of the United Kingdom and King Charles send their warm regards."

"Got that, tower. If you hear from Major Mary Sweet, let her know that the mission is accomplished."

"Wilco, Alpha One. See you in minutes. Out."

'Job well done', Brian said to himself as he moved in on the position of the aircraft carrier. 'Be on that flattop in ten minutes.' Then he keyed the satellite mic one more time. "Major Sweet, just so you know that target is a kill, do you read. The target has been destroyed."

In the bunker, Mary didn't hear the incoming call. She and her Teams were following the General's instructions as they pushed the many green, red, white and orange buttons they had finally found in concealed places all over the bunker.

"Good, very good," the General said as an Interpol medic tended to his wounds. "See? You have destroyed almost all of the MIRVs that have gotten through Western defensive shields."

McMouse climbed up onto a console that was still working and stared hard at a tiny dot that was streaking toward Moscow. Then he saw the dot split into two small blips. One tracked toward the Kremlin as the other made its way toward the Ukraine.

"What's that, General Gusto?" the mouse squeaked in its Russian voice so the General could understand. "Yes, General, now I have learned Russian just as my wife has."

"That? What? You mouse. You can talk?"

"Sure I can. What are those!"

The General looked at the console through the haze that was left in the control room. Limping to it with the help of the medic, his mouth opened and shut twice before he could speak. "Those are two nuclear warheads! One is heading toward the Kremlin and the other will impact on Kyiv, the capital of the Ukraine! We must warn the citizens of Moscow to get to the closest bomb shelter."

"It is too late, General," Putin said from his position on the floor. "Your plan for me has gone up in smoke! You are a traitor to our global cause."

General Gusto smiled down at his former boss. "No, you fool. Everything has gone exactly to my plan but not yours." Looking to Mary Sweet, the former British General smiled again. "Now, Mary Sweet. I am the one in the position to bargain. There are two warheads left and both of them can be destroyed by the single red button I now hold in my hand." He opened the fingers of his right hand and showed her the small metal housing. Behind the glass shield, she could plainly see a tiny red button. "Should I open it and destroy them both or do we wait while millions die due to your continuing foolishness."

"What do you want, General. More money?"

He laughed again. "Money? I have enough cash to buy all of England should I want to. Know, I want much, much more." He pushed off the medic from his arm and hobbled toward her. "Now. You will call the Secretary of the United Nations. I have the private number of his mobile phone and he will still be at his office in New York City. Tell him that I will destroy the warheads right now but first, he must make me the Emperor of the entire Western World. I do not want Australia or Africa or even Mexico or South America. But as for the rest? I shall be the sole Global Ruler!"

Mary considered the situation as she watched the two blips heading toward their separate targets. Reaching back into her jacket pocket, she took out her satellite phone. "General, you dial the number like this," she said as she touched a button. The phone's speaker began to shriek then quickly silenced. "Then you wait until the Secretary answers it."

The General took the phone. Looking at the complicated set of buttons, he dialled in the phone number from memory. "Now what do I do, Sweet?"

"Push that one there. Start by saying where you are and where the weapons are targeted."

The General depressed the button Mary pointed at. Placing it on his ear, all he could hear was a distant wailing noise. "It is not working. I have dialled in the number. Get him on the phone because we run out of time! See?"

Mary looked at the clock glowing on the console as she pushed a single button. The clock read, 40:00.

Still in the cockpit of his F-18 fighter, and now on the Eisenhower's deck, Brian Jones heard the satellite phone squawk again. Keying his own mic, he started to talk when he heard the Major's voice.

"Anyone listening to this conversation. This is Chief Inspector Mary Sweet. I am going to put a Russian General on the phone in a moment but first I want you to know that two nuclear warheads are heading to their targets on Moscow and Kyiv. Now put the Secretary of the United Nations on."

In his cockpit, Jones understood the simple message. "Jeez-Josephat's!" he said to himself then keyed his aircraft's mic. "Control Tower! Jones again. I need two Satellite Killer missiles on my aircraft right now! Get me fuelled up and get the rest of the squadron ready. I need to talk to my Squadron Commander. We got only minutes to take down two bogeys that will kill two large cities."

As the control tower complied with his orders, Jones got out of his aircraft. He went to the toilet then had a half a can of Coca-Cola and a bite of a ham sandwich. When his squadron had surrounded him, all dressed in their flight suits, he looked them all in the eye. "You people have never used a Satellite Killer Missile before but now's your chance. I got me two of those chicks on my wings. We've got enough in our inventory to place one each on your fighter's wings. Now get into yer aircraft. We got no time to stand here chattin'."

When the Squadron was ready, the control tower ordered an immediate series of take-offs. Climbing to altitude Jones ordered the entire squadron to maximum altitude. With the two targets on their radar scopes, Jones ordered the entire team to fire all of their weapons at once.

"Tally-ho!" a man's voice in the Lieutenant's helmet speakers yelled. Looking up, he could see what appeared to be a man on a white horse and carrying a sword charge to the east, and to the sunset. He didn't even key his mic. "Now I've gone as crazy as anyone I've ever met," Jones said to his cockpit rearview mirror where he could see his eyes covered by the tinted glass of his helmet. "That was a man on a white horse. I'm sure it was. Or I'll be damned if I'm crazy or if I'm ever going to tell anyone what I think I saw."

In his helmet speakers, Jones heard the faint cry of "Tally-ho!" again. Then the speakers went deadly silent. "I guess I am nuts, I guess. Time to get me some shore leave and go home to see the wife and kids."

In the bunker beneath the Kremlin, Mary and her Teams watched as a number of rockets streaked from the east toward their two targets. When one white target blossomed like a large daisy, the Teams all shouted and cheered. They all felt a rumble overhead. "That's one gone!" Mary shouted. "Now only one left."

They all watched as the last target began to dip and swerve. Putin began to laugh. He had crawled up to stand next to the General. Placing his handcuffed hands on the glass console, he laughed yet again. "That is my latest hypersonic missile. See how it dances and swerves to my musical orders?"

One then two then all of the missiles missed that last target. In a rage, Mary Sweet stepped behind the General and hit Putin right in the nose. "There, you murdering bastard. You'll be tried, hung, drawn and quartered. That's it I have anything to say about it."

Through the PA of the command post bunker, they all could hear a sudden cry as a voice that most of them recognised shouted, "Tally-ho! Knights, my fellow nobles. Take up your weapons one last time! Kill that deadly star that heads for the east. I have been told by Mary Sweet in her dreams last night that it will kill many citizens of what once was a port held by the last King of Judea!"

The alarm went off again. The automated voice cried, "Thirty seconds to impact." On the console, they all saw a number of strange-looking streaks of light.

"What is that, General?" Putin asked through his swollen nose. "That is not another MIRV?"

"No, you Putin rat," the General replied. "That is something I have not seen either."

"*That* is something that only the kind and generous can see," Mary said as she winked at her Psychiatric Investigative Unit. "Or, just as some will say, you have to be absolutely insane to see that man in shining armour."

As her Human Team, the PIU, cheered, the streaks of light that they knew were Lancelot and the Knights of the Roundtable moved in on that last nuclear warhead. When the tiny dog blossomed into a large circle of silver and gold, they all began to clap and cheer again as the dogs howled and the cats hissed with delight. Then they all heard puppies begin to yap as through the door, Bluebell bounded into the room with her many children.

"We missed all of it!" she growled to Mary Sweet. "All we get to do is stand duty by an empty door."

"That's perfectly all right," Mary said in dog language to the white Mama Dog. "When we all get home, I'm going to make you the first Dog Dame in all of Great Britain. That's, of course, if I'm crowned as a Queen of some country or other just as the Royal Family in my dreams has promised to me. Not that I will ever need that honour."

McMouse leaped again onto Mary's shoulder as her Team let the Russian General out the front door of the bunker and the medic, with other Team Members followed with the General.

"Job finally done and all crimes at last solved!" McMouse said to Mary. "All that's left is home for a good solid rest and to see my wife and family."

"And perhaps some sort of celebration, Detective McMouse," Mary replied to her furry best friend. "Besides, it's time for a laugh and a dance or two."

As they finally walked out the steel door into the dark streets of Red Square, Mary looked up at the glittering sky filled with the stars of distant galaxies. "Someday, mouse, we'll both go up there in a rocket or something like it."

"Rocket-schmocket," McMouse said as it yawned and stretched. "All I want now is some cheese and a soft place to sleep."

"Done, mouse. Let's go up into Putin's apartment. There are many nice beds up there."

In less than an hour, Mary and McMouse were fast asleep in the late Czar's huge bed. The curtains had all been closed and all that could be heard was gentle snoring. Then, through the ornate open fireplace, a Russian mouse could be heard squeaking, "Oh, McMouse, come out and play! I'm your long-lost cousin, Vlad McMouse the Third! We want to be in one of your next crime investigations. Please, my dear cousin. Wake up!"

But the Detective mouse from England didn't wake up. Instead, he rolled over and dreamed of a day when he and Mary sweet would voyage to the great continents of Asia where they would disembark from a tall ship near Saint Sophia in old Constantinople. "But that's another detective story, a time in the future," the mouse said as he woke up just a little.

Rolling over again he was soon fast, fast asleep.

CHAPTER 16

The Final Celebration of Mary Sweet and Her Teams of Animals, Humans and Ghosts

Now back in Merry Old England, Chief Inspector Mary Sweet and Detective McMouse were taken by a special train from a secret airbase in Scotland directly to London. When Mary stepped off the last car, she was greeted first by the Secretary General of the United Nations and a crowd of admiring London residents.

"Welcome home, Mrs Sweet," the Secretary yelled over the cheering crowds. "I am here today to present you with the Medal of Solidarity which we have created by voice vote in the most recent General Assembly." Hanging the simple golden medal shaped in the form of the Earth around her neck from a blue and white ribbon, he shook her hand then escorted her into a waiting double decker London Transport bus where Mary chose to sit on the top deck. Passing first through the Northern London suburbs, the bus stopped near the River Thames where the rest of her Teams joined her on that top deck which was now decorated with flowers.

"Welcome home, Teams!" Mary cried over the crowds shouting her name from both sides of the River. "We're home! We're finally home!"

As the bus made it's way across London Bridge, it paused for a moment at The Tower of London. Looking up, Mary and her Teams could see King Henry the Eighth, his Queen Anne Bolyn, Queen Elizabeth and Prince Philip waving down at her. "Look up there!" squeaked Detective McMouse from its position on the back of Sir Lancelot's white stallion, Goldenrod. "Mary, do you see King Arthur and the rest of his Knights? They're waving at you from those tall white clouds!"

Mary looked directly up over her head and saw the King and his Knights. Waving back, she looked back across the Thames and saw Hubert waving back at her. "Why look! It's my long-lost husband come back to me again!"

Inspector Bernie Bridgestone walked up onto the top deck of the red bus and sat next to Mary. "Hubert says a big hello and tells you he'll see you soon."

"Bernie, how is he? Is my dead husband still a human being or is he a ghost again."

"A ghost, Mary. He's chosen to go back to Heaven and hopes you'll understand. He loves you dearly but he so much enjoys being with his parents and relatives, too."

"We'll see him again, hopefully not sometime too soon," Mary said as she took Bernie's hand in her own. When she turned her face toward him, Bernie saw that she had a thoughtful expression on it. "My dear, does Hubert know how much we've worked together and how we've grown to, well…"

"Love each other? Yes, quite simply yes. And, chicken, he approves of both of us getting married again."

"Does he now?" Mary said as she kissed her friend gently on the cheek. "I hope he finds a new bride in Heaven. Somehow, I don't think it matters there if you have one or a thousand husbands or wives."

"I only want one," Bernie replied. "That's all I've ever wanted."

"Me too," Mary signed as she placed her cheek on Bernie's warm shoulder. "One is all I've ever needed."

When the bus finally parked outside Winchester Cathedral, King Charles waved to her from the steps of that grand church. When Mary stepped off the bus, a Military Guard of Honour marched her from the bus, all the way up the steps where, having bowed before him, Mary saluted. "My King, I report again to you for any other mission you may ask me. My Teams have told me that they will always be here to serve you and your Royal Family no matter where they may roam across the world."

King Charles bowed to her to. Turning to his Secretary who was holding a red cushion with white tassels, the King picked up a golden tiara studded with diamonds and emeralds and handed that precious crown to his Queen Camilla. As she smiled at Mary Sweet, a British Army officer brought out formal robes made of blue velvet and ermine. Taking off her Official Officer's Uniform jacket, Mary turned around and let the Officer place the heavy robe on her shoulders. Then a page no more than ten ran from the Cathedral door and placed a pillow of red at Mary's small feet that were still clad in her Army Regulation Boots.

"Kneel before me, Sir Mary Sweet," Charles said to her. When she did, he held up both arms and the crowd below them quieted until silence descended on the Holy Courtyard. "Will you,

Mary Sweet, accept the responsibility of becoming Queen of a new country that the European Union has created for you?"

"Your Majesty, what country is that?" Mary said quietly, unable to look him in the eye. "Sir, I am nobody, remember? Too, I'm quite insane now. I'm in no position to be ruler of anyone much less an entire country."

"Tis a small country," a Ghost said who was floating at her left shoulder. "Tis a small place down the road from me and me wife. Not far from the far western Islands of Scotland."

"Near the Faroes, Mary Sweet," King Charles whispered to her.

"You'll love it, Mary, and we'll come to visit," Queen Camilla also whispered.

Mary now raised her head and, looking up at the Royal Couple, couldn't help but grin. "So you both hear voices too?"

"Oh, yes," Charles answered. "Don't you remember how I saw and talked to my Royal mother when we were both at the Tower? And as for Camilla, well, we both see them and my father almost every day."

"Really, your Royal Highnesses? But neither of you are insane."

"And you aren't either, me Queenie good Mary," the Ghost said to that small Royal assemblage. "My name is James Larkin MacSquat. I'm of Irish descent but was raised solely on the Faroe Islands just west of the Scottish mainland. Now you listen to this here King, ya hear me? Cause you're also me relative."

"Squat? I don't think I have any Squats in my family."

"Yes ye do, and now ye'll have a yer great-great grandfather by her side, forever!"

"But, aren't you dead?"

"Naw. I'm in a bed suffering from a wee bit of Alzheimer's or something like it. What you see is me old-fashioned image and ghost of me-self!"

The Royal family laughed as a single trumpeter played three loud notes on his instrument. Then, raising the golden crown high over his head, he placed that wonderful crown on top of Mary's head.

"I crown thee, Mary Sweet, as Queen of the Peaceful Islands of Scotland. There, you shall be Ruler of your people for all time."

As the crowd roared, the King helped Mary to her feet. Together with the Royal Couple, she entered the hallowed Cathedral. "And, Queen Sweet, we have another surprise or two waiting for you and your Teams," Queen Camilla whispered to her as the Westminster Choir broke into a song of Celebration.

"A surprise? Another one, your Majesty?"

"Mary, you no longer have to call me, Charles or anyone in the Royal Family by any title. Call us by our first names now. That's a privilege that comes with being made new Royalty."

When Mary walked up to the High Altar of the Cathedral, she found Bernie there dressed in a Black Tuxedo. Then the Archbishop of Westminster stepped onto the altar with two other Anglican priests. "Queen Mary Sweet, I hear that you and this Gentle Fellow would like to be married?"

"That is so very true, Archbishop," Mary replied. "In fact, there are a few marriages that you can perform today if you have time."

Mary turned and seeing her various Team members at the front of other people standing in front of the altar steps, waved a number of couples forward. Turning back to the Archbishop and the Royal Family, the newly Crowned Queen Mary bowed low before them.

"May I present a few other couples who would like to be married for the first time, or remarried following the death of their husband or wife."

As she called out the names of the couples, they stepped up to join her on the Altar steps. When all of them were standing next to her, Queen Mary shook each of their hands and then presented them to the Archbishop.

"Sir, I have the pleasure of introducing the following couples who are also members of my Human Team of warriors. George Smith and Nurse Edith Penrose. Tony Enwenopa would like his marriage to Maria Enwenopa blessed again. Archbishop, due to the blessed intervention of God our Holy Father, Maker of all things Miraculous, Maria has come to life again after she died a few years ago in a London apartment fire with her children, Jess and Monica. Nimmy Ursula and Francis Assisi are also here to be married for the first time."

When the organ started to play a song of Holy Matrimony, Mary held up both hands. "I'm sorry but we're not finished yet!" she called to the organist. "Now, Archbishop, I'd like to present members of our Animal Team who would also like to be married or remarried. As I call your names, also come forward and stand at the Human feet so no one in the Congregation will step on you!"

As the people in the Church began to laugh, and all the animals began to bark and hiss, she called out a number of Animal names. "Chief Inspector Claws Catnip please bounce forward with your future wife, Miss Fluffy Tail Bessmit!" As the two cats bounded onto the steps Mary cleared her throat and said, "Mama Bluebell, you lost your dog husband some time ago. You want to be married to the one and only King Jack Frieze! Step onto the altar with your four paws, please!" As they walked like any dignified engaged couple onto the steps all the puppies began to bark at once.

"Please, children, keep it down!" Bluebell barked back. "Mamma Mary, please continue."

Mary cleared her throat once again and looked up as a flying white horse descended to the altar with no Knight mounted on it. "Detective McMouse, fly down here at once!" Queen Mary ordered. When the mouse hopped down from the steed's silver saddle, he landed on Detective Claw's back who only purred at him.

"Congratulations, McMouse. Have a grand day."

"Will do, Sir Claws. Now all I have to do is wait for my wife."

Mary looked back up at the Archbishop and smiled. "As usual, we're being kept waiting for a bride." When she heard a mouse begin to squeal and shout, she turned back toward those assembled in front of the Altar. "Mrs McMouse! Please hurry! You're keeping your husband waiting for your new blessing!"

When the tiny bride dressed all in white had finally joined her Mouse Husband, the Archbishop stepped forward to begin the Ceremony but Mary lifted her hand for on last time.

"Sir Archbishop. A few more marriages, if you don't mind. May I reintroduce you to Sir Lancelot and his lovely fiancé, Colonel Jennifer Markova!" As the Knight in shining armour came down again on his steed Goldenrod, Colonel Jennifer walked up to join the other Humans on the Alter steps. "May I present my husband, Chief Inspector Hubert Sweet and his bride from Heaven, Kack White. She was the wife of Nurse Jeremy, who died in a tragic accident committed by Tully Gale. These two blessed angels have found each other and now want to live together for all eternity."

A flash of bright light filled the vast spaces of Westminster Abbey as the two ghosts appeared. Standing near the Sir Lancelot and Jennifer, they traded smiles as Queen Mary cleared her throat again. "And finally, I have the great pleasure of reintroducing you to Doctor Watson who has a special announcement for everyone!"

When Doctor Watson floated up from a crypt below the Altar, he stepped up to the Archbishop and bowed to the many congregants. "Good day, everyone, and thank you for coming to be present at this Happy Occasion. As many of you may have read, Mister Sherlock Holmes has never been married. However, due to his complete recovery of his health, our detective work together, and my counsel and advice, he has finally taken a woman to be his bride forever. May I now introduce you all to the soon to be Mr and Mrs Sherlock Holmes!"

A flash of brilliant golden and orange light filled the entire building once again as Sherlock Holmes and a women dressed in a stunning golden gown appeared on the Altar. Floating toward Doctor Watson and the Archbishop, Sherlock cleared his thin throat and looked hard at the assembly below him.

"Elementary, dear Watson, elementary. Isn't that what I always said? And don't I always deduce what the facts from the falsehoods? The problem is I never had a sense of my own humanity and never had the time to find the love of my life. So take heed, all ye who hear this simple message! Take time to find someone to love and to have children with. Be not afraid of having someone special to love, honour and obey for the rest of Eternity. If you don't take my dear friend Doctor Watson's advice, you could well turn out to be as lonely as I've been for so many hundreds of years." Turning to the woman dressed in gold, he gently lifted the white veil that she was wearing. "May I now present the future Mrs. Holmes. The famous detective novelist and philanthropist, Miss Jane Marple created and made famous by that great female novelist, Agatha Christie!"

The Archbishop turned to Queen Mary. "Madam Queen, are you finally ready? We're running very late and, like all of this special assemblage, I'm getting rather hungry."

"We are already finally," Mary Sweet said. As all of the Human, Animal and Ghost couples stepped closer to the

Archbishop, the organ began to play its hymn of Matrimony as the choir sang hymns of marriage and celebration.

"I can't believe the day passed so quickly," Detective McMouse said as he walked with Police Officer Mary Sweet on their regular beat near the London Police Station. "To think of that three-day-long celebration and the medals and other awards that our Team members won! And the promotions and raises in salary! Captain Jenifer now a Colonel. Inspector Catnip now a Chief Inspector. Sargent George now a Sargent Major? And United States Navy Lieutenant Brian Jones now a Captain and a NASA astronaut."

Mary looked down at her tiny friend as they strolled through the gentle rain across the street from a park. "And what about you, Detective. You were offered a promotion and a big one at that! All the way to Mouse Chief Inspector."

"No way, Queen Mary," he replied as he waved a furry paw up at her. "You never wanted the job of Queen. So why should I take a big promotion, too?"

"Agreed, McMouse. Agreed. There's nothing wrong with taking some leave now that the Mission to find the General is finally over. I can always fly up to Scotland and take up my crown again. So said King Charles."

As they continued their stroll down the block, a large black Mongrel with a large bedraggled tail bounded in front of them. "Woof!" it said in Dog talk. "I come to you from Scotland. My name is MacWoof and I am descended from famous Irish and Scottish Wolfhounds. Queen Mary of our fair Scots Islands, I have been ordered to tell you by my great Master and your relative, James Larkin MacSquat, that you must fly at once to your new Island which has not yet been named by you except that you have called it for now, The Peaceful Island." The large dog walked toward them and put its whiskered nuzzle up to Mary's ear. "I tell you this. It is no longer a peaceful island. There are enemies there who plan to destroy England again. They are the descendants of long-dead Scottish Kings and are bent on revenge to become Kings and Queens of Scotland again."

Mary looked down at McMouse who stared up at her. "Dog, what did you say your name was again?"

"MacWoof MacSquat," the dog growled down at the mouse. "Ancestor of MacBark MacSquat."

"Ah yes," the mouse replied as it climbed up Mary's Uniform jacket. "The MacSquats. I've heard of that great barking Clan. You come from the high hills originally, don't you, MacWoof?"

"That be true," the dog said in his doggie language. "Now, I'm away but I have warned you both as I have been ordered to. Besides, it's almost my bedtime and I need my Scots broth and a bone or two to chew."

A flash of dark light filled the street as the great dog disappeared. Mary looked at her shoulder where McMouse had climbed. It sat there, chewing on a large Acorn.

"Here we go again, don't we, Detective."

"Yes, Officer Mary. Here we go again. Not that we both want to."

"But leave London now, when we've just started working the beat again? I don't know about you, but the MacSquat Clan or whatever it's called can wait for a good six months to a year."

"That's what I think too," the little mouse sighed as it stretched its tiny arms. "Besides, Mrs McMouse would have a fit if I disappeared on another secret Mission having only been remarried."

"Good, then we're agreed," Mary said as she shook hands with her mouse best friend. "Bernie would have a fit, too. Now what's say that we stop by the Shakespeare Pub for a quick half of bitter then walk on back to the Station and be done with this long day."

And that is exactly what they did. They went to the Shakespeare Pub up in north London and had a glass of great London Bitter with the Bard himself, William Shakespeare. When they were all finished, Mary and McMouse walked back to the Station and changed into civilian clothes again.

"So McMouse, that's the end of the caper, the cases and the many stories isn't it, my friend."

"Yes, but what about Putin and the General?" Detective McMouse asked his human friend. "Are they being put on trial anytime soon?"

"Not yet. In fact, I asked a judge about that only this morning. She said that it would take at least a year to gather all of the evidence against those two horrid murderers."

"A year?" McMouse squealed. "That's fine by me too! Now let's get home. I'm starved again and Mrs McMouse and the children mice are waiting for me."

"Mouse, I never asked you. Not even at your remarriage. What's your wife's first name?"

"Dolores, after her mother. She was a wonderful mouse mother to her daughter."

"Sounds good by me. I have to have dinner or lunch with my real mother again, soon. It's been a long time. Maybe, soon, we can all have dinner together? What do you say, McMouse?"

"It's a deal! We'll bring the cheese for afters and some fine English crackers."

"Deal it is. Let's get home."

As the sun set over Old London Town, the two figures—one a Human the other a tiny mouse—strolled down a concrete path together. As they walked on, another Police Officer who was now doing their beat looked down that long street and thought he saw two Humans walking hand in hand together.

"Joe, do you see that fine couple?" he said to his partner.

"Sure I do, Jack. That's, ah, well that's Mary and that other one… ummm.. good Lord in Heaven! That's McMouse! Look at the long tail on his rear end! Man how a remarriage and a new Police Officer beat can make even a small mouse grow!"

And that's the end of this tale of crime, murder and global mayhem about Mary Sweet and her many Teams of Human Beings, talking Animals and Ghosts. As the sun finally set on London Town, Mary slipped into bed beside Bernie.

"Bernie, are you upset that I was late for dinner?"

"Hardly," he replied from his place in bed next to her. "We got that cook that your mother recommended to us and my, was that dinner delicious!"

When they rolled over and tried to sleep, Mary looked up to Heaven as she said her prayers. "Hubert, you won't believe it," she whispered so as not to disturb Bernie. "But I actually miss Gertrude and that woman, Simpsa."

"Be careful what you wish for, my darling," a voice in her ear whispered back. "Gertrude actually exists, don't you know that? She was really your great-grandmother on your father's side. She was murdered in the very bed you're now sleeping in with…"

"Stop it Hubert Sweet!" she whispered into the dark room. "You'll frighten me so much I won't be able to get any sleep tonight."

"Fare-thee-well, my good wife," she heard him say.

Closing her eyes, Mary Sweet finished her prayers then rolled over. Looking at the open curtain windows, all that she could see was the dark shadow of the house across the street and the stars shining bright over its roof. "Goodnight Hubert. Goodnight Bernie. Goodnight McMouse. Goodnight stars and that house across the street. Goodnight to all of you."

She closed her eyes and after a struggle finally started to go to sleep. At the last minute she opened her right eye a little bit and said to the Moon that was now setting over the roof of the house, "Goodnight Mister Moon. I'll see you again when you rise again."

THE END

(Of the First Novel in the Mary Sweet Crime Series)

ACKNOWLEDGEMENTS

As I write this final page about me and Mary Sweet, I must inform all of you who read this that, of course, Mice, Cats and Dogs don't really talk! Or maybe they do because, like Doctor Doolittle, I love to hear animals Bark, Meow and Neigh like horses sometimes do when the talk to all of us as they try to get us Humans to feed them again.

Mary Sweet, the character, isn't real but she's based on many friends I know who are all strong, determined and precious people. Carmel Murray, Nimmy, Jin, my mother Mary…to many strong women to count. All I can say is thank-you for the honour and privilege of letting me love you and, even now, I know you love me, too.

But what about Ghosts? Are they really here? Sure, is all I can say. Ghosts are all around us and as I type, we approach Halloween. So to Jackie Harrington, the Queen of all Halloweens, I wish you a kindly 'BOO!' and hope that this short novel doesn't scare you, at least not too much.

Then there is the editor of this Novel, Francis of Assisi, also known as Frank McQuaid. Thanks so much, Frank, for editing this and I'm so glad you enjoyed it, too. To the others that have read the Manuscript before it was published, thank-you, too.

To Toqueer who designed the cover of this Novel as well as all my other Novels, thank-you again for your patience and understanding. You're an amazing permanent Member of our Storylines Entertainment Team and your hard work and attention to detail, even when you're a full-time student, always amazes me.

To the other members of the Storylines Team: Ahmed, Jinny, Larry and the other staff that are scattered all over the world, thank-you for your help and constant support. And to the new

Production Team that is currently producing the Feature Film Dolphin Song, go get 'em, Tony, Rinka and Zach! I can hardly wait to see the finished Film.

Finally, to all my good friends in Eyeries Village and Castletownbere, County Cork, Ireland, for supporting me during the almost two-years that my Partner, Carmel Murry, has been in a Trim, County Meath Nursing Home. You're constant caring ways mean so very, very much to me. And to my children and grandchildren: Kristin, Robert, Sam, Dylan, Jonathan, Aiden, Cathy, Simon, Jack, Ally and Toby: I love you all from the bottom of my heart.

I'm grateful to all of you who read this. I surely appreciate your help as we talk to each other on WhatsApp or TikTok (@tomrichardsdolphin2021), or all of my other Social Media Platforms.

I'm taking a few more days off and soon, I'll start the Second Novel of this Three Book Crime Series about Mary Sweet and her Teams of crazy and not so crazy Humans and Ghosts. A final note: except for my ancient Cat Sasha, animals are not crazy! But human beings often are, even when they're completely normal!

With Blessings to all of you, everywhere.

Tom Richards

Eyeries, County Cork, Ireland

www.storylinesent.com   Email: tomrichards141@gmail.com

14 October, 2023. Two years and a week after Carmel was forced to Leave me due to

her Early Onset Alzheimer's Disease

WHAT'S NEXT FOR MARY SWEET AND HER TEAMS?

Chief Inspector Mary Sweet and

The Great Scottish Land GrabIn this next novel, Mary Sweet and her Teams of Humans, Animals and Ghosts must go back in time to prevent the ancestors of many Scottish Clans from declaring War on England again.

In this Second Novel of the Chief Inspector Mary Sweet Crime Series, readers will again meet most of the Humans, Animals and Ghosts which they did in the First Novel. However, our Ghosts are joined by some Ghostly enemies such as the MacSquat Clan who are related to many Clans made famous by that great film Braveheart.

The novel follows Mary and her Teams as they go back in time to do what they can do to protect the Royal Families of England, as well as those Brave soldiers and warriors in Scotland from certain death.

Join us soon where, once again, you'll be entertained by another story of Ghosts, Ghouls, talking animals, bloodshed and comedy.

Published in early 2024 by Storylines Entertainment Limited. For more information, go to www.storylinesent.com